THE PRICE OF GRACE

DIANA MUÑOZ STEWART

sourcebooks casablanca

To my sisters, through kinship or friendship, for every gut-cracking joke, every moment you listened, for your intense generosity, and the loyalty and support that has kept me sane.

Published by Sourcebooks Casablanca, an imprint of Sourcebooks
P.O. Box 4410, Naperville, Illinois 60567-4410
(630) 961-3900
sourcebooks.com

Printed and bound in Canada.
MBP 10 9 8 7 6 5 4 3 2 1

Chapter 1

Gracie Parish had learned three valuable things in the last two excruciating hours driving around Mexico: The fetal position was only comfortable in the womb. Her deodorant wasn't trapped-inside-a-hidden-compartment strength. And blood circulation could be lost in your forehead.

There had to be an easier way to break into a sex-slaver's home than smooshed inside this malodorous secret compartment, while her brother and his frenemy, Victor, drove into the compound posing as mano-a-mano live "entertainers."

Sweat salted her eyes, slicked her skin. The good news? If she died, the House of Hades would feel like an oasis. A spacious oasis.

This was it. This was absolutely the last time she took part in her family's insane vigilante schemes. Ugh. Sometimes she wished she'd never been adopted into this mess. She needed a vacation on an island. A Canadian island. Someplace cold.

With a flick of her jaw, she clicked her mic. "How much longer, Justice? I'm roasting."

"Please, you've been in there for two hours. People smuggled out of Mexico stay in that compartment for days."

Days? Days pretending to be the back seat of a car, while your legs were tucked, foam padding stuck to your skin, your right arm went numb, your right hip screamed, and you could taste exhaust? "Yeah, well, not me. If my cyber skills weren't needed to rescue your boyfriend, nothing could get me into this Dante's Inferno. Nothing."

"Stop your whining. You're almost inside the compound."

Her sister scored zero on the empathy meter. Zero. "Easy for you. You're on a hilltop, stretched out, overlooking this whole scene through a scope."

"Just playing to my strength. I'm the best shot."

She *was* a good shot. *Hey. No.* "You know, this bull-poop has been going on since childhood. 'Gracie's the smallest, she can fit in that pipe.'" She mimicked a child's high-pitched voice. "'Gracie's the smallest, let her squeeze through the vent system. Gracie's the smallest—put her in the smuggling compartment so she can break out Trojan-horse style inside the compound.'"

"Bull-poop? If you cursed, you'd realize bullshit is way more satisfying." She could hear the focus and humor in Justice's voice. "And it's not my fault you're a shrimp."

"Being petite isn't a talent."

"You also have great red hair and hot underwear."

Oh. God. She'd never live that down. "Good thing. Otherwise, I'd have no excuse if they find me. Assuming they don't shoot before I explain that Tony and Victor hid me here as a surprise bonus to their sex show."

"Trust me, no red-blooded male is going to shoot you when he gets a look at that thong."

Humiliating. Circles of heat singed her already too-warm cheeks.

Should've just nodded when Justice had said, "Sure,

Gracie, pretending to be a stowaway entertainer is better than nothing, but we don't have a costume for you." Or when her sister had looked around the desolate plane hangar, thrown up her hands, and teased, "We're shit out of eight-hundred-dollar bras, and there's no Agent Provocateur in sight."

What happened after that was probably one of the top five most embarrassing moments of her life. She'd dropped her pants. She'd lifted off her shirt.

Justice had burst into laughter. Tony had sputtered. Victor had whistled. "Damn, Red, if I'd known you were hiding that, I would've been nicer to you."

Yeah. Top five. Definitely. And this, being in this car, was definitely in the top ten most uncomfortable places she'd ever been.

Well, maybe top fifteen.

"Our boys are pulling up to the compound gate"—Justice's voice was low in her ear—"so stay quiet."

The car turned. The crunch of gravel vibrated under the wheels and through her bones. "They wouldn't hear me if I screamed." Not a pleasant thought. "Seriously, I could die trapped in here."

"There's a release lever."

Yes. But the arm by the lever was numb and heavy. The car jerked to a stop. Her forehead thunked against metal.

Her headset clicked. She heard Justice's breathing and then, "There's a big *American Ninja Warrior* security guard talking to Tony and Victor. He seems to be in charge of the five men at the gate. He's gesturing our boys out of the car."

Gracie caught the sound of a deep voice, a guy with an American Southern accent. *Southern?*

The car doors opened and shut as Tony and Victor got out.

Justice snorted through the headset. "Victor just pirouetted to show he had nothing to hide. Hysterical. Man has balls."

And then some. She pictured that fine Latino pirouetting in his Magic Mike costume. Victor could fill out a G-string.

"They're going to check the car."

The front car doors opened with a squeak of hinges. Her heart rate jumped to please-God-don't-let-them-find-me pace.

Sweat rolled down her face, perched on her lips. She held her breath.

They'd find her. They'd hear her hyper heartbeat like in Poe's "The Telltale Heart," *ba-boom, ba-boom, ba-boom*. And then they'd shoot her. *Boom*.

Someone climbed into the back seat. Blood *whoosh, whoosh, whoosh*ed in her ears. Her hearing tunneled and focused in tight. Did he have his knee on her left butt cheek? Not a featherweight.

Oh Lord, please. If she survived, she'd go back to running her bar. Maybe keep her cyber-warrior stuff going on the side, but she'd stay far away from the field. And danger. And death.

His weight shifted. The padding and the springs pressed tight against her hip. *Ouch*.

No big deal. No big deal.

If they caught her, well, she'd heard that Mexicans love redheads.

Is that racist?

Gracie, stop overthinking.

He didn't register her beneath him. *Phew*. Then again, if this had been a shoddy place to hide, she never would've gotten into it. Petite body didn't mean petite mind.

The door shut with a slam. She exhaled. Thank the universe, Allah, Dr. Phil, and baby Jesus.

Someone got into the front, started the car, backed it up, drove it a short distance, and parked. The car door creaked open and slammed closed.

Had they parked the car outside the compound?

"Justice—"

"Fuck. Parked it outside the compound. You're like twenty feet from the front gate."

Fudge. She needed to be inside the gate to turn off the security. *OK. Stay calm.* "Don't worry, J. I've got this. I'll find a way inside and turn off the electric fence for you."

"You're east of the guard tower."

Honestly. The very last time I do this.

Chapter 2

Guarding the front gate of a ten-thousand-acre cattle ranch turned bad guys' hideout, Leif "Dusty" McAllister couldn't help but wonder if he had the luck of an '80s action-adventure star. John McClane's brand of bad luck.

That Die-Harder could be scarfing down burgers at a Shake 'n Steak and still run into a shit show.

Not that he was currently anywhere near that fabulous testament to his nation's culinary prowess. And if he went with the God's honest truth, he'd have to admit he'd been asking for it. Going undercover in Mexico to catch a family of American vigilantes wasn't exactly staying out of the line of fire.

Sure had raised a few eyebrows at the bureau. Uptight shoe-polish divas. If you couldn't stomach a little cow patty on your boots, you shouldn't stomp around with the bulls. But he'd spent months cultivating his relationship with Tony Parish, so when he'd offered Dusty a part in this operation, he'd gone all in. Tony was the reason he was in Mexico pretending to work for that psycho sex-trafficker Walid.

Dusty motioned for the Latino guy with the sparkly G-string and Tony, who wore a similar getup and a belt weighted with BDSM tools, to stand still while he frisked them.

As Dusty frisked him, Tony shifted from foot to foot. "Dusty."

Even though it was barely a whisper, Dusty froze. Guy was gonna call him by name? Here? Pretty stupid. Or desperate.

Dusty leaned down as he checked Tony's tools of the trade. Those and his steel-toed boots had set off the metal detector wand. Dusty got to a knee. "Take off your boots."

Tony bent down, took off his shoes, leaned next to Dusty's ear. "Gracie in back of car. Can you get her to security?"

Tony's sister was in the back of that car?

What was going on? This wasn't the original plan. How the hell was he going to get her inside without his men starting to suspect something

Dusty stood and nodded. "Put your boots back on."

He moved to frisk Tony's partner. The guy winked at him. "Take your time, big guy."

Was he serious? Walid was probably watching this whole exchange. Dusty pointed at his shoes. "Take 'em off."

Dusty checked the guy's shoes, ducked his head, hid his mouth, and murmured, "Justice?"

Inches from him, the guy retied his shoes. "Hillside. Scope."

Definitely not the original plan. His heart started to pick up its pace. She had a scope on them?

This last-minute bullshit must've been sparked when Walid captured Sandesh, Justice's boyfriend. *Damn.* Could've, would've, should've were lining up at the pasture gate in his mind.

He ran through the possibilities. Tony was going after Walid, so Gracie and Justice must be after Sandesh.

He motioned to the golf cart waiting nearby. "Good to go."

Without another word, Tony and his pal walked toward the cart that would take them to the villa. Just as well. Couldn't afford to keep talking with his men looking on. Sure, they trusted him, hard not to after months here, but they weren't total idiots. Poorly trained? Yes. Happy-go-lucky? Yes. Total idiots? No.

Now he had to get Gracie Parish inside the compound without raising suspicion, keep that hothead Justice from shooting anyone, and sacrifice one sadistic sex-slaver to the cause. Hopefully, then he'd gain an invite into the Parish family.

An invite he sorely needed to get the evidence to take down the Parish matriarch and vigilante extraordinaire, Mukta Parish.

He cast his eyes to the sky and whatever heavenly powerbroker might happen to own stock in this shit show. *Please. No more surprises.*

In answer, the alarm blared from the speakers perched on posts throughout the compound.

Thanks a lot.

The two-way radio on Dusty's belt sparked to life, security telling him the alarm had started in the dungeon—the old mine where they held prisoners. Looked like Sandesh had gotten restless.

Dusty motioned his men back from Tony and his pal, who had climbed into the golf cart. He did not want to set Justice off. The alarm had to be playing as much havoc with her nerves as his.

He absolutely had to do something though, because Walid—a raging loon since his brother's murder—was surely watching.

Adrenaline brushed its chemical magic across his blood, and the entire scene slowed, snapped into bright, glaring focus.

He ordered Tony and Victor out of the golf cart and onto their knees. Best to make it look good.

One of his guards, a recent hire, misunderstood. Deciding the alarm and these two arriving weren't coincidence, he got in Tony's face.

Newbie.

With a calm voice, Dusty spoke to the guy in Spanish. But the newbie bent down, grabbed Tony, hoisted him to standing.

And then the idiot reached for his gun. Dusty put up a hand. "No. *Para—*"

Pop. Blood splattered from a bullet hole in newbie's head. Tony wrestled out of his dead grasp and ran toward Walid's villa, with his friend a hot step behind.

Bullets started flying. Dusty ducked and ran for cover in the other direction, toward the car and the woman hidden there.

Yep. John McClane's luck. They were gonna die so friggin' hard today. All of them.

Chapter 3

THERE WAS NO WAY GRACIE COULD STAY TRAPPED INSIDE this sweaty can of a space for one more fudgin' minute.

Justice's voice came through her headset again. "Gracie. They're in. They're—"

An alarm sounded. Her heart sped up—way up. It outpaced a Ducati. She needed out of this hidey-hole *now*.

Her sweaty, numb fingers flip-flapped against the metal escape lever like a fish on the deck of a ship.

The *pop, pop, pop* of Justice's gun came through her headset before it clicked off. Why was Justice shooting? Did it have anything to do with the alarm?

Crud.

This never would've happened if she'd still been with John. She'd probably be a soccer mom, have a garden and soft moments.

Okay, stop, Gracie. Focus on squeezing that metal between your fingers. Not regret. Not the man you lost. Not the child you had to let go.

Easier said—thought and repeated again and again—than done. She thought of John all the time. And their son. Tyler. At work. At rest. At play. And now. Here in this sweaty, uncomfortable, uncertain place. Because she was afraid. And her biggest regret was losing them.

Stay calm. Hard enough to breathe squeezed inside the metal curve of this seat. Her fingers cramped, her wrist angled back, she grasped at the latch, pulled. The muscles in her wrist yelped. The spring gave with a dull click.

Breathing heavily, she pushed against the padding. The seat cracked open then stopped dead. *Fudge buckets*.

More shots. Close. Someone fired from behind the car. Someone used the car for cover. Someone fired at her sister. At Justice. Whoever was shooting at her sister was *so* dead.

She angled her knee to aid her pushing hand. The seat began to give way.

Hopefully, Justice would keep whoever was firing too busy to peer through the heavily tinted windows into the car's interior.

The car door opened. "Let me help you there, Gracie."

She flinched, banged her head. *Ouch*. Southern Accent? Southern Accent knew her name? What the hell was going on?

The car shifted. Guy must be big. There was a creak, and the seat was yanked open.

Air. She sucked it in, turned and pulled her shoulders loose. Freed. She sat up and blinked at fresh air and man.

Uhm. Oh. She stared straight into the startled face of way-too-handsome. Sunset-brown hair topped by a USA ball cap, a big, easy grin defined by the persistent crease of overused dimples, labor-tan skin, and the sexiest nose she'd ever seen. A roughly carved block, his nose added challenge and strength to a sun-rugged portrait.

Her heartbeat skittered between the dread of tense alarm and the uncertainty of unexpected arousal. Her skin heated to a temperature rarely seen outside a volcano. Of course.

The sensitivity in her body painted every emotion upon her skin in hues of red. From pleased pink to rust-colored anger to chili-red lust. Didn't matter if it was an insult, compliment, or an unexpected sexual attraction that hit her like a bomb, the result was clear on her face.

Top most embarrassing moment, please take a step down.

His eyes bounced along her body. The red-velvet bra. The matching thong. The ruby piercing snuggled in her bellybutton. The tattoo along her right side—a woman's long, elegant hand curved with vicious scarlet nails, clutching an enchanted apple, holding it out, as if implicitly offering it to the person now consuming her body.

Consuming her body with eyes of thickest amber, eyes drunk on sun, sex, sand, and Southern Comfort.

The heat from his gaze reached out and licked her. Every inch of her grew hotter. Her face. Her hands. Between her breasts. Lower.

The man reached down blindly, groped and found his two-way.

He lifted the two-way to his mouth but spoke to her before he spoke into it. "Darlin', don't be upset by this. I'm on your side. Trust me."

He clicked the radio on. In Spanish, he gave instructions for his men to go out and hunt Justice. He clicked off.

Don't be upset? Did the man realize that was her sister? Teeth clenched, she reached down and extracted her gun from the hidden compartment. She aimed at him.

A muscle along his thumb twitched, but he kept his Glock 19 down, smiled.

He smiled? Was he trying not to laugh? *Oh, buddy, let's see how quickly I can wipe that smile off your face.*

"No. No," he said, clearly reading her intent from her furious face. "Don't shoot. I'm working with Tony. I had to send those men so Walid wouldn't suspect us."

Tony? "My brother never mentioned you. And you just sacrificed my sister so Walid, a sex-trafficking supervillain, won't suspect you?"

Her finger tensed around the trigger.

He shook his head. Smile gone. His gun hand remained down. *Smart*. "I did that so Tony still has a chance. And your sister is good. Honest. Those guys can't shoot. No fooling. One of them shot himself in the foot trying to take his gun out two months ago."

"Gracie?" Justice's strained voice came through her headset.

Gracie clicked her mic on with a flick of her jaw. "Go. I've got American Ninja Warrior."

He did smile at that. "I'm Agent Leif McAllister. FBI."

FBI? Nuts and bolts. The email. The email she'd sent via a secure site to the FBI. The one she'd sent when Tyler was sick and she was helpless to go to him and it all seemed Momma's fault. The stupid email that proved her a traitor to the family and Momma's secret society, the League of Warrior Women. She swallowed a wave of panic. "FBI? In Mexico?"

"Yeah, well, I'm sort of off duty right now. No need for the agent part, actually. Just thought that would make you more comfortable. My friends call me Dusty."

"Dusty?"

"Been told I could talk a stone to dust." He reached out with his free hand. "I'm going to help you out of here. Okay?"

"You touch me and I will shoot."

His hand dropped. Good. Nothing like getting the boundaries set from the get-go.

Chapter 4

Dusty was pretty sure Tony would have an issue or two with what he intended to do with his sister. Give him the ruby. Give him the nails. Give him the apple. Yep. He wanted to lick his way down the whole damn tattoo and across that too-pink skin.

But first things first. Getting her not to shoot him. Which meant being honest with her.

Well, no. Not honest.

Telling her that the FBI had gotten an anonymous tip about Parish vigilante activities, and that he was investigating her family and using her brother Tony as means to an end, make this whole thing messy. Would cost him his job. And the person he wanted to bust most, Mukta Parish.

He'd give her his cover.

"Your brother recruited me to help take out the sex-slaver, Walid. I've been working here for months, replacing every decent shot with a lousy one, and learning this place and its quirks like the back of my hand."

She squinted, as if weighing whether or not to shoot him. "Give me your gun."

"That's a no-go." And a hell no. She opened her mouth. Probably to argue. Because after only two minutes of knowing her, Dusty also knew this was Gracie's strong suit. "If my men or Walid see you with a gun on me, things are going to get real complicated."

Her brows drew together. "Give me your gun. I'll give it back when I'm safely out of the car."

"Look"—he glanced around to make sure no one had started to pay attention—"if I wanted you dead, I'd have shot you by now. There's no time. The longer we argue, the more suspicious this looks. You need me, so risk trusting me."

She tilted her head as if to ask, *So why don't you trust me and give me the gun?*

Damn. She was going to get them both killed.

He swallowed a big helping of yes-ma'am that nearly choked him and placed his gun on the seat.

Straightening, he stepped back from the car. The SUV full of men he'd sent after Justice had pulled to a stop high on the ridge, and the men had gotten out.

At the other end of the compound, past the barn, main house, and entrance to the old mine shaft, another vehicle tore out the back gate. Road grit flew into the air as the car screamed away.

Some of his men were already abandoning ship. Just how he liked it. He took out his two-way and yelled that he had it under control and for them to stop. They went faster.

Perfect.

His Glock in one of her hands, her small-framed Beretta Tomcat in the other, red-velvet bra, colorful tattoo, belly piercing...Gracie was as hot as bourbon whiskey. With a stone-serious expression, she motioned him to the rear of the car. He took two steps back. "We don't have—"

She turned to survey the area, revealing a thong splitting an ass as round and juicy as the apple tattooed across her abs.

"Tiiii…" His voice went up like a hay bale doused with gasoline torched by a flamethrower. His blood turned to liquid lava, steamed his body, and ironed out the wrinkles in the front of his cargo pants.

He should look away.

She turned, caught him looking. He grinned. Like a fool.

A bullet thunked into the steel of the car. He dropped a hair's breadth slower than her.

Crouched by the car, adrenaline slapping him upside the head for his stupidity, he raised his two-way and told his men not to shoot.

He returned his attention to her, crouched beside him, and tried to get things under control. "You need to give me my gun. I can get them…"

Gracie ignored him, raised her Tomcat, and shot over his head. Someone cried out. He leaned in. "Don't shoot. Honestly, these guys…"

She jumped to her feet and ran up the dirt road and through the now-unmanned gate. What the hell? He was tempted to let the idiot get herself killed.

Aw, hell. Anxiety putting spurs to his legs, he sprinted after her. A woman with a gun in each hand. *He* must be the idiot.

Lady had speed. But he had longer legs and apparently more fear. "Stop. You're making this harder than it has to be. And you're going the wrong way."

She pulled up behind the guard tower, sucking in air. "Which way is faster?"

He stepped to the side, blocked their conversation from any cameras. The noise from the alarm pulsed against his eardrums. "Give me my gun. I'll convince my men I'm taking you prisoner. We can walk through here without killing anyone or getting killed."

She squinted at him. "And my gun?"

Seriously? "You'll have to give me that to convince my men you're my prisoner."

She shook her head. "If I keep my hands low like they're cuffed in front of me, they won't see that I'm holding a gun. It's dark. And it's a small gun."

He seriously could not believe her.

She handed him his gun. "I need to get to the security station to turn off the electric fence for my sister."

Great, just what this situation needed, another Parish running around.

Taking his gun, he nodded toward a building by the coal mine. "Roundish building, left of the mine—it's a yurt. That's security."

Lowering her hands, she did a fair job of keeping the Tomcat hidden. Not that it would fool anyone who looked closely enough, but dressed as she was—hot woman wearing combat boots and a thong—no one would be looking at her hands.

"A yurt. Not very secure."

No kidding. Even less secure today than it had been a few months ago. Dusty used his gun to indicate which way she should go. "Make it look good."

She lowered her shoulders, lowered her head like she'd been defeated, and started walking. His two-way squawked again, more shit going on in the mine. Damn Sandesh. Couldn't that guy just sit tight?

"My Spanish isn't great. Did they say the mine?"

He lowered the sound. They had. But he wasn't about to tell her that. She might start running again.

He needed her to stay calm and in his immediate vicinity. "No."

She looked over her shoulder at him. Her eyebrows crashed together, forming a wrinkle above her nose. He felt it then. He felt it for what it was.

The moment lengthened, drew out as clear as crystal. As clear as a blue sky on a bright, cloudless Easter morning. The decision made. The box checked. He saw it in her face. *You're lying. And I will never trust you.*

Chapter 5

INSIDE THE SECURITY CENTER THE ALARM BECAME DEAFENING. Probably because of the four large speakers mounted on the center tent pole. Around the edges of the octagonal, wood-framed room a series of computers were set up. Other than that, the room had a few stools, a coffee machine, water cooler. That was it.

Dusty had marched her in here as if they'd be encountering resistance, but the room was empty of people.

She turned and looked at him. His eyes were open wide, so was his mouth. Apparently, his men were abandoning ship at warp speed. He motioned to the bank of computers. "There," he shouted over the noise, pointing at the central keyboard. "Don't know how to turn off the alarm. But I know that's the main security computer."

As Dusty called out the password, Gracie crossed the room. She had to work quickly. Placing her gun nearby, she typed. Her fingers shook against the keyboard. Sweat slicked her palms, legs, back.

The night had cooled considerably. When the adrenaline wore off, she was going to be one shaky, chattering mess.

A series of commands later, password entered, a series of command later, and the electric fence turned off, along with that blasted alarm. Her muffled ears throbbed.

Dusty's two-way squawked with instructions she couldn't hear. He whisper-cursed "Fuck," answered whoever was on the other end, and clicked off. "Your friend Sandesh shot two of my men down in the mine. They're sending reinforcements."

He tipped up his baseball hat, wiped at the sweat on his forehead. "We need to get down there, get him, and get out before the reinforcements arrive."

Descending into a dark mine wearing next to nothing, while men with guns would most certainly be following, wasn't the best idea she'd ever heard. She wiped slick palms against slicker thighs then picked up her gun. "Let's go."

Shivering, Gracie kept her booted feet braced wide as they rode the dilapidated elevator down into the dark mine shaft. A wheel-and-pulley system, squeaking like a giant hamster wheel, fed the steel cable that slowly lowered the iron cage. The elevator was open on all sides, making the rough, sooty stone walls claustrophobically close. Gracie suppressed a coal-dust cough.

The single light at the top of the elevator cage seemed to do less and less as they descended.

Instinct screamed at her to get out of there. As they neared the bottom, Dusty pressed a button, and the cage creaked to a stop. He slid the gate open with a resounding clack that echoed up the shaft, hit the switch to lock the elevator in place, then took the lead. Gun raised and braced on the flashlight fisted in his other hand, he scanned the area.

She followed, wiping sweat from her face with her free hand. Who was he worried about? He'd already said Sandesh had killed the men down here.

Oh. Right. He was worried about Sandesh.

When they passed two dead men, Dusty cursed and said a soft prayer before continuing on. She avoided looking at them. Her anxiety levels were already skyrocketing.

Straight ahead was a stairway carved into the stone. With no lights up ahead, the steps seemed to disappear into darkness.

She followed Dusty and the cone of light his flashlight created. He was ninja quiet. Impressive for such a big guy. Her boots swished against the gritty steps, a whisper of sound compared to her heartbeat pounding in her ears.

At the top of the stairs, Dusty moved expertly into a hallway with his gun and flashlight down. She stepped out after him. He partially blocked her way, but she caught the outline of a body on the ground and someone curled up, using the corpse as cover.

Sandesh.

"Don't shoot," Gracie said, quickly moving in front of Dusty.

Looking as bruised and battered as a man who'd been held captive by a sadistic sex-slaver would, Sandesh lifted a head crusty with blood. "Gracie?" He sounded as if someone had hijacked his vocal cords and replaced them with rocks. He blinked halfway swollen eyes. "You're rescuing me in your underwear?"

Wondering how he could even see her, worried that they had to take this beaten man through a hostile camp, and a foreboding dread that told her the chances of getting everyone out alive today were slim, she shrugged. "All the cool kids are doing it."

Chapter 6

Two months later

SNUG IN BLACK LEATHER, FROM HER SLEEK JACKET TO her tight-on-the-ass pants—way too hot for summer—a matching black helmet and tinted visor, Gracie inched her low-riding Ducati Monster through Philadelphia's historic Manayunk district.

Cars and high-end stores lined the bustling block. Colorful awnings stretched over crowded outdoor seating. Rounding a corner, she got million-dollar-jackpot lucky, and waited as a car pulled out of a prime parking space.

In her rearview mirror, she spied the familiar three-story brownstone where her ex, John, lived. Squeezed among a long row of houses, his home had a balcony with a few chairs and a tier of herb pots.

Swinging off her bike, she strolled to the Italian ice cart at the street corner and lifted her visor. The man at the stand, shorter than even Gracie's five-foot-one—five-foot-three in her riding boots—with skin the rich brown of Brazilian leather, rinsed the ice cream scoop in a water-filled Bazooka gum bucket. "Wha'd yawant?"

"Watermelon."

He filled the cup, and she handed him a few dollars. She spooned the cool watermelon goodness into her mouth.

Why did people need any other flavor? Honestly, she felt about watermelon-flavored anything the way most women felt about chocolate. A fact she was careful not to share with her dozens of adopted, gun-toting sisters. Who needed that argument?

Leaning against a utility pole, she waited. It didn't take long.

The moment she saw him, her blood danced through her heart, her mouth frolicked into a smile, and the tension in her shoulders melted.

Her son.

Tyler carried his guitar onto the balcony. Curly dark hair framed his youthful, sharply angled face. Thanks to a recent haircut, she could see his green eyes, so like hers, bright against his sun-loving Mediterranean skin, so not like hers.

He'd grown about two inches over the last few months. She'd noticed when she'd trailed him through the city last week. And though, at almost sixteen, he was thin, he would definitely fill out and have his father's build.

She listened as he serenaded the block. Unless paying careful attention, most people wouldn't hear it over the street noise—people talking, music spilling from pub speakers.

There was an ache in Tyler's music. Much different from his father's, which was always full of muddled promises.

That wasn't fair. What did she know of John now that he had Ellen? Nothing. She'd probably changed him. No dark secrets to tear them apart, no family violence to rend their love.

And Tyler? Gracie knew him at two, not at three or ten or even sixteen. She'd let him go thirteen years ago, and now he called Ellen Mom.

Giving him up had been the only way to keep him and John safe from the vigilante machine that had sucked away her soul. And maybe her ability to know the clear difference between right and wrong. None of that made her feel better.

Could she have fought harder? Had she suffered enough for letting him go? Did she deserve this bit of joy on seeing Tyler?

Stop, Gracie. These questions have no answers.

She might not deserve these glimpses, but since losing her brother Tony in Mexico, Gracie was in too much pain to deny herself this joy.

The image of Tony's body lying on the floor of Walid's villa, with Justice crying over him, snapped into her brain as lethal and piercing as a gunshot. *God.*

What kind of life had Tony had? One with unrequited love and devotion. She didn't want to die like that.

Or like her biological mother, who'd reached out to her only after she'd gotten terminal cancer. They'd connected but had had so little time together.

She wanted a different life. She wanted to find a way to get back into Tyler's life. Not as a mother, that was Ellen's role, but in some small way. Problem. John would never allow any contact if he knew she still did operations for the League.

Putting aside his guitar, Tyler stood and rested his elbows on the railing. His gaze fell directly on her. She paused with the spoon to her mouth. Her shoulders drew down. Her adrenaline spiked.

He wasn't looking at her.

He couldn't be.

She was just some stranger on the street. She never

wore the same thing here. She never uncovered her hair. Heck, sometimes she took a page from Momma and wore a niqab, the Muslim veil that covered hair and face.

But he was. Tyler was staring at her. He waved. Her heart ballooned like it had been filled with helium. It rose and rose and popped, then dropped into her acid-thick stomach.

Danger.

Danger.

Danger.

She turned away, flicked down her visor, tossed her cup into the closest can, and walked back toward her bike.

What had she done? *Selfish*. The League's rules were firm. What would Momma say if she knew Gracie had broken her side of the deal? The deal where Momma promised never to hurt John or take his memory as long as Gracie could assure his silence. The deal that kept John quiet. Gracie agreed not to fight for custody of Tyler, to stay away, if John never spoke a word about the League.

The deal that let everyone continue with their lives—everyone but her.

She peeked again as she mounted her bike. Tyler was still watching her. Why had she parked here? Stupid. John came out and stood on the balcony next to Tyler.

Tyler pointed her out to him. *He pointed her out*.

A log of fear dammed her throat, blocking her breath. She'd gotten careless. Desperate and careless. John knew she rode low, customized bikes—sucked to be short—knew her petite frame.

Her heart accelerated as she drove off, adjusted and checked her rearview. John's wife had come onto the balcony.

Ellen, El, with the blond hair, who sang like a lark and worked at a popular satellite radio station. John put his arm around her waist, whispered something into her ear. She nodded.

Gracie's chest ached with a longing so sharp and hot she swore blood poured from the wound.

God, she was tired of the tension in her shoulders and the walls around her heart. She wanted a life with kittens and saucers, and sweet moments, and hot moments. Yes. That.

Taking the corner, she looked one last time. And saw the man she loved, the one she'd let go in order to save his life, and the woman he now loved, turn and go back into their home.

Chapter 7

STANDING ON A CROWDED STREET IN MANAYUNK, DUSTY wasn't sure what he'd just witnessed. Something was up.

The usually unflappable Gracie Parish had just spooked.

Hell, he'd seen less reaction from her in the middle of a firefight in Mexico. Why had she torn out of here after the weird exchange with balcony boy?

Lifting his cell, he checked the photo he'd taken of the kid, expanded it. A little blurry, but did the kid have green eyes like Gracie's? Could they be related?

Maybe. But in what way? Her file said she'd never given birth. Still, that kid meant something to her. And what of the guy, the one who looked to be the kid's father?

Dusty wished he'd seen more. Parking being what it was here, he'd only caught the ending. The kid had waved to Gracie. In response, she'd hightailed it out of there.

If that hadn't been enough to raise his suspicions, the indirect way she'd come here would've been. After she'd dropped her car off at a garage, she'd walked two blocks to another garage, then had come out dressed in leather and riding a bike.

He'd nearly missed her. Might have, if he hadn't recognized the boots. She'd been wearing the knee-high, lace-up black leather boots with a sun dress when she'd gotten in her car at the club. He'd thought that was odd. Hot but odd.

Fact was, she'd gone out of her way to make sure she wasn't followed here.

She did have a decent surveillance-detection route, proving she had training and had come here more than once. She had situational awareness but had probably grown a little complacent in her life as a club owner. She was good. He was FBI.

All that effort, she sure hadn't come for the sweet ice. Or what he'd thought would be some secret meeting.

She'd come to see the kid.

Striding through the crosswalk, Dusty went to the brownstone. It had a list of names. Pressing the button on his sunglasses, he snapped a photo.

A moment later, a girl passed him and hit the buzzer that read "John, Ellen, Henry, Tyler True."

A soft woman's voice answered. "Come on up, Lil. Ty is waiting."

The girl pulled the door open, hung far back, gazed upward, and blew balcony boy a kiss.

Huh. The boy, Ty, caught it, sat back down. Chances were the girl would join him on the balcony.

Dusty took out his listening device. He hooked it over his ear, angled it upward. It was already paired to his phone. He pretended to talk to someone while he listened.

No one could do a fake conversation like him. Every so often he'd "Yeah, honey, but..." Pause, and then "Describe where you are again..."

The door to the balcony slid open. The girl and boy embraced. She sat on his lap. They talked. A lot. Kid stuff.

This might be a waste of time. He reached for the disconnect and heard the kid say, "She came back again. That woman who keeps showing up."

Dusty lowered his hand.

"You sure it's the same woman, Ty?"

"Yeah, I told you. She's really short."

"Short," the girl huffed. "You're, like, six foot. You think *I'm* short."

"It's her. Seen her at least twice before."

He had? Bet he'd missed her a lot more times, but Dusty was surprised the kid was so observant. And smart enough not to take the bait on that *short* line.

"My dad's freaked. Finally convinced my mom we need security. He's putting up cameras."

"So, what, she's a stalker? Am I going to have to take her down?"

He laughed and snuggled her neck. They began to make out. Loudly. Well, loudly to the perv holding the microphone up to them. He lowered the volume until he heard the boy come up for air.

"Want to go to my room?"

"Your parents."

"They don't care."

She paused. "Are you sure?"

Okay, no way this conversation was going back to Gracie. He turned the device off and maneuvered through the sidewalk of people and back toward his car.

So the kid had recognized Gracie, but not who she was. That didn't rule out a family connection. Gracie had been adopted, so maybe she'd discovered a relation here and had blown it up in her mind.

Or this could have something to do with her family's vigilantism. Could she be after the father? Could she be following the kid to get a bead on the dad?

He'd find out.

At his car, Dusty's phone rang. He unhooked it from the bat-belt. Thing had near everything. A good knife, folding lock pick, mace, an EMF jammer, zip ties, but not his gun. That was inside a sheath holster concealed in the waistband of his jeans.

He took out his gun, slid into his black Malibu, and placed the weapon on the passenger seat, then put the call on speaker.

"Tell me you have something, Dusty."

His SAC, Special Agent in Charge. And he wasn't leading with patience. "Hey, Mack. I take it the Bureau hasn't reopened the Parish investigation."

"No. Officially, Parish is a dead end. Mukta Parish has a lot of fans. Doesn't hurt that that exclusive boarding school she runs is filled with VIPs."

Money folk lived by their own rules. He started the car, put the turn signal on, and pulled onto the busy street. "Even after that drone strike?"

Drones had dropped small explosive devices on the school a few months back. They'd hit targets devoid of people, doing little damage, but scared the bejeezus out of everyone.

Mack made a can-you-believe-that sound. "Yeah, even after. But a team combed every inch of the campus—even scanned the place via satellite and thermal spectral analysis. Reviewed the scans myself, and got to say, if there'd been a secret underground chamber, it would've shown up. There's bupkes."

"Come on, there's something there. We know the Parish family is running their own vigilante covert ops.

They *have* to have a secure facility to gather intel and train. The school is the perfect cover." Dusty drummed his thumbs on the steering wheel.

"Don't need to convince me. Those Parish sisters are out of control. They've got to be shut down. But where's your proof?"

"In Mexico I saw the Parish siblings in action with my own eyes—they are highly trained, lethal operatives."

"And you went undercover for months, but your prelim went nowhere. The principal was never implicated, your contact poisoned himself while poisoning the sex-slaver, and you backed off from bringing in the sisters."

Dusty rolled his stiff neck, right-lane passed a stopped car. "Backing off" wasn't how he'd seen it. Gracie and Justice had just lost their brother. Plus the email from the insider claimed the girls were adopted, trained, molded, and made into vigilantes. If that was the case, then Gracie and her siblings were victims. "These people are as loyal as Labs. I'm not going to bully them into turning on Mukta."

"I get it. That's why I'm giving you this time. If you bring me something, anything we can use, this will go from a drawer to a full-out investigation. Just ring that bell."

"Appreciate that." Dusty turned a corner. The wheel brushed against his palms as he straightened out the car. "The key is getting an invite into the family and locating the headquarters of the Parish covert ops. If it's not on campus, it's somewhere else. When I find it—that will do more than ring a bell, it will blow this thing wide open."

"Agreed. Then that's your plan." Mack paused, and

it felt like there was more there. Sure enough, after a couple of beats he said, "I have word on your dad."

Shit. His stomach did that thing that reminded him he'd once been seven years old and terrified of the man. It dropped, shrank to the size of a pea, and exploded into a ball of rage. "Yeah."

"Got something wrong with his kidneys."

His father, who'd been calling himself a faith healer for decades, was now sick. This could be interesting. Dusty jerked to a stop at the red light. A woman crossed and gave him the pay-attention glare. He tipped his baseball cap to let her know he was suitably chastised.

"What's going on there?" he asked.

"Has his whole ministry praying for him, out there earning extra money. Says a healer can't heal himself. Looks like he's been seeing a doctor on the side. I believe he's going to get himself some modern medical care."

Fucker. "If you continue to have eyes on that little part of the world, keep me updated."

"Will do."

Dusty hung up. The cold air from the vents pushed into his face. He accelerated through the green.

He couldn't believe it. His father, the faith healer who'd let so many sick people suffer—because if God didn't heal you, you didn't deserve to be healed—was seeing a doctor. And he had his followers paying for it—and praying for him.

Sure, a lot of people would say, "Those followers get what they deserve." He wasn't one. He knew what it was to be brainwashed. To be dying from a simple bladder infection and believe God had deemed you unworthy, that you got what you deserved.

It's why he was doggedly investigating the Parish family. Following up on an email from someone who also knew, understood what happened when family cut you off from the wider world and gave you a narrow, dogmatic view of it.

It's why he'd risk everything to bust Mukta Parish, the woman who brainwashed young girls and turned them into her own personal army of vigilantes. It's why he'd agreed to go undercover for Tony Parish to begin with and had worked for that scumbag sex-trafficker in Mexico. But when Tony had died, Dusty still hadn't had enough evidence or an invite into the family. And that had led him here to good ol' Bucks County, Pennsylvania.

Where he intended to step from the shadows and reacquaint himself with one Ms. Gracie Parish.

Chapter 8

As the gate swung open, Porter Jefferson Rush pulled into the driveway of the elegant stone colonial. From the back of the Navigator, his father groaned.

He eyed his father through the rearview mirror. The afternoon sun highlighted faint lines in his fair skin, showed silver in the tufts of red hair escaping the compression bandage. His green eyes were tensed in pain, shadowed under thick auburn eyebrows. The next few days were going to be rough.

"You okay, Dad?"

"Don't park in the driveway, Porter. The sun."

"Dad, you had a mini-facelift three days ago, it didn't make you a vampire."

His father's laughter cut off with a curse. He rubbed his bandaged jaw. "Don't make me laugh. Park in the garage."

Porter clicked the garage door opener and pulled into the first bay. His father wasn't really concerned about the sun. He didn't want the pariah media to spot him.

Truthfully, Porter didn't want him seen. No reason to give the media something else to mock about the Pennsylvania senator. Bastards thought anyone with six kids was a religious nut or an idiot.

The garage door slid closed behind them. Porter stepped to the back of the car and helped his father out.

Though he had his keys in hand, on a hunch he turned the knob. Unlocked.

"Dad, I told you to lock the door. Someone running for president could get himself killed this way."

His father's brows slid into a puzzled V. "I thought I had."

Sure he did. His father was a great man, a brilliant man, but he was careless in ways that annoyed Porter no end. They walked into the usually bright kitchen and stopped. The shades were drawn so his sister Layla, who sat at the table with a set of laptops open in front of her, could better see the screens.

Of the six kids in his family, Layla resembled Mother most, blond hair and fair skin. She was the swan among the ginger ducklings. And as the only girl, they all doted on her.

Porter leaned forward and kissed her cheek. "Layla-bug. How's iRobot?"

She exhaled a long breath. "My lady-in-red robot isn't working. She's frigid. All I want is to bring happiness to lonely California businessmen. Is that too much to ask?"

He laughed. Then thought about it. "You're joking, right?"

She stood, stretched. "Definitely not." With a wink she moved past him to hug their father, careful of his bandages.

Father instantly took her under his arm, a bit of comfort but also some support as he was a little unsteady from the pain medication.

Layla smiled at Porter. "I'll take this charming young man from here."

Porter glanced at her laptop screens. Looked like complicated stuff. "You sure, Layla? I can do it."

She shook her head. "I was going up to change for a swim anyway."

Layla guided their woozy father along, even as the man tossed back his insane list of things to take care of.

Agitation tightened Porter's shoulders. "I'm on it, Dad. Go on upstairs with Layla and relax. I'll be up in thirty minutes or so to check on you."

An hour later, Porter was still working in his father's office, making lists of campaign donors to reach out to. It was looking good. They had a real shot at the presidency. A real shot. He'd worked hard, destroyed his own marriage to get to this place, and now it seemed nothing could stop them. The phone rang.

He picked up it on the third ring. "Yeah."

"Andrew, I'm surprised you answered. Especially knowing I'm gunning for you."

Mukta Parish? He instantly recognized her voice. One would have to live on another planet not to. She was very political. And made appearances all over the world on women's rights issues.

How did she have his father's private number? Normally Porter would point out her honest mistake. He and his youth-conscious dad not only looked like brothers, they sounded alike. But he was curious about that "gunning for you" comment.

And this wouldn't be the first call where he'd impersonated his father. That would've been when he was sixteen.

"To what do I owe the pleasure of this call, Mukta?"

There was a moment of silence. Had he overplayed his hand? Had he said something wrong? No. He'd been listening to his father's phone calls since he was a boy playing with cars at his feet. He had the man down. So why the silence?

"Andrew." The name was spoken as one calls a dog to heel. "Have you killed the bill currently being circulated?"

What the hell was going on? Was she trying to dictate his father's policy decisions?

"I assume you're talking about the Equal Pay Initiative. The one that states a woman needs to show substantial proof that her work is equal in quality and effort to a man's before filing a suit claiming wage discrimination based on gender."

"You know that is what I mean. It's another hoop and unnecessary. The federal Equal Pay Act established in the sixties, for all intents and purposes, already makes this qualification."

"Then I don't see what the issue is. We are merely firming up the law."

"It is another roadblock to equality, one that requires a woman be grilled and subjected to gross humiliation, and you know it. Stop delaying. Kill the bill. Or I will tell the world about Gracie and end your bid for president before it even begins."

She hung up.

Stunned, Porter tried twice before managing to set the phone down on the cradle.

Gracie?

Chapter 9

THE TWO INTERSECTING CORRIDORS ON THE UPPER level of Gracie's Club When? were devoid of decoration. Or personality. Four foreboding steel doors, three of which led to work spaces, and the fourth, the only one in the second corridor, led to her apartment.

In the main corridor, the work doors led to a server room, her office, and the door she was currently behind, a tactical operations center for the underground railroad.

The underground railroad was a League cyber operation that worked exclusively in the United States. It helped locate abused women and girls, organized rescues, and placed those rescued in a new state, home, school, or job—depending on their needs.

It was here, in a state-of-the-art command center tight with computer equipment, Gracie sat creating databases to help identify creepers seeking children and vulnerable women via the dark web.

She rubbed at sore eyes. She'd been at this awhile, streamlining things so it worked not just for her, but for law enforcement. Needing a break, she pushed back from the desk, rolled her shoulders, then cringed when her cell rang. It vibrated across the shiny black surface of the desk.

She didn't need to look at the caller ID to know who it was, but her eyes strayed there anyway. Yep. Momma.

She firmed her resolve. Having Tyler wave at her

had unchained her need to be part of his life, a need so powerful she couldn't wrestle it down and leash it again. As difficult as it would be to convince Momma a new deal could be worked out, John would be worse. If he thought she was still involved with the League, he would never let her into Ty's life.

To reconnect with Tyler, she had to cut herself off from the League. And that decision, ignoring the needs of the world's women, the League, her family, was easier if she didn't have to face them.

She picked up. "Hello, Momma. If this is about dinner, I'm sorry, I have plans."

"Are they unbreakable plans? I would consider it a sincere kindness if you came tonight."

A "sincere kindness" was as good as a summons. Momma didn't make demands like that without reason. "Why?" she asked.

"Your newest sister, Cee, asked specifically for you."

"Cee is asking for me? I'm the person who said she shouldn't be adopted into our family. I know she knows this, because I said it to her face."

And Cee had a huge need for payback. Attested to by the fact that during her rescue from a sex-slaver, she'd shot and killed one of the bad guys. Sure, she said she'd done it to rescue Justice, but Gracie wasn't convinced it had been absolutely necessary.

"Perhaps that's why she asks for you. She trusts your bluntness."

Hmmm. No. Cee didn't strike her as the soft type, looking for connection. "What aren't you telling me?"

Momma sighed. "Her interest in you is unusual, I'll agree. But she sees how you live, outside the League and yet still within it. Less rules. Less attachment. She wants to know more of this. And you. Perhaps you can help train her. Your expertise in Muay Thai would be useful to her."

Less attachment was harder than it looked. She'd thought Cee liked it in the mansion, liked her new siblings. "She's a kid, Momma." A confused kid. "She needs to be a kid for a while. And I'm not interested in training anyone." She hadn't been to the gym in…yikes, a while. "Or in dinner."

Momma paused before her soft, "You have always been less active with the family, but this…is it something I've done?"

That stung. It hurt because yeah, it was.

Running a secret vigilante group that was always more important than Gracie's life was something she'd done. Threatening John's memory so Gracie was forced to send him and their son away was something she'd done. Not sharing Tony's plan to take out the Brothers Grim separately, so Gracie never knew the extent to which he'd felt ignored, was something she'd done.

"I'm sorry, Momma…" The words, like the moisture in her mouth, dried up. She eyed the dish of watermelon Jolly Ranchers on her desk, unwrapped one, and popped it into her mouth. *Mmmm.* There was no stress watermelon-flavored corn syrup couldn't help ease. Time to rip off the Band-Aid. "I just need a break from the life for a little while. All of it. The field stuff. And the family stuff too."

"Are you saying that you won't be part of the family? And will relinquish your role in the underground railroad?"

What? "No." That work didn't require her to go

out on operations. She could do that at her desk. John couldn't object to *that*. "I consider that work sacred. And I'm making some great progress with the pervert detection software I've started developing. I feel like it could one day be used by others, like law enforcement."

She was good at that, hiding behind a keyboard, not showing her face, her emotional front page, revealing more than she wanted.

"I see. So you want the protection of the League to do your work, to keep your secrets, but will disavow our work and the responsibility to your family?"

Ouch. Her neck and cheeks warmed with heat. Disavow? No. That wasn't… She did believe in the good work the League did. Not just the secret work of righting wrongs, but also the educational work of their world-famous boarding school, the groundbreaking research of Parish holdings, the charities and foundations they supported, and especially her big, crazy, loving, adopted family.

Crud. Momma always knew the exact buttons to press. "I'll be there in a half hour."

Following Momma's summons, Gracie exited her club. Yikes, it was July out here. Like stepping into a sauna. And here she'd dressed up. Sort of. Hair down, magenta sequined shirt, and black skinny jeans.

Flipping her hair back from her neck, she locked up and set the code for the alarms via her cell. When her phone buzzed, she readjusted her purse strap, turned toward her car, and with the crunch of gravel loud under her shoes, read the text as she walked.

I know you've been spying on my son, stalking him. Remember our agreement? Stay away from Ty. I'm not putting up with you and your family's craziness in our lives. Don't come around again. This is your one warning.

My son? Hurt and anger landed a punch to her lungs. Gracie stopped by the side of the car; her hands shook as she stared at the dimming screen. Thirteen years. She'd been sharing her contact information with John, waiting thirteen years to hear from him, to get one word from him about Tyler, and he'd just used that information to send her a threatening text. She took deep, struggling breaths, debated replying.

And because she was trained, because it was quiet, because her intellect suddenly recognized a threat, her ears listened of their own accord. The whoosh of a single car passing, the bark of a distant dog, and the crack of a—

She dropped to the ground a moment before the round thunked against her car. Scurrying under the car's chassis, she dropped her phone, took her gun from her purse, and flicked off the safety.

The flood of adrenaline muted everything but the sound of her heartbeat. Her eyes sharpened, methodically scanning the parking lot. There was another shot and another. Stones popped up and hit her car, tinking into steel like heavy rain.

She scooted farther under the car, came out the other side, and crept toward the rear of her vehicle, gun pointed toward the wooded area that lined the back of the parking lot.

The glow from the light poles kept her from seeing anything among the trees. A moment passed. Two. Sprinting across the parking lot, she entered the woods, ducked behind a tree. She listened to the silence, then moved cautiously forward.

It was darker in the woods, but enough light from her club filtered through the dark trees so she could see the piled dirt and leaves, the berm that someone had created. Someone had lain in wait for her here. How long had they been here? How had they known she'd be coming out tonight?

This was no random act of violence. This person was trained, so said this setup and the fact that he—or she—had used a silencer.

She bent down and examined the area, picking up shell casings. Heard footsteps. Someone moved across the parking lot toward her. She spun, raised her weapon.

Chapter 10

THE FINGER SNAP OF A SILENCED GUN BROUGHT THE SOLDIERS on Dusty's neck to attention and sent his heart into double-time. He was already approaching Gracie's Club When? but now he broke into a run.

Two blocks back, he'd realized something was up when his phone alerted him that the surveillance camera he'd set up in the club's parking lot had quit working. He'd placed it to keep track of Gracie's coming and going. It was well hidden, so either it had malfunctioned, or someone had used a jammer.

Another shot and another.

The drive leading to the parking lot was flanked by two hippie sculptures. He leapt over the first—a time-piece that looked like something right out of *Alice in Wonderland*. He jogged down the driveway, a stretch of asphalt squeezed between a warehouse and her club.

Gun out, he pulled up beside the club and scanned. No one around. There was a small crop of trees that lined the far edge of the parking lot. It's where he'd placed his camera. No one there either.

Someone darted out from behind a car. Gracie? He watched her enter a small copse of trees that lined the far edge of the parking lot.

That's where he'd placed his camera. He scanned again before heading out to give her a hand.

Nearly at the edge of the parking lot, she stepped out with her gun raised and pointed at him.

"Whoa. Whoa. Whoa. It's me. Dusty."

Her eyebrows inched up when she recognized him, but she didn't say a word. As if they were back in Mexico, she crooked her head, indicating she'd go left. He went right. After triple-checking the surrounding area, they met back by her car.

Dusty holstered his gun. "You okay?"

"Of course."

Lowering her gun, she held up a finger, as in *give me a minute*. He gave her the minute, but had no doubt she'd use that time to come up with an excuse for what had just happened.

Readjusting her disheveled shirt, covering the strap of a crimson bra but not the raspberry scrape on her arm, she bent to retrieve what turned out to be her purse and phone from under the car.

The phone and her weapon—Glock 22—went into her big bag. She opened the car door, tossed the purse inside, shut the door with an angry slam. Finally, she refocused her attention on him. "Why are you here?"

Was she serious? Not even an excuse, just a counterattack? "Because I heard gunshots, and you're jumping out of the woods with a gun in your hand."

"Some nut tried to rob me," she said, as if that were nothing to be alarmed about. Which sent off every alarm in his body. "I had a gun. He ran. And don't try to distract me. I meant why are you in town?"

"Rob you?" Uh. Huh. "With a suppressed weapon? And I'm dumb as a box of rocks."

She smiled. The kind of smile that made men drop to their knees or lose their minds.

He lost his mind.

Must have, because he was here for Mukta, the woman who adopted girls and made them into soldiers for her own war. He wouldn't be satisfied with anything less than proof of that.

So it was definitely the smile that caused the outburst: "Sure, Gracie, someone tried to rob you. With an expensive silenced weapon. Using an EMP jammer sophisticated enough not to set off your security. In a town so overconfident of the peace, not a soul opened a window to look out here. It surely wasn't more than that. It surely doesn't have a lick to do with your family and whatever shit y'all are into."

She studied him long and hard. Or maybe what he'd said. Her eyebrows crashed together. "Why are you checking up on me? Showing up in the nick of time? Asking about jammers?"

Shit. "Why don't you explain to me why someone wants to kill you?"

He stared at her. She stared back. She'd sent the letter, hadn't she? She was reaching out for something, wasn't she?

She drew nearer to him, so close his heart started its engines and revved, waiting for the green in her eyes to signal *go*.

Head inclined, her eyes flashed innocence, invitation, and challenge beneath long lashes. "Do you want to kiss me?"

"What?" He stepped back. The opposite of what he wanted to do. He wanted to wrap her in his arms, kiss her senseless, reassure his pounding heart she was safe—but not like this, not as a test, not as a game, and not when she was trying to distract him. Too bad his johnson hadn't gotten the message.

She huffed at the distance he'd created. "Guess not. Or maybe you're undercover and actually feel bad about lying, pretending to be former FBI."

She quirked her mouth, ran her tongue along her upper lip with exaggerated slowness. Oh hell, she was practically calling out his cover. He stepped forward, grabbed her by the waist, pulled her body flush against his hard-on. Her eyebrows rose in surprise. She wiggled just a little.

His head dropped before he knew what was happening. His lips slid restlessly over hers. She opened wide for him. Soft. Wet. Sleek. Her glorious tongue stroked his, sent his heart thumping in his chest.

She deepened the kiss, put her hands around his waist, grabbed the belt loops on the back of his jeans and used them as leverage to grind herself against him.

The rough friction caused his dick to strain in his pants. He seriously needed to stop, to… *Oh, good Lord. What is she doing with her tongue?*

She broke the kiss.

Head spinning. Breath hot. He kissed along her cheek to her ear and whispered a plea and a moan. "Darlin', tell me this ends with us upstairs."

She laughed, squeezed his ass. "Sure. I'm going to boink your brains out and then give away all the family secrets while you lie satiated beside me."

Boink?

She swatted his ass, stepped away. "Moron."

Wait. What?

His head cleared. Slowly.

Oh. Shit. He'd walked right into that. He'd seen the trap, watched her lay it out in front of him, pretty as a picture, told himself not to go near it, then jumped the fuck inside. She was right. He was a moron. He grunted. Put his hands in his pockets to hide his still-raging boner.

Gracie grinned. He fought his own smile. Which wasn't right, because he was pretty pissed off. "Okay, Gracie. Suppose I'll see you soon."

He turned and strolled off, unhooking his phone to make sure the feed to the camera was back on. It was. So the jammer the sniper had used wasn't destructive. He'd have to devise a way of keeping track of her that was less vulnerable to interference.

He watched her run a hand through her hair, lean against her car, and after a moment that went on long enough to boost his confidence, turn from watching his ass and get into her vehicle.

Chapter 11

Wearing workaday jeans with a button-down over her Club When? T-shirt—a giant gold question mark over a clock—Gracie knelt at the periphery of the dance floor. She took another piece of red, white, and blue foam padding from the storage box and fastened it onto the gilt rail bordering the dance floor.

Around her, the sound of workers using drills and hammers to remove old decorations and put up new decorations invaded the normally quiet morning. Club When? changed themes, based on a time period or specific event in history, every eight weeks. The new theme was the Fourth of July.

Flags and fighter jets hung from the copper ceiling panels, along with strobe lights that would add to the Fourth of July fireworks light show. As she worked, her wary eyes swept the laborers, glad for the concealed carry at her side.

How much did she know about the men working on the club changes? Sure, she'd hired the contractor, Doug, and his crew many times over the years. But these weren't all the same people who'd worked for him when she'd done her initial background check. Were they?

She wiped at her brow with the back of her hand. Sheesh. It had only taken an assassin and being threatened by an ex-lover to wake her up from the delusion that she was safe here.

She shifted as one of the workers came over to her with the framed *Independence Day* poster, an alien ship beaming an aggressive red light onto the Empire State Building. "Where you want it?"

Ignoring the hair that had escaped her ponytail and fallen across her eye, she quickly assessed any threat the man posed. He was tall, with a lanky build, but he held himself like someone who had some kind of training. Maybe former military.

This guy was one of the two men working here today whom she hadn't done a background check on. Her heart doing that tentative dance, that ready-in-a-whisper acceleration, she put her arm flat across her stomach so she could draw her gun more quickly. Paranoid? Sure. But she could live with that.

She nodded toward the picture of Prince in all his glory—between two art deco stained-glass windows near the bar. "Replace that one."

The man's eyes strayed to the spot. "You've got it, boss."

He walked away. Gracie watched him go. She exhaled a breath full of tension. Reason told her he was just what he seemed, but reason took a backseat to precaution after being shot at the other night.

Someone was watching her. Someone who had known about Sunday night dinners with her family.

John knew.

She needed to update her security. Especially the back door and parking area. The front door to the club had a walk-through metal detector, facial recognition software—hooked up to the League's servers and huge database of bad guys. And at night that door was manned by trained bouncers with military experience.

A few weeks ago, heck, a few nights ago, all of that had seemed overkill. Now, it didn't seem enough.

A loud *bam* resounded through the club, and Gracie shot to her feet. Her hand snaked under her shirt to her side holster.

Her heart pounding, she spun to face the noise. The worker who'd dropped the metal Statue of Liberty sculpture waved at her and apologized. She must've looked pissed off, because his boss started to berate him.

Pulling her hand from her gun, Gracie waved away her contractor's concern, then jumped out of her skin when her cell rang.

Yikes. Tense much? She unhooked her phone from the belt looped through her jeans, looked at the screen, and thumbed Accept. "Hey, Victor."

"How's my favorite red-headed vigilante?"

A nervous, paranoid, worried wreck. "Thanks for returning my call. I need a favor."

"Uh-oh, that sounds serious. Like you're going to ask me to put on a G-string and dance in public. You know I'll only do that if it's private. Me and you."

Victor flirted as much with women as he did with men. Normally she didn't mind the harmless flirting. Not today. "I sent you an email through our secure site. Can you check it out?"

After Mexico, they'd kept in contact. More than kept in contact. They'd become friends. And because they'd each had something to offer the other—he contacts, she cyber skills—they'd set up a secure communication site.

"Give me a sec."

She waited while she heard keys being tapped. He murmured noises as he worked and then, "Got it." A few more moments and then, “Fuck. Someone took a shot at you?”

No kidding. “Keep reading.”

He did, here and there saying a word aloud. He stopped abruptly. “So John texted you, threatened you, right before someone shot at you?”

“Yeah.” It could be coincidence. It could be. “It gets worse.”

She was glad he already knew about John and Tyler. Since returning from Mexico, they’d gotten drunk together and shared some mind-blowing secrets. Victor’s life had not been predictable. And this coming from her, who’d been raised by a super-wealthy woman to be a vigilante.

The shrill whine of a drill cut through the club and Gracie’s last nerve. She had to bite her lip to keep from yelling at the guy. She pressed the phone closer to her ear as Victor started talking. “First, I’m in. Whatever you need. No one messes with you. Second, you’re not telling your crazy-ass family?”

Here we go. “Don’t call them crazy.”

“Twenty-eight adopted kids from all over the globe. All with some horror story. Oh—and they all happen to be secret vigilantes. Yeah, I’m sticking with the crazy part.”

Well, couldn’t argue with that. Maybe they should’ve erased his memory. “Did you read the whole thing? I can’t tell them.”

“I read it. FBI guy in town. Do you think it’s that email you sent?”

Another confession her drunken self had given him. “Yeah. I do.”

"Fuck, Red. That's not good. The International Peace Team is tied to your family now."

She couldn't see him, but she heard him moving, probably pacing with that slight limp he still had from the injury he'd suffered in Mexico.

He had reason to pace. Victor had started a global charity, the International Peace Team, with her sister's now-husband Sandesh, and it was heavily dependent on Parish philanthropy. If the FBI discovered the illegal things her family did, the good work his charity did would suffer.

And if Momma discovered Gracie had sent the letter, she'd suffer. Rightfully so. But, among other things, Momma would begin to monitor her. That would ruin her attempt to be part of Tyler's life. She couldn't have that. "I know. I wish I could go back in time and not send the letter, but I can't."

After a moment's consideration, Victor said, "Only five people?"

Her email included a list of five people she thought might want her dead. John and his wife, a hacktivist she'd unveiled as a corporate shill, a teacher and sexual predator she'd chemically castrated in her wilder days, and a macho pilot she'd dated for two-and-a-half seconds. Was that all? Could she be missing someone? "Yeah. Five. Just them."

Someone came through the front door of the club. Her heart jumped. What the heck? Why wasn't that door locked? All the equipment had come in the back way. She hadn't unlocked it. Had a worker?

That was the problem with having the alarm off during the day. And with being recently shot at.

Anxiety restrained her mood like a heavy coat, or a

straitjacket. Though as she recognized the man walking toward her, she knew she had no reason to worry about him. Well, she did, just not that he would hurt her. Not physically, anyway.

Dusty skirted tables, the gold chaise lounges, workers, and ladders. That was one good looking man. It felt as if his easy gait had connected paddles to her chest and unleashed current. Her heart *ba-boom, ba-boom*ed in time to his long-legged stride.

"Red?"

Yikes. *Victor*. She needed to get control. "He's here," she whispered, though Dusty was too far away to hear her. "FBI."

"Careful, girl. I might've been out of it after being shot, but I remember the hot chemistry between you two."

He didn't know the half of it. The kiss that had immolated her soul and all previous records for sexual heat, burnt to unrecognizable ash. So not what she needed right now.

"Red? You there? Or did you melt into a puddle?"

"Uhm, can you handle the first two people on the list?" John and Ellen. "I don't have the objectivity."

"Yeah." He made a sound like regret or worry. "And there might be more people to add to that list."

That sounded ominous. "Who? How would you—"

"Take care of FBI. Handle your side of the list. We'll talk."

He hung up. With a shake of her head, she hooked her phone to her belt, and scowled. Dusty was carrying. *Fudge*.

She'd have to start leaving her metal detectors on during the day.

Though to be honest, that man was hot enough to set

off alarms without the gun. Casual jeans, a short-sleeved gray button-down over a gray T-shirt stretched over his wide chest attested to this fact. As did the sun-brushed skin covering biceps large enough to make her wonder how many pushups he could do.

Probably a lot.

She swallowed, wiped sweaty palms on her jeans.

Agent Leif "Dusty" McAllister stopped feet from her. His seductive honey-colored eyes rolled over her. Despite being dressed like a schlub, he made her feel like she wore a negligee.

"Hey, Gracie. Came to see how you're holding up after that *robbery attempt*."

Oh, that Southern accent. Even sarcasm sounded good. And as for holding up, she wasn't. "Didn't know you cared."

His gaze locked on her so intently she could not look away. "Is that eagerness or wariness in your voice?"

Eagerness? She couldn't deny it. After eighteen months without sex, a mummy could light her spark, and someone as hot as him... Best not to think about that. Way too much on her plate right now. She needed to be cold as ice. "Suspicion. What are you up to?"

He released a full breath, like she'd punched the casual right out of him. "Honestly, I was worried about you. Not just about the other night, but how you've been since Mexico."

The sincere concern in his eyes took her by surprise, reached out and acknowledged the pain that she'd hidden from the rest of the world. Except for the family, the party line was that Tony had run away. Anything else simply wasn't talked about in public.

To have Dusty recognize her grief, along with all the tension and worry of the past few days, was almost too much. Sorrow rose up and filled her throat. She swallowed. "I'm managing. Thanks for asking."

Nerves still on edge and needing to see beyond him, she moved a step to her left—he was so big, he blocked her line of sight to the front door, to any approaching threat.

He noticed and shifted too. His eyes swept the club as he spoke. "Don't blame you for being freaked out. Okay if we talk? Maybe we could go somewhere, have a drink?"

That made her smile. She gestured at the club. "You do realize I own a bar, right?"

His eyebrows rose as if just noticing. He brightened. "Excellent suggestion, Gracie. We can catch up now. Never too early. And you can even make me one of those famous drinks."

"Famous drinks?"

"Now, don't hold back on me. I'm absolutely certain a girl who spent her teen years in a bar knows a thing or two about inventing drinks. And you've probably named them too. Something like Fuzzy Panda or Starry Night."

She laughed, a laugh so spontaneous she had zero control over it. It felt good. Like something inside her had woken from a very bad dream and was stretching its back and purring.

Not good. She squelched her reaction. Forget the fact that someone was after her. Forget the fact that she needed to be on her guard at all times. This guy was investigating her family. And her. "It's called Blood and Guts. But you need some to drink it."

Ugh. She'd meant that to sound like a dismissal, not

a challenge and an invitation. Her face heated. She bit her lip, tried to think of how to get rid of him. Safely.

Dusty smiled. "That's an awful long pause, Gracie. What could you be considerin'? State of the Union? Temperature in Budapest? Last three deposits into your bank account?"

She laugh-snorted.

Obviously, she wasn't going to get rid of him that easily. So maybe she should turn the tables, find out about his investigation, what he had on her family, and if his being around could have anything to do with whoever had shot at her.

All solid reasons that had zero to do with how cute he was.

The cute thing didn't hurt, though.

She shrugged. "The club opens again to the public on Wednesday. I'm usually around."

He shivered. "Brrr. That's a climate-fixing invitation if ever I've heard one." He put on his aviator glasses. Shields up. Game on. "But I'll take it."

Chapter 12

DUSTY WAS A MAN USED TO HARDSHIP. HE'D SPENT MONTHS living his own version of hell at that sex-slaver compound. So being in this ancient house, renting a room from a gentleman simultaneously the oldest, neatest, and most flamboyant person he'd ever met, wasn't a big deal.

It wasn't even a big deal that the room had a double bed with an iron headboard that rattled every time he breathed too heavily. Or that the table he sat at smelled like compressed gypsum aged to dust. None of that bothered him as much as the mural on the bedroom ceiling.

Ducks.

Not graceful, realistic ducks, ducks he could dream of hunting. No. Happy, comic book ducks like Daffy, Scrooge, and Donald. The ducks, like the walls, had a glossy shine and were painted with every color in God's maniac rainbow.

Couldn't shake their happy gazes. No wonder he kept having nightmares.

Or maybe the nightmares had nothing to do with the ducks. Maybe it was the fact that he'd felt more like a hero before he'd met Gracie. When he'd had only the email to go on.

He pulled out his wallet and found the creased and worn printout. He smoothed the paper on the table and read, "When you're adopted into a family whose sole purpose is to train you to fight in their covert war, you lose all sense of yourself. You lose who you could have been. And have to spend most of your life fighting who they told you you were."

That had really struck him. Reminded him of his own messed-up upbringing, sheltered from outside influences, being told and taught to believe without question. It was why—years after he'd gotten free from his father and his so-called ministry—he'd become an FBI agent.

He could see how Gracie's upbringing in itself might've been a reason for writing the letter, but now he knew she had another. Or at least a potential one. Ms. Gracie Divine Parish had a son and a secret identity.

After looking into the True family, he'd come across Tyler's birth certificate. Mother's name was listed as Theresa Sylvia Hall. Trying to find her had caused him a little bit of consternation. But he'd recognized the last name. Hall. It was the same as Gracie's bio-mom. A little research, and he'd discovered Gracie had been christened as Theresa Sylvia Hall before being adopted.

Probably a sin to break into church records, but it surely wasn't his first.

That christened name didn't carry any real weight, wasn't recorded any place legally, but Gracie had used it on her son's birth certificate.

Money. Can't buy you love. Can buy you a secret identity.

Guess when your family was kind of a big deal, and into revenge, you needed to do all you could to secure some semblance of security. Not just for her, but for her kid and her ex.

He had no idea how things had fallen apart with the guy, John. Gracie didn't have contact with him now, but she stalked her son. So something had gone wrong. How pissed had he been when he'd seen Gracie stalking their kid? If he had to guess, pretty pissed off.

Could John be behind that shooting?

Maybe. The better money was on her family and their activities. Still, he'd keep looking into John. Had to admit, he was worried about Gracie. Didn't sit well with him at all that someone had it out for her. He wished she'd trust him enough to let him help with that.

Fuck. He stretched back, and his chair cracked like it was about to give way. The problem with being a big guy in a world designed for average guys, even furniture didn't fit.

He stood up, gave the chair a break. What he needed to find was a deeper way in with Gracie. Not just so he could help her out, but because she was his way into her family. She was the weak link.

Or, to his mind, the strongest one.

Strong enough to leave her family to take care of her dying mother—a woman who'd given her up for adoption. Strong enough to give up her own son, which, judging by her trip to see him, had been a deep and difficult act of love. Strong enough to see past the culture of her family and reach out to the FBI.

She'd sent the letter. Had to have.

But she didn't seem to be reaching out now. Nope. She'd closed up for sure. He'd thought it would be easier. More like her brother, Tony. He'd been pretty easy to befriend, but Gracie was a bit suspicious. And though she'd accepted his invite for a drink, he had no doubt she had ulterior motives. Like feeling him out.

To earn enough trust to get an invitation into the

inner circle, he'd need more than one drink. He'd need to become a regular at Club When?

Maybe if he got close enough to get an invite to the family, he'd work on getting her to drop that question mark in her club name. Irrational, but it annoyed the heck out of him.

He stretched his shoulders, neck, dropped his head back. Damn ducks. Hadn't seen such glassy eyes since he'd worked as a bartender in college.

That's an idea. If he needed to spend time at the club, why not get paid?

He took his cell from the table and hit the speed dial. Mack picked up with a "Yup."

"Mack, do you remember that sweepstakes promo we ran in Philly to get that guy in the Knowles case out of town?"

"The one where we gave him a free trip, so we could set you up as a temp in his job? What does that..." Mack laughed. "You want a way into the club. You're going to make it hard for the lady."

Yeah. That was the plan. He'd feel guilty except for the hope that he could spare kids the shit he'd had to deprogram from his own head.

Now, if he could just cultivate Gracie into the helpful asset he knew she could be.

Chapter 13

THE RAPID CLICK OF TYLER TRUE'S KEYBOARD FILLED his darkened bedroom. His focus on the online game was absolute. His virtual reality headset vibrated against his ears. The VR mask made every hastily fired shot and unexpected explosion seem real.

Real enough that he reflexively jerked his head at a shot to the left of his character. More bullets whizzed by, and he crouched his character by a truck, scoped the area, and dashed forward.

They'd hunted this group through the jungle of Brazil and had fought their way to the drug cartel's remote stronghold. Now he and his team raced across the compound to the rundown building where the hostages were being held.

An enemy combatant jumped out from behind a wall of stacked wooden crates.

Tyler shot. The *bam*, *bam*, *bam* rumbling in his ears. His heart rate picked up. He noted the fear but boxed it, put it off to the side so he could remain calm. The key was to feel all of it—the nerves, the pressure from his team, the overwhelming desire to free the hostages—but not let it take over.

He played with his team, implemented the planned strategy, and moved through the compound. If they failed, the group of stolen women would never be rescued.

When the message slid across his vision, he spared it barely a glance. Until he read who it was from, then his fingers froze. He missed a target, got shot, and died. Four angry voices, his teammates, yelled at him through his headset.

She'd written him back. He'd sent the email to his birth mother like a message sent out into space, a wide unknown, hoping she'd respond. And she had. She'd emailed him. Goosebumps prickled along his skin in a cold wave. This proved she cared more about him than that thing with Dad.

He didn't know what'd happened between them. Dad shut him down whenever he brought up his birth mom. When he was younger that'd been okay. He had a mom. Ellen. But it wasn't okay anymore. So Tyler had taken it on himself to find her. He'd done research, but had come up empty. Until he'd hired a private detective. Now he knew his biological mother was Gracie Parish.

Getting her email from Club When?'s website had been easy. And now she'd written back.

Tyler turned off his headset so he wouldn't hear the other players cursing at him, and opened the email. He pulled his headset down so it rested on his neck, and read.

> Dear Tyler,
>
> Thank you for contacting me. I bet you have lots of questions. I want to answer them. But these aren't answers I can put in an email. Can we talk?
>
> PS. This message will self-destruct after you're done reading it. Remember the number.

Was that a joke? He memorized the number, picked up his cell. The message disappeared. What the heck? He quickly put the number into his phone before he forgot it. He checked his email for the message. It was gone. No sign that it had ever been there.

Huh. That was weird. His mom had computer skills. And owned a bar. *Cool*. His hands shook as he pressed the call button. She picked up on the first ring.

"Hello."

His heart sank. Her voice sounded young, and she had a Spanish accent. Not his mother. He remembered enough of her to know her voice, her hair, her eyes. "Who is this?"

"Cee. I'm your mother's sister. Adopted sister."

Cee. He'd read about her. After he'd discovered who his mother was, he'd researched her family. Cee was the newest sister. "Why didn't my mom call me?"

"She doesn't want to put you in danger. I have less scrutiny on me. We must be careful in our work."

Her work? "You mean as a club owner?"

She paused. "You know of our family, our extended family?"

Our. She was including him in that. It felt surreal. It felt great. Like an adventure was starting. He loved his family. His real family. But it was so cool to be related to the Parish family, with their world-famous boarding school, private jets, private airport, and rockin' parties. He swallowed the sawdust in his throat. "They're wealthy. Powerful. Sort of celebrities. So my mom didn't call 'cause she's afraid of the paparazzi or whatever?"

Another pause, longer. "There's more to this. But

to show…uh, what we do, who we are, you must do a few things."

Anger flashed through Tyler's body. "I wasn't the one who abandoned her kid. If she doesn't want to know me, then fuck her."

He clutched his phone, thought of hanging up. Didn't.

"I'm sorry," Cee said, and she sounded sincere. "This is not what you could have expected, but if you do this, you will live a life unlike what you could imagine."

Tyler's hands were still tense. His anger still red hot. "Just spit it out. I'm done with this shit."

If she had delayed one second, he would've hung up. She didn't. "Tomorrow you go to the nearest corner. The vendor there—"

"You mean the guy with water ice?"

"Yes. He will hold a small envelope for you."

This was bullshit. And weird. But it didn't seem dangerous. Just mysterious. "Okay. What then?"

"Inside the package will be a fake ID."

Yes! "So I can get into Club When?"

"No. Will only make you eighteen."

Oh. That sucked.

"And you must never, EVER, come to the club. Too dangerous. Promise. Right now. Promise."

"Okay. I promise. Then what?"

"Once you have the ID, set up a private mailbox. Not a P.O. box. After, I'll mail you a laptop with Tor on it. Do you know what that is?"

He wasn't a total idiot. "The Onion Router. It's for surfing anonymously and for getting on the darknet."

"Yes. For dark web or darknet. Take this laptop, go to a coffee shop. Not too close to your house. At least ten miles."

"That far?"

"Yes. Once there, boot up. Instructions will appear on the screen. And that's where you will find answers. Promise. It will be worth it. Gracie, your mom, is one of the coolest people, and what we do, the family, is what you see in video games, but in real life. Okay?"

He wasn't sure but couldn't think of any reason not to give it a try. It wasn't his laptop. And it wasn't like he was being lured to a remote location. Or like he was a ten-year-old girl. "How do I get in contact with you to let you know when I have the private mailbox?"

She laughed, and before hanging up, said, "We'll know."

Chapter 14

NOTWITHSTANDING THE STROBING FOURTH OF JULY light show, the inside of Club When? was kind of a throwback. Dusty had noticed this the first time he'd come here. It had a '50s feel. Lots of shiny wood molding with gold stripes and strip lights. Behind the bar, a wall of mirrors reflected shelves of every conceivable craft beer in long, short, and goofy bottles.

The music, photos, decorations, even the drink names—names like I Ain't Heard No Fat Lady Sing—all underscored the Independence Day theme.

The club was packed. Not an empty seat at the bar. Or an empty space around it. People pushed in hard.

The chatty bouncer working the door had told Dusty two bartenders had quit. Now that was a sin. Especially since, coincidentally, a bridesmaid party and a bachelor party had shown up. They were now competing to see who could better hold their liquor. The bouncer had been taking bets.

Dusty had put a tenner on the ladies.

Behind the bar, little Miss Gracie Parish was overrun, making multiple drinks simultaneously, while she nodded to acknowledge people and instruct servers.

Only one other person was behind the bar. A brunette with tattoos, in the server's white shirt and black pants. He pulled beers and gave shots, but Dusty didn't see him making any mixed drinks.

Never say he wasn't a man to help a friend in distress. Even if he had orchestrated that distress.

He navigated his way through the crowd with care. Being as big as he was, he was well aware of his ability to intimidate without trying, so he tapped shoulders, nodded politely, and made his way behind the bar as graciously as he could.

Upon seeing him, Gracie jerked her head in surprise then smiled. Hadn't expected that. Kind of warmed his heart.

He put up a single digit, a *give me a second before you kick me out*. He leaned closer. She was a good foot shorter. "Stopped by to check on you and have that drink." He gazed around. "Looks like you're slammed. Okay if I help? Worked as a bartender in college."

Gracie's face walked the line between *yes please* and *stay the hell away*, then tipped over to acceptance. "I could use the help."

She sent the obviously relieved server back into the club, opened a couple of beers and handed them to a guy across the bar. She took his cash and smiled when he told her to keep the change.

When she turned back to Dusty, her eyes ran down him like it was involuntary. That kind of warmed him too. Warm enough to start a fire.

She pointed to a notepad. "There are two parties that have a tab, try to handle those. You can just write the drinks down. We have the credit cards, so we can tally them later."

She began making a mixed drink, efficient and calm and sexy as anything he'd ever seen. "Cash is king for you. Drink prices are there." She pointed to a laminated document held together at a punch-holed corner with a silver hoop. She winged a slice of lemon around the drink she'd made and handed it to a woman, who handed Gracie a credit card. Running the card, she gave Dusty a quick overview of the cash register.

Basically, he had to push three buttons. He could handle that and the math. "What about credit/debit cards?"

She pulled out the receipt that had just spit from the credit card machine. "I'll handle all people with cards."

"Got it, boss lady."

She smiled, and as she walked away, tossed back, "Thanks. Really."

Lady had a great ass. "Happy to help."

The beat of music pulsed under his feet as Dusty turned and did what he hadn't done since college—tend bar. He went over to a woman he'd seen trying to get Gracie's attention. "Cash, credit, or other?"

"Other. Stevenson. We've got a tab running."

He found the name in the book. Bachelorette party. "Got it. What'll you have?"

The woman smiled in gratitude, or maybe warning, and gave him a drink order that must've been for ten people.

The order was mostly craft beers, so not that hard to line up. As he made one of the mixed drinks, he asked, "Who's winning? I got money on you guys."

She laughed the laugh of the cynical sober. "As the designated driver, I can tell you it's close. My team switched to beer. They're at the point where they think that's strategic."

He laughed. "Couldn't hurt."

She shook her head. "I think those guys ingested fourteen pounds of nachos, so they've got a cushion."

Sounded like he was going to lose ten bucks. Dusty

spotted a bag of pretzels and placed them on the tray next to the beers. The woman, a dark-haired Filipino with a thousand-watt smile, lifted the tray and said, "You must really hate to lose."

He winked at her. "I just prefer an even playing field."

She maneuvered herself from the bar with the caution of a sober person in a sea of drunks.

Quick to learn where everything was, Dusty hit his stride. It wasn't hard to find people with cash or on account, so he didn't hurt for business. For the next few hours, he and Gracie worked, brushing hotly against each other as they buzzed here and there.

But, much to his disappointment, not standing in one place long enough to talk or explore that heat. The crowd kept them hopping. A few people got handsy with him and her, trying to get attention. Nothing they couldn't handle, until the big guy.

Dusty watched him. Impatient as hell, using his size to insert himself at the bar as if the crowd were an insult. He put two fingers in his mouth and whistled loud to get Gracie's attention. She turned.

If it had been him, Dusty would've ignored the guy. But he saw Gracie's eyes evaluate the guy and the situation. A smile on her face, she went right over. They exchanged a few words. She tapped the bar as if asking for his patience and began to turn.

Guy's big hand shot out and grabbed her wrist. Gracie looked at where he held her, said something, smiled like it was the only warning she'd give.

The guy's knuckles whitened on her wrist. A few people at the bar were paying attention now. Someone had taken out a cell. Gracie Parish on camera. Which meant she wasn't likely to pull any self-defense. She surely wouldn't want that all over the internet.

Dusty would've moved to help, but he was sure the lady didn't need it and wouldn't appreciate him butting in. Plus he wanted to see what she'd do.

Still smiling at the guy, she reached under the bar, pulled out a nozzle for the fountain drinks, and blasted the guy, not in the face, but directly up his nose.

Shock and the sting of it had him reeling back. The people lining the bar sprang away. Gracie backed up too but kept hold of the nozzle.

That second was all that was needed for one of the bouncers to move in for the kill. He wrestled the dude, got him under control, grabbed him by the neck. Forcing the guy's head down, he marched the soaked idiot out.

By the time the bouncer reached the front door, Gracie was already getting bar towels and handing them to customers, apologizing for the mess and offering free drinks.

Maybe feeling his gaze, she looked over at him. He'd thought he'd see condemnation, like why hadn't he hot-footed it over there and given her a hand, but she smiled. She smiled and mouthed, "That was fun."

Lady was going to break his heart.

As things slowed—the two big parties headed off for greener pastures and he was ten bucks lighter—they were able to catch their breaths. Even stood side-by-side and made drinks.

He looked down at her. She looked up and stopped dead with a bottle of rum in her hand. Did he imagine it, or was there a slight change in her face, not just the red that crept up and made her look so sweet, but another softening?

She moved off.

An hour later, the club was closed. The servers had left, and he helped clean up behind the bar. "'Cept for that incident, I had a great time tonight," he said.

She stopped stacking glasses on the shelf under the bar and graced him with a full smile. "It happens. But you did great. I'm impressed with the way you can make drinks and conversation simultaneously. You have what my biological mother called the social virus."

He laughed. "That's funny. But just so we're clear, I'm clean as a whistle."

Her face heated. She ducked her head, looked away.

This was becoming his favorite game, making her blush. He returned to wiping the bar, but even with his back to her, he was hyperaware of where she was, when she moved.

All night, the atmosphere in the club had been buzzing in him, through him. He'd assumed it was the crowd, the music, the action. It wasn't. It was her.

Pretty obvious now when he could feel her behind him, smell her, almost hear her intent as she brushed past him and began to wipe the bar area right next to him.

His body heated to tense awareness as her legs pressed closer. This was more than a softening. This was a probe of the heat between them.

He'd take that bait. "Gracie."

She stopped with the bar rag and smiled up at him, a genuine smile. The zing between them caused his blood to surge, hot and eager. She felt it. He saw it in her eyes and the way her mouth parted the slightest bit.

She stood on her tiptoes, fisted his shirt. "Don't talk." She pulled him down and kissed him, long and slow and wet. He put his hands under her ass, pressed her body against his.

Need hummed and throbbed along his skin. They were breathing heavily in no time, moaning against each other, and he was sure it could end only one way.

Then she stopped. She stepped back, stared at him. Her eyes were hungry. Her face flushed with want.

Her gaze rolled across him. "Thanks for helping tonight. I can handle the close."

A thank-you wasn't what he wanted. Needed. "You know, you keep doing that."

"Doing what?"

"Kissing me into madness and sending me away."

"That's because you are you." She waved as if that statement made total sense. "And I can't stop myself"—her voice lowered—"until I remember you're spying on my family."

This woman was one awkward honesty bomb after another. "You don't know that."

"I know you can't admit it."

Had him there. He wiped his hands on a bar rag. "I'll be by for that drink sometime."

As he moved past, she grabbed his hand and squeezed it. Her face warmed. "You're a really good kisser."

Lord help him, but he wasn't the only one not going to sleep tonight. He lowered his head, close enough he could whisper hot sighs in her ear. "It's not just kissing that I'm good at."

He heard her breath catch.

Oh man. The red creeping up her face. His heart jumped and bucked like a bull released from a chute. As bulls went, he came equipped with only one horn, but it was hard and determined and rarin' to charge at her.

Aw, hell. This might've been a mistake.

Chapter 15

Inside her pristine upper level office, Gracie yawned and punched another key on the computer keyboard. She hadn't slept well last night. Having someone who wanted to kill her had turned every noise in her apartment into a threat. And since she'd been awake anyway, her mind had turned to Dusty.

He was a really good kisser.

It's not just kissing that I'm good at.

Ugh. The man was wheedling his way past her defenses. And it was somehow working. *Thanks, hormones.* This was getting messy. She hated messy. Attested to by her upstairs office—orderly white walls, white desk, rounded white grandfather clock, and white leather chairs. Neat and clean.

Everything here was where it should be, and it made her feel better. It reminded her she had control. Things were bad, scary, but she'd set up new security protocols, added panic buttons behind the bar, and had planned a refresher course in threat response for her employees. It was a bar, so they'd take the changes seriously but wouldn't find them suspicious.

She looked at the time on her cell. Almost eleven a.m. Victor said he'd call at eleven. She needed him to call. Still in sweats, she had to dress and head downstairs to handle lunch. But doing that seemed ridiculous when her list of would-be killers was downright unnerving.

Well, actually, it was the two names left on that list that unnerved her—John and El. Because how could she defend herself from them, take them down, and not hurt Tyler? She couldn't. So, what, let herself be a sitting duck?

Her cell rang. Her heart picked up its pace and every nerve in her body rushed forward at the same time. She fumbled with the phone. "What do you have on them?"

Victor answered her anxious tone with, "They seem like a stable couple. Well respected. But there was an unusual transfer of money, ten thousand dollars. I tracked it. It went into an offshore account."

Gracie froze. Her face. Her heart. Her muscles. Her breath. Her vision dimmed to the point where she had to remind herself to breathe. "When?"

"A week before you were shot at. Think you can use your cyber skills to track it down?"

Probably. "Yeah. Send me what you have."

"Will do. How'd you do with your list?"

"One dead. One in jail. One happily married and on a reality TV show. That leaves your two." *It can't be either of them. It can't*. "I need to go back and see who I'm missing."

There was a weighted silence. "About that. What do you know of your biological father?"

"My father? Not a thing." The import of that question hit her. "What do *you* know about him?"

He sucked in a breath through obviously gritted teeth. A snake made less of a hiss. "Well, that's the interesting part. When Sandesh was trying to discover who the family traitor was, he asked me to look into Justice's closest siblings. You were on the list."

She was probably top of that list. She'd been pretty mean to Sandesh. But it hadn't been her. It had been Tony. "And you found out about my dad?"

"Yeah."

She felt a twinge of expectation. Growing up in a dynamic household full of adopted kids, many of whom didn't know or didn't want to remember their families, it seemed almost wrong to ask where she'd come from. And when her bio-mom had come back into the picture, it seemed twice as bad to ask. She'd had an embarrassment of riches, after all. Two mothers who loved her. And though she had wondered over the years, she'd instinctively known that if that information hadn't been painful for her bio-mom, she would have shared it. So she'd told herself she had way too many family members to go looking for more. But now? "Tell me about him."

"First go to CNN. They have a live feed, click on it."

Her fingers flew over the keys. At the site, she clicked on the live feed button. The screen burst into action.

The scroll below the video said, "From the Hyatt Bellevue in Philadelphia, Senator Andrew Lincoln Rush to announce his bid for president."

A man with a lean physique walked onto a stage filled with a group of people as backdrop. He wore a classic blue Armani suit. Music played. His supporters clapped and cheered.

She leaned close to her monitor. Her stomach squeezed. He had red hair and green eyes. *Fudge*. "Is that him?"

"Yes. That's your father."

She wet her suddenly dry lips. The clapping, cheering, clicking of cameras, and talking slowly died down.

Rush welcomed everyone. His microphone squawked. He adjusted it with a smile.

"Are those his kids behind him?"

"Yeah. Five boys. One girl. And his grandkids. There's ten."

"So many."

He snorted. "You can't be serious."

"They're so clean-cut. Kids and grandkids."

"Yeah, it's like a Fashion Week photo shoot back there. The blond woman, the older one, nipped and tucked, she's his wife. The boys range from your age, thirty-two, to the oldest, forty-two. They all have some presidential name, either middle or first name."

"And the girl?"

"The youngest. Layla Eleanor Rush, twenty-seven. Mom kept trying until she had that girl. *Parenting* magazine did a cover story on it, years ago. The article's over-the-top, acting like the mom was Sarah from the Bible and the kid was sent from heaven."

Layla was beautiful. Dressed in an iridescent green silk baroque-style dress. The kind of dress that took confidence and money.

Gracie ran her hand over the monitor. Would they have been friends? Would the boys have teased her? Like Tony?

Unexpected emotion tightened her throat, moistened her eyes. The senator began to talk about one of his sons, Porter Jefferson Rush, who was also his campaign manager. The camera zoomed in on the tall man in the back, who looked exactly like his father. Honestly, it was like they were twins.

Unlike his father, Porter did not appear to like the

spotlight. Sweat ran down his face. He wiped at it, leaned back, waved off the praise. But as his father encouraged the crowd to clap louder, Porter left the stage.

Whoa.

Looked like some family strife. How tight-knit was the family? Could they be one bad news day from falling apart? "Do you think an illegitimate kid, an illicit affair over thirty years old could…" She stopped. "How old is Andrew Rush?"

It was hard to tell. He looked very young.

"Sixty-eight."

Sour saliva flooded her mouth. "My mom was barely nineteen when she had me. Rush would've been thirty-five."

"Okay. So she was a lot younger than him, but still of age. And an affair isn't the reputation killer it used to be. You add in three decades and the fact that you landed in a good place…it's weak motivation."

True. She'd been adopted into a wealthy and respected family. "He's conservative. Maybe he wouldn't want ties to the Parish family."

"Could be. Your lot does have a reputation. But he's dipped a toe into the feminist waters a bit over the years. It hasn't really stopped his career."

If it wasn't fear over the political fallout, assuming Rush was the one who sent the hitman, maybe… "Maybe he's worried about his wife, his family. Maybe they'd turn against him if they found out. That would make running for president a lot harder."

Victor made a noise of agreement. "Good point. That's a big family. Lots of personalities. I'll investigate the lower half."

"I'll take the upper half. Thanks, Victor."

She hung up. A lot of ifs and buts, but enough possibility to send her gut churning. Her list had just grown by eight. She'd have to enter their faces into the club's facial recognition software. If any one of them ever came through her front doors, she wanted to know.

What a crazy morning. First the money transferred from John's account. And now it turned out she might be someone's dirty little secret.

Chapter 16

Porter knelt and cleaned up the vomit from the floor of the hotel bathroom. Great. A thousand-dollar gray plaid suit absorbing gruel from his stomach.

His father knocked on the door again. "Porter? Porter? Are you okay?"

Porter stood. "Go away, Dad."

God, he sounded like a teenager, not a man of forty-two. He tossed the soaked washcloth into the wastebasket and went to the sink to wash his hands. Wetting a hand towel, he bent and wiped the knees of his suit pants.

"Porter?"

"A minute."

God in heaven. The problem with running his father's campaign was that he had to deal with the man whether he wanted to or not. And right now that meant dealing with his father's dirty laundry.

Things had gone from bad to worse to worst. *Bad*. After Porter had intercepted the phone call with Mukta, his father had admitted that he had an illegitimate child. *Worse*. Mukta Parish had a video recording of the woman, girl—now dead—detailing how the senator had drugged and raped her. *Worst*. Mukta had been using the existence of this recording to blackmail his father, influencing how he wrote policy for thirty years.

His father had confessed to the content of the tape

this morning, moments before the press conference. Porter's stomach still rocked.

The handle to the bathroom door jiggled. Porter rinsed with the hotel-brand mouthwash, took a deep breath, and opened the door.

He pushed past his father and went straight to the suite minibar. He grabbed a bottle, twisted the cap. He drank without looking. *Scotch*. He exhaled the heat of the drink. Grabbed another.

Even if people could forgive the "affair," there was no way his father's supporters would ever forgive the fact that Mukta Parish had been initiating policy, directing research and funding for her causes for decades.

A man who was supposed to be strong and principled had been the puppet of a rich, outspoken woman. Porter shuddered.

And Mukta had been devious in the way she'd blackmailed his father. She'd cherry-picked—on votes, personnel decisions, even the focus of the many committees he'd chaired, including Senate Appropriations. Nothing overt enough to cause someone to raise an eyebrow. But if someone went looking for it, knew what they were looking for, they'd see the pattern.

His father grabbed his arm. "Porter, what were you thinking, leaving like that? You have the entire family worried. Layla wanted to come up here. I convinced her and Mother to stay downstairs and entertain at the luncheon."

Porter jerked out of his grasp. He would've preferred Layla. "Go downstairs, Dad. A five-thousand-dollar-a-plate lunch. You need to be there."

"Your sister will handle things. Half the people there are her hipster Twitter followers anyway. Let the campaign go for now. I want to talk to my son, not my campaign manager."

Porter let out a breath. "Trust me, Dad, you don't."

A long moment of silence filled the room. That pause was long enough for Porter to get up his courage. "It was just the one, right, Dad? You didn't do it to anyone else?"

His father took a step back. He visibly composed himself. Sure, the man had had three decades to get used to the idea.

"Just her. Your mother and I were… She wanted a child, a girl. You know. She didn't want me. She needed me. I felt like a tool. Not a man."

"I can't hear this." His poor mother. This would kill her. The personal and social humiliation. Not to mention the national and global scandal.

His father shook himself, shook off the memory or the confession or the guilt. His voice came out as the candidate's voice. "I sincerely regret the decisions I made as a brash young man."

A brash young man? He'd been fifteen years older than the woman he drugged and raped. Next, he'd tell him everybody makes mistakes or that she shouldn't have been alone with a married man.

Porter had to get himself together. Manage stuff. "When was the last time you heard from Mukta Parish?"

The blackmailer, the woman who, when Andrew Rush was elected president, would own him.

"Yesterday. She continues to insist on a cabinet position for her eldest daughter."

Not just a cabinet position, a crucial cabinet position. And why not? She didn't need the money, but she sure as hell needed the power. Especially after learning, through much personal sacrifice and humiliation, there'd been an investigation by the FBI into the Parish family. Suspected vigilante activities. Global vigilante activities. *Christ.*

As if he could read Porter's mind, his father said, "Thank God that FBI friend of yours discovered the case against Mukta was closed. Who knows what secrets would've crawled out of that kind of investigation."

True. The daughter was one problem. Mukta an entirely different one. One that needed a different strategy.

"That's it. We press there, the investigation. Threaten to expose Mukta if she doesn't back off."

His father shifted his stance, massaged his temples. "I've told you, Porter. I can handle this. There is no reason for you to get involved."

Involved? God, the man had no idea. Porter was already involved. Involved to the extent that he had sold his soul. His mental health. For a country that might never appreciate it. But he'd come this far. There was no turning back now.

Chapter 17

HAVING CHANGED INTO A BLUE-PRINT SUMMER DRESS under a light-blue blazer, Gracie made her way through her bar to the corner table.

Dusty sat there wearing cargo shorts and a hunter-green T-shirt. He was eating a burger topped with plantains—the chef's special. Looking *so hot*. That hotness, also a problem. His cute disabled her intellect. She moved a chair and sat next to him at the table. *Not* because he smelled so darn good.

It was the best place to observe the entire club.

The corner of his mouth tipped up when she sat, but he said nothing. Swallowing another bite, he sipped the drink she'd made him and coughed. He eyed the swirly blue mixture with surprise and took another swig. He put the drink on the table and grinned in approval. "Blood and Guts. That's a game changer. And the burger… unexpected but tastes great."

Her heart fluttered, as light and breezy as a butterfly's wings. "I'm glad you like the drink. And the burger."

He lifted the burger to take another bite, stopped. "Thought it'd be less busy during the day, less of an eatery."

She looked around the club. Not the same teeming masses as the night but fairly full. "I accidentally hired a great chef. People started coming in for lunch. Knew a good thing when I saw it, so I expanded the kitchen. Hired another chef."

He put the burger down, swallowed his bite. "Guess that feels like a problem when you're under threat." He nodded toward the front entranceway. "Noticed the new security measures. Metal detector on. Got a guy working security during the day. What else is new?"

Oh, just that her father was a senator with a huge family who might want to kill her. And John and El had transferred money to an offshore account right before she was shot at. "Security is a little personal. Don't you think?"

He stared at her. And heat pushed through her body so fast and hard she was surprised her shoes didn't blow off. "I wish you weren't hot enough to melt my panties."

And there she went.

He barked unexpected laughter. "And that's, what? Impersonal?"

His eyes gleamed with amusement and more than a little lust—and that heat called to her sense of daring. Her brain felt giddy, drunk on hormones. "I just meant couldn't you have some gross ear hair or a less perfect rear end or a less masculine nose or a horrible Philly accent instead of that killer Southern one?"

He wiped his hands on his napkin. "The accent. It always gets them."

"Yeah." She played along, running her eyes up and down his muscular chest. "The accent is what gets them."

He leaned toward her, licked his lips, and in a voice that dripped sex, said, "Smart move with the entrance. Get any info from the security camera footage out back?"

Sheesh. That accent was the devil. She leaned back. "Before you leave, I'm going to insist you come to my office and let me pay you for working last night."

He lifted his eyebrows. They exchanged a long look. His said he understood she was dismissing him. Hers asked what he was going to do about it. The red in her face said something entirely different.

He nodded, crumpled up his napkin, and stood. "Man should never turn down an honest day's pay. Lead the way."

Gracie led Dusty through the club to the back hall. As they passed the men's bathroom, a man came out and nearly crashed into her.

She backed up, reached for a weapon that wasn't there. *Customer*, she told herself, and forced her hand back down.

The man, a big guy, shaggy, grease-darkened hair, an unruly beard, dressed in a hoodie and jeans, eyed her with an intensity that set her heart racing. He drew up short to let her pass.

She watched his big hands flex in his pockets. Every intuitive nerve in her body tensed, readied to respond.

The man's eyes jumped over her head to Dusty. She saw something visibly shift in him. "Sorry," he mumbled and walked past them with an oddly disjointed gait.

What had that been? Maybe she was being paranoid. She turned to Dusty. He was turned, watching the man, who was walking away. Maybe not.

Boxing off the moment for later, she led Dusty through the swinging door that read *Staff only*.

He followed, and in a voice that might've been a bit strained or distracted, said, "Shame about losing both night bartenders. What are your plans on that?"

Another worry. She'd hired back a bartender who'd worked for her a few years ago, but that wasn't going to cut it. "Still forming, actually. At least I learned my lesson with the last two. Never hire people who are romantically tied."

She looked over her shoulder at him. His eyes jumped from her backside to her face. He'd been looking at her butt. A thrill of delight rolled through her, but she reprimanded him with her eyes.

His face warmed. He shrugged in apology. "Ah, so they broke up and neither could take showing up for work?"

"No. The opposite. They called me from the airport. So sorry, but it was the opportunity of a lifetime. They won a two-month cruise."

"Two months?" Dusty choked. "That sounds awfully expensive."

She laughed. They passed the corridor with the steel door that led upstairs, and she hoped he wouldn't notice.

"Steel door? Security pad? That's high-tech."

Of course. Hard to hide the fact that you were a spy from a spy. She grinned at him. "I live upstairs. There are drunk people downstairs. I like to protect myself."

And she had a bunch of servers up there that stored and sorted information for the League. Her only connection to her family right now seemed to be computerized.

He gave an exaggerated, skeptical nod. "Tell me, for that security pad, do you have one of those under-the-skin do-hickies? Some kind of access and tracker, right?"

Ugh. Tony. He must have told Dusty about the Parish GPS, monitoring, and security clearance all in one. And, yeah, she had one embedded in her wrist.

The familiar smell of fried food in the air, she stopped at the door leading into the kitchen. "What else did Tony tell you? You wouldn't happen to know anything about my embarrassing teenage drama?"

He shook his head. "Naw. He was tight-lipped, that one. A good man who seriously wanted to do good. You know he wanted to keep you all safe, right?"

She knew. He'd betrayed the family to stop Justice from making lethal mistakes. It hadn't helped. In the end, he'd sacrificed himself. And Gracie's last words to him? She'd called him a traitor.

That hollow place in her chest, the one that belonged to Tony, opened with a great lurch, echoing with cries of pain and regret that sent physical offshoots into her body.

Stop. She mentally shook herself and whispered, "Must not feed the dragon of grief."

"What's that?"

"Sometimes I wonder if the world survives off pain. If it secretly eats the electric impulses that shock our human hearts."

His face paled. Too honest? Too dark?

"My father used to talk about how the world was alive," he said, "a great snake that had swallowed us, a literal living hell. Claimed we're all being tested to see if we can escape and go to heaven. Me, I think that's an excuse, a way to let pain shut you down. And to do that is to blaspheme the beauty of this world and the gifts we've been given. The grace."

Usually she hated when people used her name as a pun. Not this time. His words felt like an invitation, like he was reaching out. She wanted to reach back, needed... Maybe it was time to live again. Live with the pain. Maybe in spite of it.

Stop it. Of course he's reaching out; he's trying to cultivate me as an asset.

Feeling foolish, played, she sent him a lethal look. A look she hoped hid her fear, her hope, her confusion. "You pretend to care. You genuinely seem to care. But you barely knew my brother. And though I know you'll deny it, and this has to be a game we play"—a game that she knew well and couldn't completely fault him for—"we both know you were using him to get at my family. And now, you're trying to use me."

Chapter 18

STANDING IN THE BACK CORRIDOR OF CLUB WHEN? Dusty felt the biting chill of Gracie's words. Not with her "barely knew my brother" comment, but with the "using her" line.

A server came through the exit side of the kitchen double-doors in a puff of fried onion smell, eyed the two of them, and went on her way.

Part of him sorely regretted not being able to explain why he was here. That he was trying to save people. Her included.

"Your lack of trust seems a shame considering I saved your life in Mexico and all. Apparently, you've forgotten."

She shook her head. "I haven't forgotten. Not that first moment I saw you. Not how you helped save my life. Not how you helped us all get safely away, bundled me into the SUV, and went back and buried my brother." She turned and pushed through the steel swinging door with a whispered, "I'll never forget."

The door swung back and forth as he stood there, dumbstruck. Damn, she'd done it again. Her honesty. It blew him away. Somehow drew him close and kept him apart from her all at the same time. He followed her through the doors.

The kitchen was newer than he'd expected and bigger. Stainless steel sinks, fryers, and large stainless-steel cooking and prep area. Must be part of the expansion she'd talked about.

After Gracie introduced him to her kitchen staff, she led him into a small, pristine, poorly lit office with no windows. A few photos of family and the like, some official-looking framed licenses. A large wooden desk with a single chair behind and one in front of it. Not even a file cabinet.

She shut the door behind him, and he heard her inhaling deeply. Was she sniffing him?

He pivoted toward her, raised an eyebrow. As the skin on her cheeks blossomed with red, she ducked her head and tried to move past him. "I'll get your money."

Naw, he wasn't letting that go. He stepped in front of her. "How do I smell?"

She shrugged. "Not awful or anything."

The heat in her face grew three shades darker, a take-me-against-the-desk red. Or that might just be his warped interpretation. "Hot in here?"

"It's an office adjacent to a kitchen, what did you expect?"

He leaned toward her. "That's not the heat I was referring to."

Wide, angry eyes snapped up at him. "Yes. I get it. I'm desperately attracted to you. You're hot—scorching. I can feel you when I'm alone at night, naked, in my bed. And that makes me afraid, because I'm pretty sure you're using me. Just like you used Tony."

Her honesty was as sudden and disarming as a tsunami. He swallowed. He wanted to be straightforward with her, wanted to tell her something that would make her less suspicious, less afraid. But right now, that felt wrong.

And since the invite was there, he bent down, slow enough to let her know his intention.

She closed her eyes and lifted her lips. He brushed his own slowly across hers, and she made a sound that called to every primal response in his body. His hands snatched out and pulled her against him, fisting a handful of her sundress, dragging it up high enough to get his other hand on that fine ass.

The kiss deepened. And…the woman was wearing a thong. He squeezed the round globe of her ass. Best day ever.

Chapter 19

On tiptoes in her ground-floor office, Gracie moaned against the lips of the hottest man she'd ever met. Electric tingles danced across her tongue. Her entire body hummed, thrummed.

Such a good kisser. His sure, skilled lips drove away inhibition. Drove it away and parked it on the moon. She needed to get closer. She needed him under her.

Ugh. Why wasn't there a couch in here?

Desk. Right behind him. She pushed against his chest. For a heartbreaking moment, he misunderstood. He pulled back, dropped her dress, took his scorching-hot hand from her butt, tried to take his lips away.

No!

She grasped his shirt with one hand, kept his lips to hers, probed his mouth with her tongue. He moaned, deepened the kiss again. *Yes. That. So good.*

She pushed him again. He got the message this time and let her steer him backward until he hit the desk. He sat on the edge to keep from falling.

She kept up, never losing contact with the expert sweep of his tongue. She could not get close enough, not have enough of him near her.

Bracing her hands on his shoulders, she lifted up and straddled him.

He didn't miss a beat. His hands snaked around to grip her butt again, held her against his hard body. *Fast learner.*

She slid her hands up and under his T-shirt, running her hands up and down the silk-skinned muscles of his back. So many muscles. So hard. Speaking of hard…

She lifted for a second, reached between them, unbuttoned his shorts, and freed his cock. She stroked the tip of him. He groaned. "That feels good."

He was big.

She tried to get her hand deeper into his shorts, get all of him, but it was impossible. She made a frustrated whimpering sound. He smiled against her lips, lifted her up with one hand, pulled his shorts down with the other. Their lips never lost contact.

He sat back on the desk. She dropped onto his arching body, like she'd missed him for a hundred years. A thousand. More. She rubbed her wet core against the length of him. The soft, saturated silk of her thong barely kept them apart.

He moaned into her mouth. "That feels amazing. Slick. Hot."

It did. She ground against him, and his lips took hers with fevered need. Their breathing picked up, creating a different kind of music, hot exhales.

He felt so good. The hardness of him. She moved faster, a frantic, pulsing action that made him suck in a breath. He tried to pull back. "Gracie…"

She was so close. The coil of energy building, teasing with the pressure. She kissed him with a fiery intensity, begged with desperate moans in the back of her throat.

"I've got you," he said. He helped her along, using his hands to bounce her ass in a way that increased the heat and friction between them. Oh. That felt so good.

The tension, like the rhythm of their bodies, built to absolute madness.

He whispered about how hard he was and how good she felt, and all the ways he intended to have her.

She gasped with his dirty promises and moaned with the absolute need for him. And she came, right there in her office, her core slick against him, the electric current throbbing through her, releasing waves of pleasure.

Chapter 20

DUSTY SAT ON HER DESK, GRACIE—HOT, SWEET, AND wet—straddling him. His orgasm hit him so fast and excruciatingly good he arched against her, gliding her sleek wetness back and forth against his cock. It wasn't until the last shaking bit pumped out of him that he realized where he was, what they'd done.

Damn. He hadn't come from dry humping since he'd been a teen in high school. That's what a woman hot enough to burn flesh and a six-month dry spell got you. *Embarrassing*.

And yet a good time had been had by all. Then and now.

Breathing heavily, but always a gentleman, he whispered to her about how good she felt, how good she made him feel, and how he still very much wanted to see her naked.

For a moment, her head tucked into his shoulder, her breath hot against his neck, she almost purred, but then she put a hand on his chest, pulled away.

"Uh. Thank you, Dusty."

"And thank you for allowing my hands to make the acquaintance of your sweet ass."

He squeezed said ass. *Incredible*. Did not want to let go.

She blushed and avoided eye contact. "So I'll get you your money now."

He snorted.

She seemed to realize what she'd said and began

to stammer. "I mean, you know, for bartending the other night."

Reluctantly, he released her, lowered her feet to the floor. Woman knew just the temperature of water to throw on him. Cold.

He took some tissues from a box on her desk and a minute to clean up, pull up his boxers, cargo shorts, and zip himself into respectable.

She watched him do all this, straightened her dress, licked her lips once. Her face was a soft, satisfied pink. Her eyes a warm shade of green. Lord, but that had been fun. She didn't seem to want to talk about it, skipped over it like you would roadkill.

She moved behind the desk and sat. He turned to her, realized he could barely stand, put his fists against the desk for support. *Damn.*

She opened a locked drawer in her desk. Was she…? "Gracie, I'm not a proud man, but if you pull out money right now, I will lose my shit."

She closed the drawer, picked out a candy from a dish on her desk. A dish packed with watermelon-flavored Jolly Ranchers. He noticed her hand tremble as she unwrapped it and popped it into her mouth. "What do you want?"

He wanted another shot at her. One where she didn't climb him like a monkey and dismantle every bit of self-control he had. He shrugged, trying for casual. "You need a bartender. I need a job."

Her head snapped up. Her eyes widened. "You want to work in my bar?"

"No. I want to work with your family." *Get access to your momma.*

Her fine red eyebrows crashed together, weighted, it seemed, with heavy suspicion.

"Hear me out," he continued. "I left my job to go undercover with that scumbag Walid to help with your family's vigilante activities—"

"That was Tony's ball of wax."

"For someone so honest, you sure do lie a lot."

She made a stunned sound, as if he'd goosed her.

Huh. Maybe he could've been a little less direct. "Look, I cleaned up a bunch of your family's mess in Mexico. It raised questions at the bureau and got me fired."

He paused to let that sink in but got no reaction. She just watched him expectantly.

He exhaled. "And since I know your family does the kind of work I believe in—the kind that changes lives—and since I know they can afford my fees, I'm trying to find a way into your organization. But since you're not the trusting type, I figured we could start small."

She scoffed. "Don't mistake my lack of self-control for a lack of intelligence. You're investigating my family. Looking into something that doesn't exist." Her eyes darted down and away. Her face heated to a powerful red, a lying-through-her-teeth red.

Well, that made two of them. Despite the smell of their honesty, cum, and sweat thick in the air. How fucked up was that? "Gracie, why would I tell you I'm ex-FBI if I'm undercover investigating you and your family?"

"I wondered."

"Got an answer?"

She bit her lip. Damn, that was sexy. He shut down the replay of the last ten minutes. Not easy.

He bet she did have an answer, and it was probably

pretty accurate. Her cyber skills and family connections were good enough to penetrate any cover he could've come up with. That's why he'd gone with a truthful lie.

She leaned back and stared at him like he was seven layers of chocolate cake and she was on a diet. "Fine. With everything going on, it's better to have you where I can see you. We can call it probation. See how you do."

He processed what she'd said. Couldn't help the big ol' Southern grin. "Probation sounds like one step away from where I'd like to be. I'm happy to take you up on that offer. And any other offer you might want to make me. Boss."

He winked at her.

Her face heated again, but this time with genuine embarrassment. He couldn't help himself. He laughed, a loud burst that prodded a smile out of her. A beautiful smile. A we-both-know-the-truth smile and I'm-still-one-step-ahead-of-you. Was she?

"When do I start?" After all, he had a cruise to help finance.

Chapter 21

Nearing midnight on Sunday, surrounded by the steady quiet of her clean upstairs office, Gracie worked on identifying her enemy.

It was late, but her schedule was tied to the bar, so it didn't feel late to her. Even if she'd been tired, she couldn't have slept.

She'd managed to hack into the offshore account that either John or El or both had funneled money into. It was registered to an LLC. The company was a shell. Impossible to trace. So far. But the money had been used to purchase Bitcoin. And that Bitcoin had disappeared into the dark web.

So, that sucked. It didn't necessarily mean they, or even one of them, had hired a hit man, but if she'd been an average person, without siblings who were assassins, she might go to the dark web for a hit man.

Maybe she should close the club.

No.

Closing the club would bring Momma and Leland around faster than she could say Benedict Arnold. And they didn't mess around. They'd discover the looming threat on her life, including what she had on John and El. And any investigation would definitely lead them to Dusty and her letter.

Her shoulders slumped. Momma would not take any of that lightly. There would be anger and attack and retribution. But the problem wasn't just about her writing a letter; the bigger problem was she had no idea how all of this might impact Ty.

The ungodly loud sound of her phone playing the *Legend of Zelda* theme blasted through the quiet office. She rubbed at her eyes, picked up. "Yeah."

The voice on the other end was a whisper with a soft Spanish accent. "It's Cee."

Cee was calling her? The kid hated her. And it wasn't like she was into random acts of forgiveness. Not with her background. Cee had grown up in El Salvador. She'd lost her father, her only living parent, a few years ago. She'd been thirteen. Her uncle had inherited her father's Salvadoran wealth—and her. He'd squandered the money, sold their house, then sold Cee to a human-trafficking cartel. She'd been fourteen.

Justice had rescued her nine months later. "Cee, isn't it late for you? What are you up to?"

"I'm in North Philly."

"Philly!" *Okay, stay calm. This is not how to get your new teen sister to open up*. "Are you okay?"

"Can you come get me?"

"Of course. But tell me what's going on so I don't have a panic attack the whole way over."

A long pause. "I fight with Momma. And decide to go on my own."

"You ran away? From campus?" *Impossible*. Sure, she and Justice had done it—fifteen years ago. Security had grown more sophisticated since then, and after the drone attack Cee now lived in one of the tightest security zones in the country. "How?"

Cee sighed. Oh, sure, this was annoying for *her*.

"Took out my chip and left it in my room. I hid in the trunk of a car leaving school."

Ouch. She'd removed the GPS chip from her own wrist? Kid was creepy. And brilliant. She'd learned from the League in months what it had taken others years.

Momma had even had her IQ tested and discovered this kid, rescued from an illegal brothel, might be one of the smartest humans on the planet. Still, maybe because of that, she was also one of the most traumatized.

"Okay. Text me the address. Are you in a safe spot?"

A hot sigh. "I'm not a child or an idiot."

Temper. Temper. "Well, you got one of those right."

Gracie hung up, pushed her chair back, grabbed her car keys. As she exited her office, the steel door shut behind her with a clang that sounded final. It locked automatically with a whirring of steel pins sliding into place and a beep. Like all doors on this level and the one leading up to this level, it was blast proof.

She marched down the hall and turned the corner to her apartment to change into her mission gear and concealed carry. Not just because she'd been recently shot at, but because this was no ordinary kid.

Chapter 22

Sitting at the table by the foot of his bed, Dusty stared at his laptop screen. He'd been staring intently at Mack's message for the last few minutes. Made no sense. According to Mack, a DC agent had been looking into the information Dusty had compiled on the Parish family, specifically Gracie Parish.

Why would this guy want to know about her? She was a side player in all of this, not a principal. Up until Mexico, she'd seemed the Parish kid most distant from her family. And though her file contained more information now, including the fact that she had a kid, nothing there explained this guy's interest.

Time to dig into the DC agent. He set to work. A short time later, he'd gotten the basics but dove deeper.

An hour later, he'd found lots of interesting information. The agent was from a wealthy family, had tons of political ties. He pulled up a photo of the guy's lacrosse team. At least three of his teammates were from political families.

Dusty expanded the picture to look at each of them. Nothing remarkable. Except maybe Porter Rush—and only because he had *her* on his own mind.

A lot of people had red hair and green eyes. Still, Rush could've been Gracie's brother. They looked that much alike.

Dusty paused with his fingers on the trackpad. When

he'd looked into Gracie's biological mother, Sheila, hadn't there been something about her involvement in politics? Born in Tasmania, she'd come here interested in the American political system.

She'd worked on a campaign back in the day. If he remembered correctly, it'd been Senator Rush's, right?

It was a coincidence, had to be. Yet…

He set to work. Two hours later, and he had a firm connection between the Rush family and Gracie Parish. Specifically, her biological mother, Sheila Marie Hall and Rush.

A photo of a young Sheila at Senator Rush's campaign headquarters, thirty-some years ago, when he'd first run for and won his seat.

Dusty sat back. Did Rush's son Porter know his dad had an illegitimate daughter? Could be. Porter was running his father's bid for the presidency. He was probably involved with vetting his own father.

So Porter finds this out somehow and then asks his old friend and teammate, the DC agent, to find out what he could about Gracie.

Why?

Could this be the reason a sniper had tried to kill Gracie? The way these political boys got around an illegitimate kid didn't seem so bad, but add in the fact that Gracie's mother had been young, Rush's conservative background, and the weird mythology that had sprung up around Rush's daughter Layla—like the good Lord himself had blessed the family with a girl after five boys—then maybe.

But the agent had also asked about Mukta.

Mukta and Rush. They ran in some similar circles.

And she'd adopted his illegitimate kid. Did Mukta know it was his kid? He'd bet she did. Made for some awkward party talk, surely.

Come to think of it, Gracie's adoption was an anomaly. Gracie had been adopted as an infant, but Mukta Parish adopted only older kids, damaged kids, kids with some sad backstory.

Might be the sick way his mind worked, but it seemed Mukta could benefit a lot by holding this information over Rush's head. Politically a lot. Businesswise a lot. What might a man do to get that kind of monkey off his back?

Fuck. Gracie was in serious danger.

Dusty jolted at the annoying *beep*, *beep* of the alarm he'd set to go off whenever Gracie left the club.

He checked his phone. Sighed. Was it too much to hope she'd sit still for one night? *What are you up to, Gracie?* He rolled out of the chair, grabbed his bat-belt and his keys.

A quick visit to the bathroom, and he headed out of the private entrance and down the wooden steps leading from his room to the driveway.

He jumped into his car, turned the ignition, and checked the tracker on his phone. He'd slipped one onto her phone last night. *Huh*. She was headed toward the turnpike.

He left the driveway and glanced at his gas. *Shit*. He'd forgotten to fill it. *Damn*. This woman was running him ragged.

Chapter 23

Gracie steered her Ford down the well-lit North Philly street lined with duplexes and parked cars. She drove slowly, hoping Cee would respond to her text and run out.

She didn't. Fishing her cell from the cup holder, she tried calling. No answer, but as soon as she hung up, a text popped up on her phone: I'm still inside.

Really, Captain Obvious? She was tempted to double-park, run up and drag her out. *No*. Her training wouldn't let her hang her car out to be marked by anyone who came along.

She circled the block and pulled into a space that hadn't been vacant the last time around. Parking karma. After locking her car, she quickly jogged back to the house.

Baseball hat and sunglasses hiding her face, she skirted the small metal gate and reached the ajar front door. *Ajar?*

Her adrenaline woke up like a spooked pit bull. Hearing sharpened. Awareness increased.

Ducking her head, she reached under the brim of her hat and yanked down the silver, light-distorting face mask sewn into the lining. With her face covered, she pocketed her glasses, slipped on her gloves, unholstered her gun, and crept inside.

Three people, two men and one woman, blindfolded, tied up on kitchen chairs that had been dragged into the center of the living room. All three were out cold. She rushed over and checked pulses on each. *Steady*. Looked like they'd been drugged.

What was going on? The entire floor was a mess, strewn with thumb drives, laptops, and piles of DVDs.

She scanned the area. The room smelled like skunk weed. And ramen noodles. Where was Cee? A startling crash from the basement cranked up the pace on her already pounding pulse.

Gun raised, she stalked into the kitchen—four half-eaten Styrofoam cups of ramen noodles on the table, and the basement door wide open.

Soundlessly, she approached the door, crouched, and sighted around it. The steps down were wooden, thin, worn, and dark. She couldn't see the bottom. Going down there would be stupid. Dangerous.

Her breath hot against her face mask, she started down the stairway. Instead of using a flashlight, she let her eyes adjust. The worn boards creaked under her feet no matter where she stepped or how lightly she trod. Halfway down there was a chill. And the sour, overwhelming stench of layered body fluids. Piss. Sweat. Vomit. Blood. Cum.

Her heart raised an all-hands-on-deck, all-units-report-for-duty, SOS, and Mayday alarm all in one. It was pitch-black on the last step. Tentatively, she reached forward and hit a heavy felt curtain that hung across the basement entrance.

Pushing it aside, she entered quick, quiet, and ready. The room was large but broken up in sections of wood framing. A red light hung from the rafters.

She scanned what looked like a small studio. A bed

and camera were set up with lighting, obviously for filming. A computer monitor on a tall table flashed obscene pictures, screaming women, bloodied, sexual torture.

And by the back door, a heavyset man in all black wearing a face mask trying to get out. He wrestled open a series of locks, including a rusty lock chain.

Gracie aimed at his head. "Hands up."

Her voice came out as deadly serious, as angry, as she felt. The man froze and slowly raised his hands. Gracie ordered him down onto the cement floor. He backed up and got onto his belly.

How many other people were here? Where was Cee? Gracie moved over to the man and began to check him for weapons. Pressing along the sides of his back, her hand sank into padding. *Padding?*

"Gracie, it's me."

Gracie jumped back. *Cee?* She pulled her sister to her feet and leaned in close enough to see her fire-brown eyes through the black mask. "Is anyone else here?"

Cee shook her head. "No. Just those perverts upstairs."

Perverts? Oh God. It all fell into place. Cee was on a mission. The stacks of DVDs on the floor. The people tied up. Cee had set them up. Set them up for who? "What—"

Heavy pounding on the front door ricocheted down into the basement. Cee looked at the back door. "It's the police."

Police? She'd called the police while she was still in the house? The sound of police entering. Their loud footsteps echoing on the floorboards.

Toots on toast. They could not get caught here. In a house obviously used for seedy activity, with three people tied up. It would be all over the news. Momma would kill her. Them.

Gracie reached out and quietly undid the rusty chain, opened the basement door. A quick scan of the area showed no police. She looked back at Cee, who nodded that she was ready.

Flinging the door open, Gracie ran, with Cee a step behind. She heard a gruff female voice call from somewhere behind her. "Police. Don't fucking move!"

Chapter 24

THE OFFICER'S COMMAND ECHOED AROUND GRACIE and Cee as they sprinted across the fenced-in backyard.

Dodging refuse—old sink, mattress, a toppled birdbath—Gracie pivoted so she ran behind Cee, offering her body as some protection to the teen. Not much. The kid was taller.

Cee grasped the rusty fence handle and slid open the six-foot-high wooden gate. The cop yelled again, then shot.

They slipped into the alley. Blue lights flashed at one end. A police cruiser. They turned and ran the opposite way. Police lights bounced into the alley at that end.

Sitting ducks.

They were between two approaching cruisers in an access alley lined with tall wooden fencing. Nowhere to run. Nowhere to hide.

The cruisers inched forward. Had to go over. She turned to tell Cee. She was already scaling the fence, huge fake torso and belly halfway over.

Mad skills. Terrible teamwork.

Spotting an old tire, Gracie ran, hit the rim, and hoisted herself over the fencing. Thank the powers that be she didn't have her belly ring on right now. That would've hurt.

She flipped over the side and landed inside a rectangular patch of yard. Hearing the low warning growl, she had just enough time to grab Cee and yank her back hard. The bull mastiff jerked against his chain. Through her face mask, Cee's eyes were as wide and surprised as someone woken from a nightmare by ice water to the face.

The dog barked and growled like it hadn't eaten a person in three weeks. A light went on in the house. The sliding door screamed open, and a slender man in boxers rushed onto the deck.

Crud. Gracie pivoted and ran. A step behind Cee who was already running. The man's eyes must've adjusted, because he two-finger whistled and yelled, "They're over here!"

Gracie put on her speed, jumped up, way up, and grabbed the edge of the fencing. She swung herself over and landed on the other side a second before Cee. They sprinted across the next yard, over the next fence and the next.

When they had a little distance, she grabbed Cee before she sprinted away again.

"Is the padding dissolvable?"

Cee nodded. *Good*. She'd done that right at least. Gracie pointed toward a covered boat in the yard. "Take off your clothes, ball them in the padding. We'll shove it under the tarp, let it dissolve away any evidence."

Cee crouched by the boat, pulled off the top layer of her clothes, balled them in the padding, and used a penknife to break the seal inside the padding, releasing the liquid.

She shoved the package under the boat's cover. It was already breaking apart in her hands.

Cee wiped her hands on the grass, looked to Gracie. "What now?"

"They're searching for two people, one short, one heavyset. You're neither of those." Gracie pushed her car keys into Cee's hand. "White Ford Fusion. Hail-damaged." She stopped for a minute. "Can you drive?"

Cee's sweat-drenched face looked offended. "Of course."

Of course? Kid was fifteen. Gracie pulled her jacket sleeve over one hand and scrubbed Cee's face, brushed out her hair with her fingers, then pushed her toward the gate. "Wait for me at my club."

Cee pushed back, slowing herself. "I can't leave you."

"Yes, you can."

"I don't..." Cee trailed off as the flash of a cruiser's lights bounced off the fence. They crouched face-to-face. For the first time, Cee looked like a kid. Scared. Vulnerable. Stubborn. "How will you get back?"

Now she was going to try and be a team player? Would've helped if she'd told Gracie what she'd be walking into. "Uber. Now go."

Cee stood, peeked out of the gate to make sure it was clear, and walked out, looking nothing like a big, fat felon and everything like a wayward teen in jean shorts and army boots.

Gracie stood and ran in the opposite direction.

Chapter 25

THE NUMBERS ON THE DENTED AND DINGED EXXON GAS pump ticked rapidly up. Dusty's attention was split between that, the homeless guy wandering the gas station muttering and cursing, and the tracking app on his phone. Gracie hadn't picked up on this one yet. Though she had found the one he'd put on her car.

Tank full, he handed the homeless guy a couple of bucks, climbed into the driver's seat, pulled out of the lot, and headed toward where Gracie had stopped a minute ago. Only a few blocks away.

He turned up his police scanner. It had been filled with casual law enforcement chatter when he'd pulled into the gas station, but things had grown serious. An anonymous phone call. Suspicious activity at one of the duplexes rented by college kids.

Someone had called in an incident on the same block Gracie had gone to. He'd bet money Ms. Gracie Parish was heavily involved and that this had something to do with her family's illegal activities.

For such a little thing, Gracie sure was a big pain in the ass.

He drove past the street she'd been on and spotted a police cruiser. For a split second, maybe a half second, he considered and then made the decision, the box checked.

If she needed him, he'd be there. He'd do whatever he could to help her get out of whatever situation she found herself in. And he'd make damn sure she knew who'd helped her. This could be the thing that got her to open up to him.

Coasting around the North Philly block, Dusty wasn't sure how he'd ended up going from a comfortable, if slightly hot, bedroom two hours ago, to running interference for a woman whose family he was trying to stop.

There was that shaky edge of undercover morality again. Help the bad guys escape the good guys to stop the head bad guy. Confusing.

But here he was. He'd just seen Gracie and a heavyset guy vaulting six-foot fences like Olympians, while the cops began to give chase.

Couldn't have the cops catch her. Not just because she didn't deserve to be in jail, but because it would send her family into further lockdown. He'd never get anywhere near them, and months of investigating would go down the toilet, just when it was getting interesting.

He continued to weave his way through the neighborhood and spotted a cruiser backing out of an alley. It took off. Pulling the wheel left, he slid up to the curb in front of a fire hydrant—no other place to park around here—and flicked off his lights.

With a bit of hope-this-doesn't-come-back-to-bite-me-in-the-ass, and gratitude he wasn't technically on the job, he took his radio jammer off his bat-belt.

To get extra juice, he plugged the black box, with its four antennae, into his car's power outlet and switched it on.

The chatter on his radio instantly died down. *Okay, Ms. Parish, you do the rest.*

Chapter 26

GRACIE FLUNG HERSELF OVER ANOTHER FENCE AND dropped to the sidewalk. Two cops were nearby. She waited to be spotted. One of the officers looked over.

She ran. Not too fast. Behind her she could hear the creak of leather gun belts and the clink of metal and the orders to stop. She picked up her pace.

Through yards and across streets, she ran. Jumping fences and zig-zagging to change direction, she ran.

The footsteps of those behind her began to grow distant. Blood whooshed in her ears. She kept her eyes focused ahead, knowing at any moment the reinforcements would arrive and cut her off.

She rounded a corner and saw no one. Somewhere behind, she heard one of the officers curse and with heavy breath radio in her direction. She climbed over another fence. There was a shed by the edge of the yard. Jumping up, she grabbed the edge, hoisted herself onto the low roof.

Squatting there, sweat plastering her face mask to her skin, her disbelieving eyes searched the area.

Where was the cavalry? Sure, they couldn't keep up, but she'd heard someone call in her direction over the radio. No reinforcements?

This was too good to be true. *Patience. Hold.* Forcing herself to take slow, deep breaths, she waited. A minute later and still nothing. If she waited longer, they might stumble upon her.

Crawling across the roof, she jumped and landed outside of the yard, in another access alley. She ran.

At the end, she altered course on instinct, heading toward another neighborhood. No one behind her, no one ahead. With a sense of detachment, she picked up her pace. This was almost fun.

Not almost.

She vaulted a hedge, ran across the yard. Muscles burning, she ran until she exited the neighborhood, ran down the road, and came out onto Bustleton Avenue.

She stopped beside a boarded-up corner store. Hidden in the dim area behind it, she pulled off her hat and face mask, set them on the ground. She yanked off her long-sleeve shirt and vest, balled them up, and tucked them in her hat. She shoved the whole thing into a packed Dumpster.

Now wearing a white tank top and black cargo pants, she shook out her long hair and started walking. Her phone vibrated in her pocket. Expecting to see Cee's number, hoping the kid was okay, she unzipped the pocket and pulled out her phone.

The number on the screen wasn't one she'd expected. *Dusty?* Her newest employee must've saved his number to her phone. Curious—make that suspicious—she picked up. "Yeah."

"I'm in North Philly. Near Red Lion and Northeast Ave. Need a ride?"

Huh. He was no more than a half mile away. Better than Uber. "Yeah. I'm on Bustleton. Head north. You'll spot me."

Jaw tense, she hung up. There was only one way he could've known she was in Philly. He'd put a bug on her. Not just her car. She'd spotted that one. Spotted it and hadn't bothered looking for others. Sloppy.

A short time later, he pulled up to the curb. The car door unlocked with a click. Yanking it open, she slid into the seat, strapped on her seat belt, and saw the jammer settled between them.

Her eyes rose and searched his. He shrugged. He'd saved her? She wasn't sure how she felt about that. Well, grateful. And something else. Something she'd think about later. Right now, she was also really annoyed. He pulled away from the curb and began to drive.

She adjusted the vent toward her. "You put a tracker on me?"

"Inside your phone case. Last night at the bar."

She closed her eyes. Hopefully disguising how much that hurt her feelings. And insulted her professional expertise. She knew he was after her family; how had she forgotten that? It was all that damn hotness and fun. And look where it had landed her.

Where had it landed her? Seated next to him in an air-conditioned car that smelled pleasantly of Dusty's aftershave. Probably something called Ocean Breeze. She refocused on the jammer. "You ran interference?"

"Yeah."

He wasn't very chatty tonight. "I'm going to need you to stop tracking me."

"I'm not sure I can agree—"

"Promise. Right now."

He shifted in his seat. "Okay."

That made her feel better. Stupid, but he sounded authentic. "I need to call my sister."

"I saw your car take off. Not sure who was behind the wheel. She looked young."

She leaned her head against the headrest. "She is. She doesn't even have a license."

His hands tensed around the steering wheel as the car slid to a stop at a light. He said nothing. Not chatty at all. She dialed Cee's number.

Her sister picked up right away. "Gracie, are you okay?"

"Yeah. How's the driving?"

"I can't move the seat back, but it's okay. I'm"—she paused as if checking something—"forty minutes from your club."

"Okay. I'll be there about forty minutes after you. Don't talk on the phone and drive."

She hung up.

Dusty accelerated with the light change and turned up the air conditioner. Felt great. She was drenched in sweat and stank of it. "Thanks."

"I've got you."

Now why did that comfort her? Like she wasn't alone. Like he really cared. She closed her eyes, waited for him to say something, question her. He didn't. He adjusted the radio to a country station, and they rode with the twangy music playing around them.

After a short time, he whispered, "It's okay to sleep."

The man was some kind of magician, or vigilante whisperer, because her body relaxed instantly, and she drifted off.

She woke later when she felt his warm fingers against her cheek. Her eyes blinked open. Her head was turned in his direction, and he was close enough to kiss. Smelled good enough to kiss. Like man, that Ocean Breeze, and heat.

As if hearing her thoughts or seeing them in her eyes, he leaned forward, kissed her lightly on her lips.

Fire shot through her body. Something in her called out for more. He pulled back, watched her. His sunburst eyes held her. There was kindness there. And more.

She had to know. "You didn't ask. Not one question."

His lips quirked, a little sadly. "I didn't want to get into it. Not tonight. You know?"

Strangely, she did. She didn't want to play the game either. The one where she lied and he lied. And they both pretended that the lies, even though the other knew they were lying, didn't matter.

Without her permission, her heart softened a bit. "Thanks." She swallowed, but her heart still felt too full. "For helping me. For not asking. Thanks."

She moved toward him, toward those lips.

There was a knock on her window. His eyebrows lifted. Gracie turned. *Cee.*

Chapter 27

STRETCHED OUT UNDER THE PLUSH WHITE COMFORTER OF HER bed, in a room with air conditioning set to arctic cold, Gracie blinked open crusty eyes. She had no desire to get up. Her handcrafted California king, a gift from Momma, was hard to leave on the best of days. Today wasn't the best of days. Her body ached.

Mmm, the smell of pancakes and bacon. Her stomach grumbled. With her stiff arms complaining, she dragged off her summer-weight goose down, exposing her white tank top and green silk boxers.

She braced and wrenched herself out of bed. Her legs screamed. Her back screamed. Her butt screamed. Time to head back to the gym.

After going to the bathroom and splashing cold water over puffy eyes, she shambled out to her family room.

Cee had had to sleep on Gracie's sofa. She felt bad about it, but she didn't have an adult-sized bed in her other bedroom. Just a crib and tiny toddler bed shaped like a car.

The blanket and pillow she'd given Cee were folded and piled on the arm of the silver leaf couch. In the kitchenette, the white cabinets were ajar. Dishes, bowls, a frying pan, an egg carton, and pancake mix took up the limited counter space. Gracie usually cooked downstairs.

Cee had done the hard work of cooking over an electric stove with only two small burners. And then setting up all the food—orange juice, plates with pancakes and bacon—on the breakfast bar.

Cee sat on a swivel barstool, feet propped on the stool next to her. She was dressed in Gracie's white cotton T-shirt, staring at her phone. Her hair was jet black, so dark the recessed lights made streaks of purple in it.

Gracie nudged Cee's legs out of her way and sat next to her with a hiss escaping her mouth and a hot *you suck* from her thighs. "Good morning," she said.

Cee lowered her phone. "What took you so long to get home last night?"

Oh, I don't know. I was busy trying to avoid being captured. Gracie took a strip of overcooked bacon and began to chew. "Don't cop an attitude."

Cee's sharp jaw extended as she pursed her lips. "I thought *cop* meant 'police.' *Cop* also means 'to have'?"

Whoops. She kept forgetting English wasn't the kid's first language. "Yeah." Gracie took a couple of the scorched pancakes and added them to the plate in front of her. "Where's the syrup?"

Cee blinked at her. "I couldn't find it."

"It's in there." Gracie pointed at the fridge. "I can't stand without shock waves, so do you mind?"

Cee got up, walked around the bar, and retrieved the syrup. She put it down and flounced back into her seat. "You might need some better conditioning."

Said the kid who ran a quarter of what she did. Still, she hadn't been to the gym in...well, since Tony. They'd trained together most weeks.

Gracie poured syrup on her pancakes. "You're welcome for the rescue, by the way. Who were those people last night?"

Cee began to fill her own plate. The kid had been waiting for her to eat? Kind of sweet.

"Six months ago, the two men you saw drugged and brutally raped a girl. Someone who went to their college. She was lured by a friend, the girl you saw last night. That is their way. They use a girl to lure another. The girl who'd been raped tried to go through normal channels, but she was drunk and using that night. So that disqualifies her from humanity and justice."

Gracie cut her pancake. "How'd you find out about her?" She put a piece of pancake into her mouth. Not bad.

"Someone who went to the Mantua Academy happened to know the girl. She told Jules about the case. When I heard about it, I did some research. I organized the mission."

Jules. Another sibling. She and Cee were in the same unit—so they trained, learned, shared a hall, formed a bond. And though Cee was acting like it was all her idea, she doubted that was true. Cee didn't have the computer skills to pull this off. More likely it was her, Jules, and Jules's twin, Romeo. Swallowing another bite, she said, "That's against the rules."

"Research showed the victim had filed a police report. The police had interviewed her. It seemed it would move forward, but then was dismissed. My research also uncovered more. The proof I left on the floor of that house. This is not, how you say, a single incident."

"Isolated. You mean an isolated incident." Gracie used the bacon in her hand as an accusatory finger. "And I meant you went against the rules of engagement. You went in there half-cocked. Tied people up. Drugged them. You could easily have left evidence that leads the police to us."

"I was so careful."

"Was getting me caught part of your 'careful'? If I had been a little slower, and you a little faster, I would've been caught while you got away."

Cee poured syrup over her pancakes, speared one with her fork, lifted it, and bit the dripping edge. "I didn't think..."

"Exactly. I need you to send me all of the information you've collected. You can't start a splinter vigilante group within our already illegal vigilante organization."

"Thomas Jefferson said, 'When injustice becomes law, resistance becomes duty.' I was merely doing what I came here to do."

Great quote. "And that's why you fought with Momma?"

"I'm not a child. I want to go on missions. I want to do the job. Unlike you."

Gracie finished chewing her bacon, swallowed some coffee. Whoa. Dark as Cee's hair. Like Justice's hair. Cee reminded her of Justice in a lot of ways. All that anger. Too bad there wasn't an off button for aggression. She wished she could make her new sister understand. Anger was useful on occasion, but when it became the go-to emotion, it poisoned. It ate you up and turned you around and made you see the world as your enemy. And Cee deserved better, an opportunity to live a life free of that. As much as that was possible.

"Okay. So you got mad, pulled out your chip, ran away, and decided to go rogue. So why call me?"

Cee took two large bites of her pancake and took a long swig of OJ. She chewed, wiped her mouth with her hand. She had her attitude set to block and parry. "Because I wasn't sure you'd come."

"Meaning?"

"Meaning if the one person who didn't want me anywhere near the League came, then..." She shrugged, swung her legs back and forth.

Gracie's throat grew tight. The kid had decided that if she could trust the person who had admitted she was openly against Cee being adopted, then she would give the family another chance. That hurt.

"I deserve that. And I'm sorry. But does Momma? Why go through the adoption process, just to run away the moment things get uncomfortable?"

"You do not understand." With a clang, Cee tossed the fork full of half-eaten pancake on her plate. She curled her hands in her lap and fisted the baggy tee she wore, revealing the jean shorts underneath. "I am here to fight. To rescue. To save. I can't do that in my bed by ten. I can't take out the bad guys if I'm studying math."

Gooseflesh winged across the expanse of Gracie's skin. She understood how the League could make you feel—not just that you could do something about the injustices, but that you should. Needed to. "The rules are for everyone's good. This isn't about you, about one person. If you don't want to play by the rules, tell Momma you've changed your mind."

She was so young. She should know that she had a choice. She could change her mind. "If you don't want adoption, that's fine. It'll be fine. We can set you up anywhere. I promise. We'll take care of you."

Cee's cell beeped. She picked up her phone, texted something. Was her lip trembling? She looked back up with eyes as fierce as a tiger and as attentive. She stood up. "I am not leaving my family. I am where I want to be. I am a Warrior Woman."

Pulling off her T-shirt to reveal her jean shorts and the tight blue tank she'd had on last night, she marched toward the front door.

Gracie stood. What had she said to make her so upset? She was trying to help. Cee was the one who'd run away, taken out her GPS chip, said all the stuff that indicated she wanted out. "You can't leave here without me putting in the code. I'm the only one authorized to allow unchipped people in or out of this level."

Cee paused with her hand on the door. "What about the elevator? It's just password protected, right?"

Kid couldn't find the syrup, but she'd found the secret elevator? Gracie's eyes strayed automatically to the inset bookcases flanking the window seat. Both bookcases were stuffed to the brim with books. And behind one of them was a hidden compartment.

"No, you can't use that either. It only leads to the basement." To the tunnel there that led to the warehouse.

Cee frowned, frowned the way a smart person does when they come across something that makes no sense. Gracie waited for her to ask. She didn't. She crossed her arms over her chest. "Then let me out. I'll call Momma. She'll send a car."

She wasn't going to let Cee make her feel guilty. Curds and whey on a big hairy spider. She did feel bad. "You want to do the work? Let's start with training. I'm going to go through last night's mission on the way to Momma's. Step by step. I want you to know exactly what you did wrong."

"You're driving me?"

"Yep."

Gracie wasn't sure, but she thought she saw the barest

hint of a smile, the repressed hope of a hardened teen, flit across Cee's face.

Someone in a light-blue Toyota Camry had followed Gracie to the Mantua Academy when she'd dropped Cee off. Thankfully, Cee hadn't seemed to notice. That would've been bad. Cee would've asked questions, mentioned it to Momma.

Disaster. Momma and Leland would not only have asked questions, they'd have gotten answers. Answers that would lead them to John and El, to Gracie stalking her son, to the threat on her life, to Dusty and her email. Her betrayal.

Shudder.

Momma and Leland and the League would go on the attack. Gracie had no idea what the blowback might be on Tyler, but it would probably end her attempt to become part of his life. Once her family was involved, this would be out of her control. It would get messy.

She couldn't let that happen.

Gracie carefully checked her mirror as she continued up the long, winding road. Yep, the light-blue Camry still followed. And whoever drove that car had no stealth. Either he wasn't very good at his job or he wanted her to spot him.

The disturbing idea that she was being herded flashed through her mind, but she dismissed it as grandiose. Even if someone could've worked out her reaction to a tail, few people knew the Mantua Academy owned a hundred acres of heavily wooded, uncultivated land in Bucks County. It was where the family practiced drills, basic survival skills, and tactical maneuvers. And it was where she'd confront her tail.

Crud. Backup would be nice. Challenging this guy in the isolated woods was dangerous. Not as dangerous as letting this surveillance continue. Time for a showdown.

Hands sweaty against her steering wheel, she reminded herself it would be okay. Her knowledge of the land and her stealth—judging by his driving he had none—would give her the upper hand.

She turned her car into the hidden drive. At the lift bar that blocked access to the property's dirt road, she got out and waved her chip over the lock. It clicked open. She undid the chain, swung up the bar. After rolling her car inside, she put the gate back into place.

If this guy was intent on following her, he'd have to do it on foot.

Her car bounced along the dirt road for nearly a mile. At the barn, a rickety wooden structure worn with age and greened with moisture, she pulled onto the grass and hid her car behind it.

A quick visit to her trunk, where she fished out a camo shirt and hat from her bugout bag and grabbed some zip ties.

Her heart and her hope ticked up a notch. This was it. An opportunity that felt like action instead of reaction. A real lead, a chance to get answers. She needed this to end. The longer this went on, the longer the threat on her life was out there, a looming unknown, the greater chance things would escalate, the greater risk this could impact Tyler.

Crossing the clearing, she used one gloved hand to push past the archery range netting and into the woods.

The wail of cicadas, buzz of bees, and chirp of birds

masked her movements over uneven ground, thick with brambles and heavy with vines that snaked around trunks like anacondas. she had some stealth. She made her way as silently as possible over the uneven ground, thick with brambles and heavy with vines snaking around trunks like anacondas.

With the skill of a cat stalking a mouse, she circled back and snuck up behind the guy.

She heard the man before she saw him. He was big. Not as big as Dusty. But tall and muscular with a peculiar, duck-like way of walking.

Wait. The way he walked… It was the guy from the bar, the one who'd given her the evil-eye after coming out of the bathroom.

Slowing her footfalls, her heart picked up its pace. Adrenaline spiked, her focus tightened on the man. Dressed in nondescript, dark clothing, his hands clasped in front of him. *Toots*. He had a gun.

She'd been moving up, closing in on him, but drew up short, creating more wind than noise. Still, he stopped, spun in her direction. She ducked behind a tree. Bam, bam, bam. One shot vibrated through the trunk.

He missed every other time. Not a great shot. She could lean out and shoot before he knew it.

But she didn't want him dead. And if she had to injure him, she wanted to do it in a way that allowed him to still communicate.

She broke from her cover. Zigzagging into the woods, another bam, bam followed her.

The ground dipped, she crouched used the dip to cover her progress. Ahead. A dead tree.

Sometimes being petite didn't suck.

She dropped down, shimmied inside, through wood shavings, spider webs, and crunch of roly-poly bugs. Gross. Moss laced every inhale. A moment later, he crashed after her, slid down the embankment with a curse. He slowed, scanning, breathing heavily. His loafers wet with grass and mud stopped not more than ten feet from her.

Her heartbeat which usually normalized quickly after exercise, kept up its frightened Muppet-arms in space pace. She needed to be fast.

As fast and deadly as her training, she burst out, rushed forward. He turned. Not fast enough. Her fist snapped against his side and carried the full weight of her body.

He cried out, lost his weapon, grabbed at his side. She kicked his kneecap, sent him to the ground. Securing his wrists behind his back with a zip tie, she picked up his gun and searched him. No cell phone. No wallet. So not a total idiot.

Pocketing his weapon, keeping her own out, she moved around to his front.

He lifted his head. "This is not legal."

No kidding. She got him to his feet and began to march him deeper into the woods. Never can tell when family might show up. "What's your name?"

"Wilkes. James Wilkes."

"You are on private property, Mr. Wilkes. There are *no trespassing* signs all over."

"So call the police."

He tried to turn; she put her gun into his side. "Call and tell them what? That I stood my ground? You came on private property and shot at me, after all."

"Call them," he insisted. Panic worried his voice into a higher octave.

He should be worried. A woman who feared for her safety, the safety of her family, of her child had a gun to his side on private property in the middle of rural-as-an-outhouse USA.

Once she'd marched him far enough into the woods, she slammed her fist into his kidney. Wilkes buckled like origami. On the ground, he curled onto his side.

His face was beet red and tears leaked from his eyes. He rotated his face against the earth. He sucked in a breath, drawing in a bit of leaf and dirt. He coughed it out, wiped his lips on his shoulder.

She squatted beside him. "Why are you here, Wilkes?"

"Porter Rush," he wheezed, "wanted information on you."

Gracie nearly bit her tongue in half in the aftermath of her shock. Sure, this wasn't Austin Powers, and she didn't need to ask him three times, but who gives up the ghost on the first question?

Which meant he could be lying. But for who? Gracie grabbed the guy's shoes, dragged them around, forced him to sit up. He cried out, gasping for breath.

She put her hand on his bent knee. "Why you?"

Sagging over his knees, he whispered in a voice minted with mud, "I work for him, for the campaign."

"Rush's campaign?"

"Yeah. I do deliveries and stuff."

"Volunteer or paid?"

"Volunteer. I'm on disability. It's something to do."

Disability? Crud. "What's wrong with you?"

"Bone cancer. Could you take your hand off my knee?"

Gracie pulled back her hand like it had been lit on fire. Cancer. The way he walked… It'd been pain. She winced, remembering how much pain her mother had been in before cancer took her life. "Why did you agree to this? Why not let him pay someone? He's got the money, you know."

"You can't trust no one in this business. They're all out to get you. Porter knew he could trust me. I owe the senator my life. What's left of it."

She was sure there was a longer story there, and she was interested in any good her father did, but she couldn't be distracted by those things. "So you took it on yourself to kill me?"

"I didn't… You startled me. I… just reacted."

Maybe. Or maybe he was lying. "What did he ask you to find out about me?"

"If you visited anyone. You know, like a boyfriend or maybe someone you cared about seriously."

That was a very bad thing for Porter to want to know. A thing that meant he was thinking about going after those she loved, not just her. "What did you discover?"

The guy's face was only splotchy now. His tears dried. The dirt on his face mostly drifted off with his movement. But he still held his shoulders hunched and looked like he'd been defeated. Gracie had to harden her heart. Not think of this man trying to do something he thought was good, trying to live his life despite the pain and…

"I know you have a kid."

Her heart froze solid. "Did you tell Porter this?"

He looked away, as if he didn't want to answer, but shook his head. "Not yet."

She was going to have to make sure he never did. "How'd you find out?"

"I've been following you and the girl."

Gracie let out a breath that vibrated with relief. This man had no idea how close he'd come, how close she'd come to having to… "I don't have a kid. That was my sister."

His eyes widened. "Oh."

"You suck at this."

"I know."

She went around behind him, sliced off the zip tie with her pocket knife. "I'm going to let you get back in your car and go. You tell Porter that we need to talk. I'm not a threat to him or his father's campaign." Unless, they threaten me. "Let him know that. And don't follow me again."

She came around to his front, helped him to his feet, caught and held his eyes with her own. "Understand?"

"Yeah. I got it. Thanks."

Stepping back, she indicated which way was out and watched him limp out of the woods. Porter would never call her. But at least she knew a few things. He knew about her. He knew she was his sister. He wanted to find out more about her, about who she loved. That meant he was planning something. Threatening her?

But why send a guy who was not only incapable but sick? That made no sense. If he'd already hired a sniper to kill her, why send this random guy after her? So risky.

Unless… He could've wanted her to know that someone was following her. Distract her while he came at her from a different direction, plotted against her elsewhere.

That was really paranoid.

So why did it seem like she was on the right track?

Feel that way in her gut? No one ever talked about how a political figure's affair might affect his family. And Porter, who had so much to lose... *Poop*.

The truth was, if she wanted to end this nightmare, go back to trying to find a way into Tyler's life and make herself respectable enough to deserve that opportunity, she was going to have to fight for it.

Chapter 28

Early afternoon sun and the July heat wave screamed against the hood of Dusty's Dodge and front windshield. He wiped sweat from his face, deciding whether to turn the car back on.

He was already at his destination, the partially full parking lot of Club When? And would've gone in, but his cell was ringing. Mack.

Too damn hot. Turning the engine over, he picked up the phone. "Secret Agent Man," Dusty said, "got something for you."

"Good to hear it. But first, something personal. Your dad's in a hospital in California."

Dusty's hand flexed around the phone as the air in the car started to cool. "That fucker. He let my mom die." He'd nearly let Dusty die too. Not to mention torturing all the other followers of his crazy ministry with his *let God heal 'em* policy. "Getting treatment?"

"Yep."

This was it. This would do it. His ministry would shut down. "Tell me his followers have wised up."

"Some. Not all. He told them he had a vision. God told him the exact man who would heal him, gave him his name and everything, so it's like God's healing him. Crafty SOB."

Same boat, different river. "Thanks for the update, but from now on, I don't want to hear unless he kicks it."

"Understood. What you got for me?"

Dusty pushed his sunglasses up on his head as he watched a group of people get out of a car and walk around the side of Gracie's club, headed to the front door. "I think Gracie Parish's biological father is Senator Rush from Pennsylvania and the front-runner to become the next president of the United States. And I think he's being blackmailed by Mukta Parish."

Mack was silent for a long moment. "Keep going."

Dusty quickly explained to him what he suspected about the connection between Gracie, Sheila, Mukta, and Rush.

"Did you send me any of this?"

"Not yet."

"Good. Don't."

Don't? "Okay."

"How sure are you about this blackmail thing? What is Mukta Parish getting from Senator Rush? She obviously doesn't need the money."

No. She didn't need the money. "It's only preliminary. But recently, Rush pulled a bill he'd sponsored that would've raised the bar on women proving workplace discrimination. Came out of nowhere. It's the kind of bill Mukta Parish would've openly disdained."

"That's a bit mild. Almost influence peddling."

"Not so mild. Some of the senator's key decisions have resulted in benefit for her companies and power for her family."

"Like?"

"He supported one of Mukta's daughters, helped get her a judgeship for the Eastern District of Pennsylvania."

Mack whistled. "Okay. You've got me interested. If

you're right, we could take out Mukta. And expose these crazy bitches."

"Hey. Dial it back." *And don't call Gracie a bitch unless you want my fist in your face*. "What about getting Rush? He's in this too. Could be after Gracie Parish."

"Yeah, well, thirty years is a long time to be someone's lap dog. He could help us here."

"What? Hold on." Dusty watched a woman from the club wobble across the gravel parking lot to her friend's car. Heels, gravel, and lunchtime mojitos didn't mix. Maybe he should talk to Gracie about paving. "I'm not convinced that what Mukta has on Rush is just an illegitimate kid. Let me do my job."

Mack grunted. "You think she has something else on Rush? Something dark enough to get him to initiate policy for her for thirty years? Something that made him want to kill his bastard child?"

He did. Because in this instance, going after Gracie felt personal. Or maybe it was just that he took it personally. He intended to find out. "You interested in knowing for sure?"

"Yeah. Let's step on some toes. I'll work my end. See what you can uncover between them. And, Dusty, this is it. Get the job done."

"You picking up the tab now?"

"Yeah. But let's keep this between us."

Between them? This was it? Mack was worried. Seemed like time was not on their side. "Will do, Mack."

Dusty hung up, switched off his car, got out, and faced the heavy fists of July heat as he headed into the club. He'd come to town looking for one case and had stumbled onto something entirely different.

Chapter 29

Gracie held open the back door of Club When? to let one of her chefs, Jack, wrestle boxes of meat through. Once he passed her, she picked up her own box and let the door shut.

They'd had to pick up from her local supplier, because the farm's delivery truck had broken down. Normally, that wouldn't be a big deal, because Gracie padded her deliveries, but she'd been distracted lately by the threat of death, and they were running unusually low on supplies.

After putting away the meat, she apologized to her chefs and returned to her office near the kitchen.

She sat down at her desk to make a record of what they'd received, and her cell rang. *When it rains…*

She picked up. Leland's gruff voice greeted her with, "Where did you find Cee?"

Ready, set, avoid. "Philly. She regretted running away and wanted someone to come get her. At midnight."

Leland gave an exasperated sigh. "She's a handful."

Yeah. Which was why they didn't usually adopt that late, but she wasn't bringing that up again.

"Why'd you go to the fields yesterday?"

Of course. Gracie considered the bowl of watermelon goodness on her desk. Even went so far as to pick one up, twirl it in her fingers. "I was just reconnecting with nature. Needed a break from the bar."

A heavyweight pause. A pause that weighed as much as Mike Tyson and Tyson Fury combined. "You've changed security protocols at the club. Something we should be aware of?"

Yes. But nothing she'd tell them. "I had an incident in the club. No need to worry about it. Been planning to change things up for a while anyway."

"Gracie, you know we're on your side here, right?"

Gracie's heart sank. Normally, that would be true. Normally, there wouldn't be any doubt in her mind who could protect her, help her, support her when she was in trouble, but not now. The League was still reeling from the drone attack and the loss of Tony in Mexico. And the truth about the danger she was embroiled in was messy. And somewhat her fault. "I know. Thanks, Leland."

She hung up. And her cell beeped letting her know the facial recognition software out front had identified someone. She opened the screen. *Toots on toast*.

John.

A moment later, the door to her office creaked open. She looked up. Her heart jumped into her throat. She pushed it back down with a swallow as her fingers fisted around the Jolly Rancher.

John walked through her door, closed it. She froze. Not just deer-in-the-headlights froze, Neanderthal-trapped-in-ice froze. Only her eyes moved.

He looked the same and different. Still thin, with a runner's body, but no longer the wiry teen she'd once known. He'd filled out. He was wearing a blue suit, tailored and tapered and too trendy by far. His dark hair slicked back. His dark eyes focused.

And she felt…nothing. Not the stirring of lost love,

not the longing that had held her for a decade, not a spark of lust.

John's perceptive brown eyes traveled up and down her black-and-yellow Club When? T-shirt, scholarly bun, and the startled look on her face.

He nodded. "Hello, Gracie Divine."

Crud. That was a jab, saying her first and middle names. As if her name were contradictory. He used it when angry, had done so ever since that day she'd told him the shocking truth about her family's activities—her activities—a shock that had destroyed them.

She sat forward. "It's been a long time. I wasn't expecting you."

Oh, good. Her voice sounded normal. That normalness steadied her breath and her mind. She might be able to get through this.

He ran a hand over his face and through his slicked-back hair, then let out a breath deep enough to dispel old feelings or push them into the past. "I didn't want to give you a chance to prepare."

Gracie discreetly reached down and checked the gun attached to the bottom of her desktop. "Prepare for what?"

"I'm here to get you to stop. Stop with the computer. Stop coming by my house. Stop stalking my son."

They'd detected the backdoor she'd made for Victor on their computers? *No way*. "I stopped—"

"Don't lie, Gracie. We saw you."

Lie? She'd stopped going by after his text. Even though it had killed her. "Was it so wrong, wanting to see him?"

John leaned against the door, as far from her as he

could get and still remain in the room. He shook his head. "You don't get to see him. That's the agreement. I stay quiet. You stay away. You get your precious League."

This was it. Her opportunity to tell the truth. And to fight for a chance to be in Ty's life. "Let's stop here." Her heart paddled the breaststroke into her throat. "I need you to know the truth. I didn't want you to go. After I told you about the League, there was blowback from Momma and Leland." This felt like betrayal, but it needed to be said. She exhaled a deep breath. "I sent you away, told you I chose the League over you and Ty to protect you—"

"Stop." John adjusted his tie, coughed. "You asking me to leave was a relief. After you told me about that chip thing under your skin..." His forehead pinched together. Disgust? "I'd planned on going and taking Ty."

The candy she'd been holding dropped from her hand and onto the desk, cracking inside its translucent wrapper. He'd planned on taking Ty away from her? "You planned on taking Ty away from me? But I thought... you loved me."

His dark eyes flashed with something—a spark, a memory—and for a moment she saw the young man she'd fallen in love with. "We were young. What did we know of love?"

Like a decade's worth of candles being blown out, her old image of John vanished in a puff of smoke.

"I loved you. I gave up my son to keep you safe. To keep you whole for him."

He stared at her. "For me?" He shook his head. "Leland and Momma knew I was going to go. I told them if you fought for custody, I'd reveal what I knew about their illegal activities. If they told you something different, gave you some story..."

For a moment, Gracie's world tilted on its axis. Everything she'd thought she'd known about giving up John, about being forced to give up John, suddenly shifted. Like when she'd found out Bruce Willis was dead in *The Sixth Sense*, her mind began unraveling all the clues she'd not seen before.

And the undeniable conclusion. John had threatened Momma and Leland. When Momma and Leland had offered her the choice to take John's memory or let him go, they were letting her decide what they should do.

She flushed a red so hot it felt like someone held a live wire to her skin. Her cheeks were flames of distress. She'd been an idiot. "So if I'm no longer involved with the League, just a woman who owns a pub, and Ty wants to see me?"

"Come on, Gracie. You have to know that..." He hesitated, and then, "There's no way I will let Ty anywhere near you or your family. I don't want him to know what you all do."

"What we do? Rescue people? Stop pedophiles? Stop abuse? Defend those without power?"

"That's not your job."

She honestly could not get enough air into her lungs to tell him about her creeper detection software, her work. He disapproved of her. Not Momma. Not the League. Her.

Her stomach roiled with sticky tentacles of regret. "We need to talk about this, John. I'm not going to go away this time."

"Don't say that." He surged forward, hands balled into fists. The crisp blue suit, polished and professional, contradicted the impulsive anger behind the action. "I'm not putting up with any of that craziness in Ty's life. I have another son. A wife. Don't come around. Don't test me."

"Are you threaten—"

"No. No. But I will do what I have to do to protect my family. Remember that."She hadn't recognized when he'd taken Ty what he'd been capable of. So what was he capable of?

"You realize that's a threat, right?"

He glared at her, turned, and stormed out, slamming the door behind him—on her, on their past, on the lies—with a firm click.

She sat back and clasped her trembling hands tightly between her knees.

Chapter 30

Entering Club When? Dusty noticed a guy coming out the front door. He held the door open for him. The guy's eyes traveled up, widened at the sight of Dusty. That made two of them. Gracie's ex, John.

Dude looked pissed. What was he doing here? Probably none of his business, but that didn't mean he wasn't going to find out.

Passing through the club, Dusty went into the kitchen. The smell of French fries reminded him he hadn't eaten this morning. He shouted hello to the chefs, gave a thumbs-up to the distracted dishwasher before heading to Gracie's office.

The door was open a crack. He toed it with his boot and it opened the rest of the way. Gracie sat behind her desk, sobbing into her hands.

Shit.

She looked up and immediately buried her face in her hands again. "Go way."

She probably meant away, but that's not how it came out, so…

He closed the door, walked around her desk, spun her chair toward him, and took a knee. He leaned close enough that his shoulder practically kissed her forehead. "Gracie."

She slumped forward, dropped her head onto his shoulder. He put his arms around her shaking body.

His own heart picked up its pace. What had John done? What had he said?

He lifted her up, brought her onto his knee, and held her tighter. "What's wrong?"

For a few wracking minutes, she sat there crying. Her tears dripped onto the shoulder of his gray henley, her fingers dug through the fabric into his biceps. Then her breathing evened out, her tears slowed. She slid off his knee and into her chair. "I'm not sad. I'm angry."

He shifted onto his haunches, reached over to the tissue box, got a tissue, handed it to her. "At what?"

She blew her nose, tossed the tissue into a can beside her desk. "At myself." She looked him directly in the eyes. "I gave up my son to protect his father, who could not have cared less."

Her stare was a direct challenge. If he admitted knowing she had a son, he as good as admitted to investigating her. Her family. And after what Mack had just said…time was not on his side. His throat grew tight. Aw, hell. "Tyler. Your son. You gave him up to protect John."

She closed her eyes in what looked like relief, exhaled, opened her eyes, and told him the story. Well, the bones of it. Her family didn't "get along" with John. He didn't approve of some of their "business practices."

After saying that, she blushed a red so deep he could feel the heat on his own face. "How did John find out about those particular *business practices*?"

She shrugged. "I told him. I know it sounds hard to believe, but I was naive."

Not hard at all. "You'd been educated in the Mantua

school, adopted into the Parish family. All your experiences, schooling, spirituality, had been filtered through that world. You got out and fell in love. Wanted to share your truth with someone. Not so hard to believe."

He adjusted his position. Gracie stood so abruptly, he had to grasp the desk so he didn't fall over. She moved around the desk, got the chair there, and dragged it to him. "You look uncomfortable."

Now why did that make him want to hug the stuffing right out of her? He took the chair, set it beside the desk, and sat. "Thanks."

She sat down again, swiveled so she faced him. "You're right. I was sheltered enough that it was almost culture shock to find out what I'd been taught was dogma and not necessarily how the rest of the world worked."

"What had you been taught?"

"You know, it's my responsibility to fight for others, to seek out injustice, to right wrongs. Marvel superhero stuff."

Sounded like she was mocking herself. "So you got out into the world—to a bar, no less—and saw people drinking, screwing around, having fun, realized you'd been sold a bill of goods, and said—this is the teenage you, now—fuck this?"

She shook her head. "No. Never. The responsibility was too deeply ingrained, but that fact—that I couldn't give up the fight—made me F-word mad. I'd never been given the option of just worrying about my own problems, having a family, making money, taking care of my business. It didn't seem fair."

"And then John showed up."

"Yep. An opportunity to just be me."

"You got pregnant."

"And for a while it was actually good. I got to be Gracie in love. Gracie pregnant. Gracie as a mom. Until, in a hormonal lovefest, I spilled the beans to John." She bit her lip. "I guess you can say I'm not the least emotional of people."

So said the memories of her riding him in this very office, her boldness in Mexico, her tears right now. "So not-the-least-emotional-of-people tells her first love she comes from a family of"—he paused, adding secret weight to the words—"*businesspeople*. And all hell breaks loose. Family's pissed. Boyfriend's pissed. And Gracie Parish does what she can to make it okay."

Gracie's shoulders slumped. "Not that simple. But, yeah. And everyone went back to their lives."

"Except you."

She nodded. "Ty was two when I gave him up. So I still remembered the smell of his baby skin, the feel of his hair against my cheek, the way his laugh made the world better. Naturally, I tortured myself with memories."

Her hands simultaneously swept tears aside from under both eyes. "Then a few years ago, Ty got sick. He was in the hospital for a month. During that time, I kind of lost it. I couldn't be with him. Hold his hand. Brush back his hair. I blamed myself, a lot. But I also blamed Momma. I stewed on that anger. Then I did something to get back at her."

She stopped there, looked at him. Though she'd never admitted to sending that email to the FBI, he could see that confession in her eyes. He nodded. "Got it."

She let out a breath. The tears came again. He reached across the desk to the tissue box and pulled out another and handed it to her.

She took it, wiped her eyes. "Ty's getting sick made me realize I could lose him without even knowing him. So after Mexico, after Tony…I decided to try to live a different life. I thought I could return to being in Ty's life. Not as his mother. But in his life."

He could see where this was going. "John came by today and told you that was never going to happen."

She nodded. "Yeah. Guess I can't blame him."

"I can."

She shook her head. "You don't get it. My life is dangerous."

Like hell. He was investigating her mother for vigilante activities, and he understood better than most. Naw, he just couldn't square a man who'd keep his son away from a caring and loving mother. "More dangerous than a cop, a detective, FBI or CIA, a solider? Lot of parents with those jobs."

She rubbed at her forehead.

"Gracie, when your biological mother showed up, after giving you up for adoption, Mukta, your momma, let you go live with her?"

"Not without stipulation—I returned for classes, training, Sunday dinner—but yeah."

"You think that was okay?" he prodded. "Sheila had lymphoma. That wasn't going to end well. And she was taking you away from everything you'd ever known, to a bar, no less."

Gracie blinked, squared her shoulders. "Wait a minute. Momma let me go because she loved me. She wanted me to know my mother. And all of that judgmental stuff didn't matter."

"Why not?"

She stared at him. "Love matters more."

He stared at her. "Yep. Love matters more."

Hearing her own words echoed back to her, she drew in a shaky breath. She reached out, as slow as if she were approaching a dangerous animal, and rubbed a thumb over his jaw. "I really like you, Dusty." She dropped her hand. "But I still can't trust you."

He leaned forward. "Don't trust me. Don't." He let that hang there a moment, acknowledging that she was right. It was a moment in which the lies, like wisps of an old spider web, clung to him. "Don't trust. But let me help you. That's why I'm here."

She balled up the tissue and put the fisted hand to her forehead; bits of white tissue poked out from her fingers. "I don't need rescuing."

"What do you need?"

She dropped her hand. "Right now, I could really use some Motrin."

He nodded, leaned the rest of the way forward, and kissed her lightly on her cheek. "Okay, then, we can start with that."

Chapter 31

Off nearly every surface of Club When? the light show flashed red, white, and blue. Music pulsed from the speakers. People crowded onto the dance floor, bumping and grinding.

Dusty had to admit, he liked working here. A lot. The rhythm of the bar, the way the air began to buzz as people streamed inside. One second prep work, the next he ran around, exchanging pleasantries with people from all walks. And then there was Gracie.

Though she'd started the night in a haze of gloom, her mood had lifted. Now as she worked, she swayed those hips, that ass, in a way he was sure God himself deemed to be one of the most pleasant sights on this planet.

Damn, being here with her felt right.

It felt right when she bent to get something from a fridge and his eyes found their way to her fine, round ass. Made his palms itch.

It felt right when she caught him looking, smiled without reprimand, and all that guardedness, all the hostility meant to ward people off was suddenly not there.

It felt right, so right, when Gracie, rocking her hips to one of his favorite songs, shot him a *what-are-you-waiting-for* look, and he forgot for a moment those things called boundaries.

He put an arm around her waist and drew her back against the front of his body. He'd expected her to elbow him hard enough to give him second thoughts, but she moved with him. Against him.

People hooted approval. He dipped his head to her ear, and sang with "Make You Feel My Love."

And when she turned to him with a blush? Oh, he liked how she blushed. He could make a game of it—all the ways he could get Ms. Gracie Parish to blush.

It felt right, so right.

Until he remembered exactly why he was there. Then he felt like shit. He had to talk himself into focusing on his investigation. Remind himself of exactly who he was after and why.

As the night wore on, he had to remind himself again and again. Especially when Gracie whizzed by him smelling like candy and whiskey. Nearly bit his lip in half. Nothing could be more irresistible.

Too quickly, the evening of laughter and drinks and darting here and there quieted down. The music switched off. The lights came up. And the club went into standby mode.

As he put away bottles, Gracie sat at the bar with a clipboard, taking stock. She looked so damn earnest. Not a "trace"? of makeup. Hair pulled back. Chewing on the tip of her pen and closing one eye to evaluate her paperwork.

Dusty waved goodbye to the last of the servers and returned his attention to Gracie, who'd turned her attention to him. She took the pen from her mouth. "Where did you come from?"

Why did the fact that she wanted to know about him cause his heart to beat faster? Finished cleaning, he began to count the register. "I thought that was obvious. Kentucky."

"Not so obvious. Let me guess. Your dad is one of

those typical Southern fathers, super into his family and God and horses."

"Well, I could ride a horse long before I could ride a bike. But my dad was more interested in himself than family or even God. He was a faith healer."

Gracie cradled her chin in one hand. "That sounds pretty religious to me."

Finished counting, he wrote down the number before answering. "The way my dad operated had nothing to do with God. He was a fraud."

The corners of her eyes creased. "So you never saw any miracles?"

He shut the register. "I saw what he classified as miracles. People pretending to be healed, because only unworthy or sinful people didn't get healed."

"Pretending? If someone shows up and can't walk, you can see if they've been healed or not, right?"

He raised an eyebrow. Funny she should choose that example. He moved over to her, picked up a rag, and wiped the bar. "I once saw an old woman who couldn't walk. We're in this big meeting hall. Folding chairs set up, fluorescent lights, incense, and Tiger Balm."

He finished with the rag, put it in the bucket under the counter, leaned against the bar. "Dad came over to her. Now he's a big, powerful guy. The kind of fellow who can intimidate with mannerisms and voice. Dad puts his large hands over hers, and his voice rings out." Dusty raised his hands to demonstrate. "Walk."

He lowered his hands. "Moments like that you could feel his power, feel the tension in the room, everyone standing up from their folding chairs, looking. It was something.

"This lady's feet began to move spastically. My heart started to pound. It was going to happen. I knew she'd walk. People oohed and aahed. Everyone praising God. My dad commanded louder that she rise. His powerful voice gave me goosebumps.

"Her feet went twice as fast, she put her bony hands on the armrests of her wheelchair and tried to lift herself. Her arms shook, her legs gave, and she fell back into her seat with a cry."

Gracie's face followed the story, showing interest, then puzzlement, then sadness. She got it. Some wouldn't.

"Dad told her, told all of us, it was her fault. She'd done something in her past, some wrong she needed to be forgiven for. If she repented and trusted God, she'd be healed. She began to cry. The whole congregation, including me, blamed her."

"That's awful."

"Yeah. But back then, because I'd never been taught to think any other way, I believed him."

Gracie rubbed at her arms. "When did it change for you?"

"I was seven. Nearly died from a bladder infection. Dad's thinking was if he couldn't heal me, or anyone in his *ministry*, and I use that term very loosely, then God had deemed us unworthy."

Her face showed stark disbelief. "That's crazy."

"It seems crazy to me now too. Back then, trembling and sick and dying, I thought, 'Why did I lie about that cookie? Why did I forget to say *yes, ma'am*? Why won't God let me live?'"

Her face softened with empathy, not sympathy. He appreciated that. Nothing to feel sorry about. That part of his life had helped make him the dogged, determined man he was.

"I've never heard you say *yes, ma'am*."

Had to smile at that. "You Northern girls beat it out of me. Nothing harder than trying to explain to some hot thing you're trying to make time with that *yes, ma'am* is just upbringing."

She laughed. Got serious. "How'd you survive the illness? Did you get better?"

He looked past her to the empty bar, the strip-lights along the dance floor. "My mom went against my dad, reached out to my uncle Harvey. He worked in law enforcement. Showed up with his gun and his partner, threatened an investigation if Dad came after us. An idle threat, but the old man wasn't so well-educated. He agreed. Uncle Harvey raised me, helped deprogram me. Thanks to him, I came to see the world differently. Maybe got a bit of a chip on my shoulder for people who try to force their views on others."

She lifted her eyes to his. He could tell she knew what he was saying. It was out there. Why he was here. Why he was investigating her family. Why he cared.

Ball was in her court.

Chapter 32

Seated at the bar, her chin propped in her hands, in the after-hours quiet, Gracie absorbed what Dusty was saying about his father. A manipulative and abusive man.

She let his statement "*Maybe got a bit of a chip on my shoulder for people who try to force their views on others*" expand into the quiet between them. She let it echo inside her. He was sending her a message about Momma, about the League, and his motivation.

Though she wanted to, she didn't feel the need to respond immediately, to fill the silence with her side. Their eyes met, stayed locked. She enjoyed it, the way his sun-soaked eyes heated her.

"We had similar upbringings, but not exactly the same. Your father would've sacrificed you for his own sense of self-importance. Momma sacrifices herself to save others." Gracie saw that more clearly since John's visit. For years Momma had taken Gracie's anger over John. When in truth John had planned to go all along.

He leaned toward her. "I certainly am interested in learning more. Mind if I ask some questions?"

Oh boy. Time for a subject change. "Your breath smells really good. Did you eat one of my candies?"

"Way to avoid the question. And yeah, I ate one." He licked a too-pink tongue across his lips. "Thought about you as I sucked on it."

Whoa. The statement and the sweet Southern sex

dripping from his voice stimulated every hormone in her body. She needed him and that tongue closer. "You have to have sex with me."

His eyebrows shot up. *Whoops*. Had she, his boss for all intents and purposes, just ordered him to have sex with her? Lowering her head, she squeezed her eyes closed tight. "I mean, that didn't sound right. Of course, you have a choice."

She raised her head. *Dusty? Where did he—*

She grabbed the sides of her barstool as it spun. Dusty stood before her, staring down at her, a little too serious, a little too close, a lot too hot. "Got a choice, do I?"

He leaned in. "Pretty obvious to me the only person here who needs a clear choice is you, so I'm going to ask. Knowing all the things you suspect about me, about why I'm here, are you really, really sure you want to sleep with me, Ms. Gracie Parish?"

Oh. Man. He was not messing around. His breath was warm and sweet against her face.

Gracie, you need to say no. Tell him you don't sleep with the enemy or something equally self-righteous.

"I haven't been with a man in eighteen months."

That wasn't self-righteous. That was an invitation.

He smiled, a smile full of promise. "Got me beat. It's been six months. But at least I'm clean."

Six months? Why did that turn her on so much? She hooked her feet around his legs, pulled him closer. "I'm clean too. And on the pill."

He let out a breath that was part moan, and she caught his lips as he dipped his head toward hers. She slipped her tongue into his sultry, eager mouth and reveled in the taste of him.

Tugging her T-shirt free from the waist of her jeans, his hand snaked under and cupped her breast. They groaned simultaneously. The sound vibrated against their tangled tongues. *Now*. This had to happen. *Now*.

They came up for air, the smell of whiskey in her nostrils, and their labored breaths loud in her ears. She needed him inside her. But not here.

Dusty moved his mouth up to her ear. "Upstairs?"

She couldn't take him upstairs where she kept the servers for her family's operations. He'd all but admitted he was investigating them. *Mood killer*.

She shook her head. His eyebrows rose. He looked around the bar, as if judging the strength of the tables or the softness of the chaises. Maybe...*Um. No*.

Dusty, as perceptive as he was hot, reached behind her and grabbed his keys from the tray where he'd put them earlier. He jingled them. "My place is real close."

"Text me the address. I'll meet you there."

Chapter 33

Driving through the deserted streets of what the locals called The Borough, Dusty answered his cell on the first ring. Gracie's voice came through the car's speakers as soft and sexy as the whisper of lingerie against skin. "I've been dreaming about having you in my mouth."

Holy… He grew hard enough to split denim. Least that's the way it felt. "I like where this is going. What do I feel like in those dreams?"

"Thick and hard." She certainly had him headed in the right direction. She paused, and he bet she was every shade of red. He couldn't wait to see how deep he could get that red to go.

"I dream of taking the tip of you in, sucking, and using my hand to stroke you while I take all of you into my mouth."

Lord. There were way too many lights on this street. His johnson began to hurt. He shifted, pulled at his jeans. "Just inside your mouth?"

"No. Other places too. But in my fantasies, I have a fondness for sucking you off."

"Good to know." *Seriously*. She was killing him.

"I have this thing about wanting to give a blowjob on my knees. That's probably kind of submissive and not feminist at all. But I've actually never tried it."

Never? He gunned his car through the yellow. Who designed this street? A light every ten feet. "Gracie, hun, I'm all about making your wishes come true."

She laughed, low and pleased. "I'm so wet just thinking about it. Thinking about you sliding into my mouth, sliding between my legs, and then pumping into me fast and hard. I want to see you lose control."

He was getting dizzy from lack of blood flow to his brain. "Darlin', I'm not sure my insurance will cover collision-by-boner."

She laughed again. "I'm here."

She drove like a maniac. Thank the good Lord. "That's a good sign."

"It is?"

"Yep. I intend to make sure that isn't the last time tonight you get where you're going before me."

He pulled up a minute behind her.

There was one major problem that Dusty could think of as he led Gracie up the wooden fire escape to his apartment's private entrance. The ducks.

No grown woman wanted to have sex while google-eyed ducks peered down at everything. And the things he intended to do to her required she be comfortable with vulnerability. Not happening if she got a look at that awful mural. *Judgy ducks*.

Checking that the wireless alarm he'd installed hadn't been tampered with, he unlocked and opened the door. Gracie peered inside, then at him. "It's kind of dark."

He grasped her hand and pulled her in after him. "I'm sensitive about the lights."

Kicking the door closed with the toe of his boot, he pulled her close. They came together like fire and gasoline. His lips found hers and laid claim with kisses as long, hot, and needy as what he'd soon be pushing deep inside her.

Her soft fingers fumbled under his shirt, ran hungry nails along his abs, back, down to the waist of his jeans.

She startled, realizing the entire head of his johnson was poking out from the waist of his jeans. "Oh."

This woman out and out murdered him. "Impressed?"

She rubbed the tip, the moisture there. *Fuck*. His eyes rolled back in his head.

"Very," she breathed. "In my office… I hadn't…" She trailed off, unbuttoned his jeans, unzipped, put her hand around his length, stroked as if to convince herself that was all him. He thrust into her hand. She made a small whimpering sound.

He bent and nuzzled her ear. "That makes two of us."

"Strip," she said and, squeezing him tight, added, "Hurry."

She let him go and he sprang to action, pulled his shirt off over his head, tossing it into the room, stripped off boots, and stepped from his jeans like he was hot-footing it across a black-sand beach in July. Not fast enough. She was already naked.

Soft lights from outside filtered through the blinds, revealing the curves of a body so ripe and beautiful, he swore the nine choirs of angels themselves sang along with him. *Hallelujah*.

Those breasts, hips. Thighs. The gentle V of her… Lord. She was perfect.

He had to… He sank to his knees, wrapped his arms around her, palmed each cheek of that fine ass, and put his hot, needy mouth to her center.

She gasped.

He moaned against her. She was as sweet as she was soft, slick, and salty. He licked her, growing painfully hard with every flick of his tongue against her clit. She grabbed his shoulders for support and made soft moaning sounds that quickly turned into sharp, needy cries.

Was there any sweeter sound than the desperate moans of this woman while he went down on her? Nothing. He wanted more of that. As much as he wanted to have the heat currently against his mouth around his dick.

That knowledge made him crazed as he teased and stroked, licked and sucked. Releasing the grip he had on her fine ass, he slipped a hand between her cheeks, slid fingers forward, crooked one, two inside her. So fucking soft and wet.

"Oh, that..."

He picked up the pace. She let out a low, throaty moan. The fingers on his other hand slipped back and forth against that smooth skin that led to her ass. He slipped one inside the tightness there.

Her nails dug into his shoulders. She rocked her hot silkiness against his eager tongue, writhed against his quick, exploring fingers. "Yes. Please. Oh, please."

He could feel her tension building, feel as this perfect woman reached that perfect point, felt... She cried out, screamed his name as the orgasm took her.

Warm liquid. So sweet the choir lifted their voices. He lapped her up, his johnson hard and full between his legs, so ready for her he nearly came.

When her tremors slowed then stopped and he could tell by the way she braced hands against his head that her legs were ready to give out, he scooped her up, carried her to the bed.

Chapter 34

GRACIE'S HEAD STILL SPUN FROM THE INTENSITY OF that orgasm, her body singing with how he'd touched her, played her with his tongue and fingers.

Dusty lowered her onto his bed. She hadn't even been aware that he'd picked her up. She was boneless and her legs naturally spread wide for him.

He was hard, rigid, as he stood there and took a long, lingering look. "You are so beautiful. So perfect."

Bending over her without dropping onto the bed, his hands explored, caressed, appreciated her curves, her breasts. His touch was a hot worship. She pushed her chest up and he answered her, fondling her sensitive breasts, lightly pinching her nipples.

She groaned and he took one pink bud in his mouth. He sucked on it, moaning as if he had just tasted the best dish in the world. And she thrilled with the sensation, writhed with joy and need as he sucked, squeezed, and teased.

"Dusty…Dusty…now."

Lingering for a moment on her breast, he let the bud pop from his swollen lips with a hotly whispered "Perfect," then crawled onto the bed. His hard body aligned over her soft one. They kissed. Hungry. Demanding. Imploring. Her lips tore at him. Her hands dragged at him. His cock throbbed against her, begged to move into her.

Wanting him inside of her, she arched into him.

"It's okay?" he asked and thrust just a little.

She meant to say *yes*, meant to say *hurry*, but she hissed, a sound of both pain and pleasure, at the size of him.

He groaned. His breathing ragged, he gave her a minute. Sweat slicked his skin. She could see his pulse working in his neck. Hear his heart pounding. He put his lips by her ear. "Gracie, if this is too hard on you…"

She laughed. "Pun intended?"

"Nope. Not enough blood in my brain right now for puns."

She wrapped her legs around him, tightly. Tight enough that he pressed deeper into her body.

His eyes sprang open, mouth worked soundlessly for a moment. He looked down at her, visibly battling for control. "Grace." His voice was strained, awed. "So hot. So fuckin' tight."

She was pretty sure her tightness had more to do with his size. She pressed her legs against his ass and arched into him. Given the green light, he kissed her again, the scent of her own body on their lips, and pushed all the way inside her.

She grunted. He grunted. Her slick warmth locked around him. This time he didn't stop. With his body shaking, he pulled out slow and thrust deep. And just like that, she began to come. She cried out. "Faster."

With a deep chuckle, he whispered, "Yes, ma'am," and pushed fast and hard, sending fire shooting through her body and electric tingles bursting across her nerves.

His large cock rubbed against the sensitive zone outside her body, hitting her just right, causing powerful shocks to explode through her. She dug nails into his back, bit wherever she could find skin, on his shoulder, bicep.

Each of his deep strokes met the desperate

encouragement of her rising voice and rising hips. She cried out, "Yes. Dusty. Yes. That!" as she came apart around him.

She rejoiced in the power of him, the way he filled her, took her like he was making a point, like he'd found his home, like this would be the start of something that continued every day from here on out.

He lost his rhythm. Thrusting madly, he cursed and broke inside her with a warmth she could feel pouring into her as he whispered a pleading "Grace, Grace, Grace," into her hair.

After a moment, he rolled from her, palming her hip, the wetness of him dripping between her legs, the feel of him spent, warm against her. Nothing could've prepared her for how good that had felt, how quickly she'd climaxed with him. It was just something about the way their bodies fit together. Perfect.

It took him a moment to catch his breath, then he kissed her ear. "I have no words for you, Grace. None." He kissed her, open-mouthed and deep, sending her blood to boil again, then pulled back. "Thank you."

She couldn't help but grin up at him. She wanted to say a thousand things. Two thousand, but all she could manage was "You took my breath away." And then, "Are those cartoon ducks on your ceiling?"

He laughed, wiped the tear that had slipped from her eye but didn't mention it. Not one word. "Ignore the judgy ducks." He dropped his hand lower, traced the barely visible—thanks to the lack of lighting—tattoo on her hip, the apple, the hand holding the apple. "When'd you get it?"

Her tattoo. It had been a long time since she'd

thought about the crazy two weeks that had led to it. She and Justice had run away. "I was young. Fifteen."

"Fifteen?"

She smiled as he nuzzled her neck. Dusty, it turned out, liked to cuddle after. Usually she wasn't a cuddler, but with him it was different. She really didn't want to think too deeply about how wonderful his attention felt right now. "I'd snuck out with Justice. We were wild. And I wanted something that symbolized how dangerous I felt, dangerous enough to change the world with one bad decision, with one wicked offer."

She turned to meet his eyes, which were filled with wild need and honest interest. They lay face-to-face. "And since, in fairy tales, a hand offering someone an apple always seemed to start the most trouble, that's what I wanted for my tattoo."

He kissed her nose. "Thank you for sharing that with me, Grace."

Grace. Not Gracie. She'd noticed the change. "I like when you say Grace. It sounds…warm. But why the change?"

He exhaled a steady stream, causing a fan of her hair to play across and tickle her cheek. She tucked the strands behind her ear. If it was possible to be completely comfortable and utterly nervous all at once, that was how she felt.

"Because I don't know any other way to show my gratitude for the bounty you shared with me than to say Grace."

Oh. Wow.

"Except, maybe, to also give you the truth."

The truth? Her mind perked up and began pacing the inside of her skull. She knew what he was going to say. And she didn't want to hear it.

Chapter 35

Gracie wasn't sure how to get Dusty to shut up. Had his room gotten hotter? It felt stifling.

"Some time ago, I received an email at the FBI," he said. "An email I'm fairly sure you wrote."

She held her breath as her mind screamed for him to stop talking.

Oblivious to her tension, or maybe because of it, he ran his hand affectionately up and down her arm. "Read that thing a thousand times. Got it memorized."

Oh. Her throat grew tight. She'd sent that letter in the hopes of reaching someone, sharing a pain that seemed too great for herself. And he'd gotten it. He'd gotten it and come to her.

And that was so sweet. Except it put everything in danger. Whatever this was between them. Her relationship with Momma. Her siblings. The Mantua Home. The work the League did. The important work. All in danger.

"I guess you can say I became a little obsessed with taking down the woman who would train children to be vigilantes."

Her eyes widened. Her heart lurched. *What? Momma wasn't just that. The letter was unfair. Stupid and unfair.*

"I worked on the case for a few months. Set myself up with Tony, gained his trust, and tried to work my way inside."

He'd suggested he hadn't, but Dusty had used Tony.

"When Tony asked me to help him take down sex-slavers, I figured it would be the perfect cover and gain me the access I needed to get to Mukta. Didn't work out that way."

Of course not, because I'd bet my last dollar Tony had known what Dusty had been after. But he'd needed someone at the compound in Mexico who wasn't family. He'd used Dusty back.

"Grace? Say something."

Gracie exhaled. Inhaled. Her heart beat an anxious rhythm in her chest. Terror. Dread. Loss of control. Was this what a panic attack felt like? "You're after Momma." Heavy breaths. "You're trying to lock her up." Panicked breaths. "Take her away from my sisters—from me—based on the email I sent?"

"Whoa. Hold on now." He slid his arm across her stomach. "Grace, are you okay?"

Okay? She wasn't okay. Her vision started to dim. Of course she'd known he was investigating her family, but that he was specifically after Momma felt like a punch to the gut. She'd been lying to herself. Thinking she could control all the horrible things that could result from that stupid email. And now she realized she couldn't.

She'd risked her family. Momma. And if that wasn't bad enough, slept with the man who was after them. Would she ever learn? Forget about trusting someone else, she shouldn't trust *herself*.

She had to leave.

She tried to slide out of bed. His arms tensed around her waist. He let out a breath, this one troubled. "Grace, don't leave. I want to share things I've uncovered. About your dad. You know him, right? Rush?"

He knew about her father? Of course he knew. He was investigating her to get at Momma. She nodded, waited to hear what he had to say.

His voice quickened. "I believe Mukta is blackmailing Senator Rush. I think she's using your existence to control how he directs government funds, votes on legislation, among other things."

Blackmailing? Over her? Was this his case? Was this how he'd set Momma up? "Why are you telling me this?"

He put his other hand on her chin, turned her head. Once she looked directly at him, he brought his face close to hers. "Grace, I want to help you. Whoever is after you hasn't gone away. Chances are they'll let things cool off and will come back hard. I want to stop that from happening. And here's the thing—I'm willing to give up my case, to trust you, trust that your momma isn't who I think she is. But I need to see for myself. I need to talk to her, ask her some questions."

Gracie's stomach rolled so fast she was pretty sure it twisted into a knot. A complicated Gordian knot. "Are you seriously using this moment between us, my fear over the fact that someone is after me, to try and get in to question Momma?"

She knew she should be cooler than this, better at controlling her emotions, but that stung.

He shook his head. "Don't do that. Don't write me off that way. I'm willing to trust you. Are you willing to trust me? Trust that that isn't my motivation here?"

Her heart sank to her feet. Trust him? He'd just admitted to a thousand lies. "Do you have any idea what you're asking?" Why did he need to question Momma? Was he going to arrest her? Would that change things for him like it had with John? "I can't just march a fudgin' FBI agent into my fudgin' family house like it's no fudgin' big deal."

Especially when she'd sent the email that had launched his investigation. But if he was telling the truth, if this meant he'd stop his investigation... Or was that a lie? "I need to think. I need"—*to get away*—"a little time, space."

She sat up. He sat up too, grasped her hand, twined his fingers with hers. "Grace, let's talk about this. I can't help if you won't let me in."

She shook him off. "You can help by giving me space."

A moment of pain, of rejection, flashed across his face, but he quickly schooled his features to FBI-empty. He nodded. "So when I show up for work tonight?"

"You no longer work there."

She climbed out of bed, dressed without turning around, and left without a word.

Chapter 36

Gracie pulled into the parking lot behind Club When? feeling confused, worried, heartsick, and tired. She hadn't slept all night and probably wouldn't get to sleep today.

She yawned, pulling her keys from the ignition. Absently, she dropped them into her purse and dragged her body toward the club. The six-a.m. summer sun was up and brightening the sky. It warmed her hair, her skin. Didn't warm her mood.

She had an honesty headache. So much had changed since this time yesterday.

John had told the truth. And in doing so, upended something she'd held against Momma for over a decade.

She'd told the truth to John. And in reply, he'd ripped away her naive notion that she could become respectable enough to be allowed in Ty's life. Not that she'd let John have the last word on that.

And Dusty had told her the truth. He'd specifically targeted Momma, not the League. That was a knife to the gut she hadn't expected. She felt sick with guilt for sending the email.

Waving a wrist over the security pad, she put in her personal code. After the beep, she went inside, flicked on the light switch. The florescent lights blinked awake. The lingering smell of fried food and booze hit her nose. Home sweet home.

Boxes of booze from yesterday's delivery lined the hallway. Going to be a busy day.

Kicking off her shoes, she pushed them under the lime-green bench outside the kitchen and walked inside. *Food. Protein.*

She dropped her purse by the cooktop and collected ingredients for an omelet. No sooner had she done that than her cell rang. Her heart picked up its pace.

She pulled her cell from her purse, equal parts hope and dread. Not Dusty. "Hey, Victor."

Was that her voice? Sounded deeper. She sprayed cooking oil into the skillet, turned on the burner.

He hesitated. "Red, I'm going to want every salacious detail of last night's sexcapade, but first we got a problem."

Stupid moaned-sore throat. "What problem?"

"Another fifty thousand went out of John and El's account and into an offshore account."

I will do what I have to do to protect my family. Remember that.

"Sugar." She turned down the burner.

"That's not all. I've gone through security footage outside your club and spotted El sneaking around, taking photos."

Gracie's stomach rolled. "Momma could be blackmailing Rush," she blurted out. "Using my existence to get him to support legislation and her agenda."

An agenda that often clashed with big businesses with deep pockets.

"Shit. Looks like we have a winner in the explosive news department. Not that we can totally rule out John and El."

No. Not yet. Not after that weirdness with John.

"Porter also had me followed. I confronted the guy he sent after me. Sent back a message."

"Damn. Porter coming out of the woodwork kind of blows away everything else I was going to say about the suspected Rush kids."

"Tell me anyway."

"Well, the youngest Rush boy, George, has a sick kid. Spends a lot of time in the hospital. One of the boys, Quincy, is a heart surgeon. Rich. Married. Kids. Two mistresses. No time for murdering you. Got some great sex tapes of your half brother, by the way."

"Gross."

"The daughter is some kind of celebrity in the geek world. Two million Twitter followers. Hot chick who works artificial intelligence."

That's interesting. "Can you learn more about her?"

"Sure."

"It seems, except for Porter, the family members all have their own lives. Even Rush's wife has her career as an interior designer."

"Yeah. And Porter probably wouldn't want the fact that his father plays ball with Mukta Parish in the news. Donors especially wouldn't like that. Your mom isn't exactly beloved."

Yeah. If Dusty was right, the blackmail changed everything. Porter's entire career, livelihood, was tied into his father's. And she knew from her own investigation that he had some personal issues, recent ugly divorce, so his career had to be his number one concern right now. "I'll handle Porter."

"I'll take John and El. Plant a bug. Listen in. Dig more into the sister."

"Thanks, Victor. Anything else?"

"Yeah. Since you're sleeping with that FBI guy—"

"How did you—"

"Be careful. He's not playing straight with you."

She knew that. Boy, did she know. But was that what Victor meant? The hair on Gracie's arms stood on end. "What are you saying?"

"I spotted something in the security footage you sent me. It's blurry. Can you let me see footage from farther back?"

Cradling the phone against her shoulder, she broke some eggs one-handed, whisked them in the heated pan. "Why?"

"Not ready to share with the class just yet. I might be wrong. Let me investigate my suspicions first."

Sure, she'd just trust everyone all over the darn place, take them into her home, into her heart. "Fine."

"Thanks. See you tonight."

Tonight?

Victor hung up. She looked at the dimming phone screen. Did he expect her to let him upstairs to look at the security footage tonight? That sounded bad. She put her phone down, rubbed at her arms, and watched the omelet bubble.

That's when she heard it. Well, not heard it. But sensed it. Her someone-else-is-here bells rang on five-alarm.

She turned off the burner, removed her gun from her purse, and crept along the dim corridor that connected the kitchen to the bar.

Inside the club, she spotted her at a table, eating a bowl of Cheerios, judging by the big yellow box. Gracie lowered her gun. "Cee. Are you crazy? I could've killed you."

Well, wounded anyway. She wasn't the kind of shot Justice was.

Cee took a sip of what better be plain OJ. "Sorry. I didn't want to interrupt your call."

Yikes. Had she said anything important to Victor on the phone? "When did you get here?"

"Early. Around four."

Gracie resisted the annoyance igniting her cheeks. How did she keep getting out of school? What were Momma and Leland doing over there? Why hadn't her security system let her know that someone had entered? She should've gotten a text. This kid. "How'd you get in?"

Cee waved her wrist. "I used my chip."

No. It didn't work that way. Unless? "Who programmed your chip? Who gave you the code to get in here?"

Cee's eyes grew wide, guilty. Gracie changed the code every week. Only Leland and internal security had the codes. And only one person in Cee's class, the only other boy adopted into the family, Romeo, had those kinds of cyber skills.

Oh boy. This was turning into a ball of wax. Cee's unit, Vampire Academy, was testing every boundary. And Cee seemed to be leading the charge.

"All right." Gracie held up a hand. "Let's unpack all of it, but first I'm starving."

"I bet."

Smart mouth. "Wait here."

After putting her weapon away and making her omelet and a cup of tea, Gracie sat down opposite Cee.

"You and Rome have to stop messing with the security chips. Leland is going to come down hard on you. And—"

Cee slammed her hand on the table, causing the silver spoon in her now empty bowl to jump. "They already have. But no one does anything about the group I found!"

Whoa. Angry much? "League operations are shut down because of the drone attack. We have to protect our people too. And it's not like we're doing nothing. We do a lot in other areas." *Like blackmailing a senator to support our agenda.*

Cee fidgeted. "I can't forget them."

"Who?"

She sat forward. "The other girls like me—they're scared, uncertain. Not understanding how men's desires reduce us to just a body. As if we had no souls." Her lips tightened for a moment and then released. "Please. Allow me to do the work. Please."

Gracie felt a tug on her heart. This was the first time Cee had shown her a motivation that didn't seem prompted by anger or revenge. Her eyes were slick with fierce intensity. She wore the force of empathy on her face, the sincere longing to help another.

Gracie knew that look. Had worn it. She knew what it felt like to believe that what you were doing, what the League did, was the only way to fight back. She could almost hear the thud of that other shoe dropping. Because as much as she complained about the League, her time in the world had only made her believe more in the work they did. And yes, sometimes Momma's tactics were questionable, even hurtful, but her intention was to help, to free, to rescue others, especially girls like Cee.

Fudge buckets. She'd risked all of those good

intentions, her entire family, when she'd sent that email. If she further exposed them to Dusty and he betrayed or rejected them, it would devastate her. A lot more than if he'd just betrayed and rejected her. "Let me drive you home. I'll talk to Momma." She looked around. "Do you have stuff?"

Cee nodded, looked away. "Yes. Upstairs."

Upstairs? A finger of foreboding swept down her spine. She'd gotten upstairs? "You and Rome have got to knock it off, Cee."

Cee stood up, stomped her foot and glared. "Do you want lions or rabbits in the League?"

"Neither. We want foxes. Cunning. Not rage. You need to stop being so angry."

"You need to stop being so afraid."

What? "I'm not."

"Yes, you are. Of being one of us. Come out from behind your computer and do the work. You might find that people"—she paused, swallowed what seemed to be a genuine emotion—"are worth it."

Gracie's face flushed with heat. *Poo. The kid was right. Still...* "Look, I get it. You want to make a difference. And you can. But for today, you're in a safe place. Let that sink in. Relax."

Cee shook her head. "No place is safe." She looked around at the club. "This place can't protect you. It won't. Nothing will."

Gracie balled up her napkin and tossed it onto her plate. "Just get your stuff."

Chapter 37

After taking a bus ten miles from his home, Tyler walked down the street to the shipping store where he'd rented his private mailbox. The owners, a woman and her husband, were busy behind the counter bubble-wrapping some kind of large glass bowl. They barely stopped long enough to nod hello.

He nodded back, pressed the code on the gleaming painted golden door—like something you'd see in anime. He imagined opening it to see a too-pale doll with stringy hair, giant eyes and tits. Nope. Not this time. He pulled out the silver and black laptop and slipped it into his backpack. He'd done this enough times it now felt like routine.

Backpack on and weighted by the custom laptop—the Parish family didn't mess around—he left the store and avoided the Starbucks at the end of the street. Cee had told him to vary his routine. Seemed stupid, but he'd been followed before.

Although he'd been followed by his mom. Biological mom. Not the mom that lived with him, took care of him, and annoyed the heck out of him.

No. The mom that had given him up. He couldn't wait to meet her. Talk to her. And she wanted to meet him. According to Cee, she'd given him up when he was younger to keep him safe from the scary life of the Parish family.

He didn't find it scary. It was cool. It was real. Like

really helping people. No bullshit. He stood in line at the window for the juice store, got a watermelon smoothie, paid with a crumpled ten, and sat at an outside table with a neon-red umbrella.

He booted up his computer, hooked into the stand's free Wi-Fi, sipped his smoothie, and checked the mailbox Cee had set up for him. Ten emails. Looked like she'd been—

Ah. Brain freeze. He shut his eyes.

Once it passed, he took a more cautious sip of his smoothie and went through the emails, starting with the oldest. Most were things Cee had already told him. Things he'd done. Getting a burner phone. Making sure he had a face mask to block facial recognition software. When he got to the more recent emails, he found each one had instructions that built on the last one. By the time he'd followed all the instructions, he found himself in a secure chat on the dark web.

An instant message box popped up. Check it out.

Gruesome images of naked women tied up on chairs, drugged, being raped, tortured, appeared.

What the hell? He looked away. Closed the window. *Damn.* He double-checked that even though his back was to the building, no one could see his screen. They couldn't.

He didn't open the box again. His hands shook. *Shit.* That was so messed up. Like the way the women had been tied, bruised. The paleness of their skin, cuts on their…

There were some sick people in the world. He wasn't going to look again. But this proved it. He was doing the right thing, lying to his family, sneaking around. It was the right thing to do.

Another message popped up: The money you sent is going to stop this.

He typed: It's enough? Fifty thousand seemed like a lot to him, but he'd never funded vigilantes before.

Yeah.

He let out a breath. When can I meet my, he hesitated, deleted, retyped: When can I meet Gracie?

Do you have access to the cabin? Can you make sure no one will be there?

His fingers began to twitch. His heart to pound. Finally. This was it. He'd done everything they'd asked. Yeah.

Then soon. Put the laptop back in your mailbox. You won't need it again.

Why not? He ran his hands over the expensive laptop's glowing red and black keyboard. This was his connection to the group, to the plan to take down bad guys.

This was the way his mother would contact him to be part of the family and the League of Warrior Women.

Did they really need the women part? Couldn't it just be League of Warriors? Kind of sexist the way it was.

He typed: How will I know the plan?

I'll text you the next steps on your burner.

Chapter 38

NOT MUCH COULD RUIN A STROLL THROUGH THE CHARMING sidewalks of Bristol, Pennsylvania. Antiques stores, homemade ice cream, pancake places, mom-and-pop coffee shops, bookstores, and taverns along the Delaware River, cute as all hell.

Too bad Dusty's brain wouldn't let him enjoy it. Kept replaying Gracie's reaction that morning. Shaken. Breathing hard. Angry. Pretty much obliterated cute as hell. Made his chest hurt that he couldn't even call her.

She wanted space. He'd give it to her.

Space sucked.

Skirting an antique washboard with a rusted grill and an old pram doll carriage in front of one of the shops, Dusty went two doors down and entered a restaurant. Reminded him of a New York diner—thin, rectangular, with two-person booths, steel-poled barstools, and a long Formica countertop.

He automatically noted the number of people inside and where they were sitting. Not too busy. Practically empty. Two women in a booth. Three guys at the counter. Waitress. Cook.

He swung into the last blue-plastic booth, back to the wall, with a view of the front door, kitchen door, and reflection of the restroom doors in the mirrored glass behind the counter.

The waitress, a middle-aged woman with a been-there,

done-that smile, handed him a menu. He thanked her. Told her he was waiting for someone.

Always liked to arrive early. Take in the surroundings, make a note of things. Recon never hurt anyone.

It was a good twenty minutes before Mack showed, wearing a suit as trim as his lanky frame. In all the time he'd known Mack, he'd never seen him put on an ounce. Not of muscle. Not of fat. He was immune to both, apparently.

In his dark suit, with his *Mission: Impossible* shades and his swagger, Mack couldn't have looked more fed if he'd had a bard follow him around singing about his Quantico exploits.

Guy could tone it down. Look less uptight. Huh. Maybe Gracie and her vigilante ways were rubbing off on him. She sure had last night. He pushed the hot image of her away, far away.

Mack slid into the booth. "You look distracted."

No shit. Dusty shook his hand. "No more than usual. How's the fort?"

"Still secure. How's the investigation?"

Here we go. "Investigation stalled. No leads. Getting nowhere with the asset."

Nowhere he could put in a report, anyway.

Mack's eyebrows rose. The waitress showed up, dropped off two glasses of water, and tried to hand Mack a menu. He shook his head. "Burger. No bun. No fries. Black coffee."

"You're going to live to be a thousand, Mack. And not one day is going to be even a tiny bit fun." He handed the waitress his menu. "Give me the same with cheese fries and a sesame bun."

She smiled at him before leaving. He took that as approval for a healthy appetite.

Mack's dark eyebrows pinched together at the bridge of his nose. "Kind of surprised you admitted that about the investigation, Dusty. That's part of why I asked you to come today."

It was?

"I think you should let this case go."

Dusty opened his mouth to argue, object. Closed it. Mack had just rolled a girder off his shoulders. After the last year working his way in with the Parish family, getting to know their business practices, getting to like the family—more than like some of them—he'd been fighting a growing sense of wrong. Judging by Gracie and Tony, those kids were raised to care for others and themselves. And what they did outside the law was a drop in the bucket compared to some. A drop that weighed toward justice.

Dusty clenched and unclenched his hands. The relief nearly staggered him. Mack took his silence the wrong way.

"I know what you're thinking. You put it all on the line. Your job, your life, your own money, and ended up with the same results. Could've just stayed home."

"Way to cheer me up."

Mack grimaced. "Sorry. But I think you've got to face facts. We're never going to get them on the vigilante stuff. Whatever they were doing, they're not doing now. They're spooked from the drone attack, from having our guys all over them. They've gone underground."

True. Plus Gracie had pegged his cover the day he'd strolled into town. But it was over. His heart began to beat faster. His mood to soar. Couldn't wait to tell her, see her face. They could start fresh. Find out what this was between them. She had to know, way down where it mattered, that this was more than sex. He could set up shop in town for a while, help protect her.

Mack turned his water glass, as if sizing up its cleanliness. Satisfied, he removed the paper from his straw and took a sip. "Look, all the doom and gloom silence isn't necessary. It's not a total loss. I want you to concentrate on the blackmail."

Dusty sat up straighter, like someone had shoved a steel pole up his ass. "What?"

"I know what they have on Rush—or pretend to have. Mukta Parish has an old video of Gracie's mother claiming Rush raped her. After he drugged her."

Rush drugged and raped Sheila Hall? Did Gracie know? "How'd you—"

"Digital copies were anonymously sent to the Chester office last night. No sooner did I hang up with you than I had that proof in my hot hands."

"Anonymous copies? As in more than one?"

"Yeah. Turns out Mukta has been extorting multiple government officials. They've been doing it for ages."

Dusty leaned forward. His heart rate picked up. "Explain how they do it."

"Take for example Rush."

"Yeah. Start there."

"Rush slept with that woman—"

"You mean Gracie's mom, Sheila? The woman he raped?"

"What if it wasn't rape? What if she lured him to sleep with her? Then the Parish family makes a tape with Sheila, looking so young and innocent, claiming Rush drugged and raped her."

Looked like Mack had already condemned Sheila. "Who's to say he didn't?"

"Exactly. Except he wasn't the only one the family set up this way. I don't know how many, but I've seen a couple of these recordings. Same girl, Sheila. But each recording accuses a different man."

"So you have recordings with Sheila Hall claiming different men drugged and raped her?"

"She never mentions them by name. There's someone asking her leading questions. She answers the questions."

"So the interviewer asks was it this guy, was it that guy?"

"Yeah."

"So different questions, different names, but the same answers?"

Mack nodded.

"And you have proof this was sent to other men besides Rush, proof the Parish family blackmailed them all? Along with men willing to say so?"

"Not yet. The videos are thirty years old. Out of the recordings we got, Rush is the only person still in government. The only one who apparently produced a kid. Two of the blackmail victims are dead. One had a heart attack six months ago. The other shot himself in the head two weeks ago."

Victims? "Anybody else?"

"That we know? A federal judge. No longer on the bench. Got Alzheimer's. I went to see him this morning. Saddest shit ever. Kept asking for his wife."

He'd been to see the judge? Investigating on his own? "So except for Rush, none of these recordings are currently in use. And there's no way of corroborating the other stories? Sounds like a convenient way to get Rush off the hook for something pretty damn heinous. He could've altered the recording sent to blackmail him and sent them to you. Had to suspect the truth might come out. Might be trying to muddy the waters. Have you had the tapes authenticated?"

Dusty leaned back as the waitress put their food on the table, asked if they needed anything else. He smiled at her. "No thanks."

She looked at Mack. He waved her off, picked up his fork and knife. "Give me a day or two. You're being a little hostile considering I'm giving you what you want. The Parish matriarch will go down for this. She's been controlling government, changing laws, diverting government funds to support this crazy women-centered agenda. I just need more proof. As you pointed out, so far this is weak."

"So the answer to that is no."

Mack sliced his burger, delivered a bite to his mouth with the fork. For such a dainty action, he didn't seem to care about talking with his mouth full. "The recordings are copies. I got the lab on it. We'll see. But I'm pretty sure we'll need the originals to determine that shit."

Dusty pushed his plate away. He couldn't stomach food right now. "Any other proof?"

Mack gestured with a fork full of meat. "Years ago, someone filed a lawsuit worth tens of millions against one of Mukta Parish's companies. The case was thrown out by the same judge, Judge Roberts, that I mentioned. Months later, Roberts was photographed at a fundraiser with Mukta Parish. It shows her and the judge in what looks like an intense conversation."

"That's light beer mixed with water. Weak."

"Yeah. Well, like I said we're just getting started. Mukta Parish is devious, but we can get her on blackmail."

"You sound pretty sure."

Mack cut another triangle of meat. "Last night, I reached out to Rush's son, Porter. Talked to him. This morning he got back to me. His father might be willing to testify against Mukta."

He'd reached out to the guy who, along with his father, might be trying to kill Gracie? "He's willing to testify? Admitting he's been Mukta's puppet will ruin any chance at the presidency."

Chewing, Mack shook his head. "Not necessarily. He never played ball with her. Any decisions he made for legislation aligned with his values. It wasn't until she tried to secure a cabinet position that he came to us."

Dusty leaned back in his seat. What was he saying? Of course, Rush and his son would love to play victims fighting back. Standing up for what was right even if it might cost him the presidency. Mack knew that. He had to. "And you think his constituents will buy that?"

"Buy what? Rush is taking on people like Mukta, women who would use and abuse the system, claiming victimhood in order to gain money and extraordinary rights. He's standing up to them. Let's face it, his base will eat up the idea of Mukta getting her comeuppance."

Fuck. Mack was all in. People always imagined informants as lowlifes, but it was the assets in high places that rated. No higher place than the presidency. "Mack, tell me you aren't trying to free up a candidate for president," *at the expense of Mukta's family*, "a guy who once in office would be beholden to the bureau?"

Mack stopped with his fork halfway to his mouth. He lowered it. "What do you care? It gets Mukta and a couple members of her family off the streets."

Looked like Mack had found a way to go from a so-so career to being upwardly mobile. "Hold on a sec. What do you mean a couple members of her family? I thought this was about Mukta."

"Mukta and anyone else involved in the bribery."

The hairs on the back of Dusty's neck stood on end. "Are you trying to tie Gracie Parish to this whole thing?"

"Tie her to it? She *is* tied to it. It's her father. We have evidence that she has hacked into the senator's home computers. And other things."

She thought the guy was trying to kill her, of course she did research. Dusty leaned into the space that Mack had just left. His arm rested far over what could be considered the table center. "What things?"

"Don't worry about it."

"Who's investigating who sent the recordings? You?"

"Leave it."

"No. I won't. You're putting Gracie in more danger. Ignorant people might hate Mukta—she wears a hijab, is overly-educated, wealthy, and viciously outspoken—but Gracie isn't so easy to hate. She's as American as apple pie, beautiful, and runs her own business. No matter what evidence you have, Rush won't want her out there speaking for herself, speaking against him. You just made her even more of a target."

Mack's eyebrows rose. "You seem to be getting a little agitated. And paranoid."

"You're the reason, Mack. You're the reason people don't trust us, don't trust us to do our job, don't trust that we're making decisions based on our roles as defenders instead of what's best for our institution. Or what's best for our own careers. You're what's wrong with this country, the bureau."

Mack stood up, threw down a ten-dollar bill. "Why don't we touch base after you've had some time to digest?" He gave Dusty a disappointed look then walked out of the restaurant.

A moment later, Dusty's cell beeped. He looked down at the screen. You're off the case. If you do anything to jeopardize this investigation, I will have you arrested.

A fistful of angry strides later, and Dusty was outside on the pleasant streets of Bristol, Pennsylvania, delivering his resignation to the swell of Mack's too-straight nose. And jaw. And thick skull.

The sizzle of a Taser hit his ears a blink before fifty thousand volts squeezed his body. He dropped to the sidewalk. His jaw tightened. He went board rigid.

Fucking Mack. Couldn't throw a punch to save his life.

Chapter 39

MUSIC PUMPED THROUGH CLUB WHEN?'S SPEAKERS, pounding rhythm through the gyrating bodies that bumped and writhed on the dance floor.

Behind the bar, Gracie mixed a mojito. The erotic push and pull, the wild abandon of her customers, usually thrilled her. Tonight it made her miss Dusty.

Work was a little duller, a little lonelier without his good-natured humor and easy-going manner. *Yikes*. She had to stop thinking about him.

She focused again on making the servers' drinks. She had two bartenders dealing with the people pressing forward and leaning across the bar to order drinks. One was in training, a replacement for Dusty—there she went again—and cousin to the other bartender she'd rehired.

He seemed like an okay hire. Hard working. But—

A little niggle in her awareness alerted her to his presence. She felt the wave of desire and heat light up her insides. Forcing herself to finish, she poured a beer and put it on the tray before glancing up. Dusty leaned against the end of the bar. "I need to talk to you."

The little butterflies in her stomach winged up her throat where they fluttered and danced.

Dang, he was so good-looking. Heat kissed her cheeks. All she could think about was the force of him entering her, seizing her, bringing her shaking and writhing to pure bliss.

This was a problem. When someone could make you

feel as good as he made her feel, they had power over you. She refused to be powerless.

Wait. Hadn't she asked for space? She picked up the next drink order. "You'll have to wait."

His honey eyes flashed. His voice lowered. "Grace."

Her breasts perked up and paid tight attention. *Way to go, tattas, why not send up an I-want-you-bad signal flare*. One that matched the hot patches of red now marching across her face and down her neck.

Really hard not to seem affected when your face was as telling as Pinocchio's nose. Too bad he didn't have such a tell. Anger flared in her chest. And pain. *Control. Make the drink*. She turned on the blender.

When she was done with the order, she turned back to Dusty. *What the what?*

A beautiful young woman with dark hair stood at Dusty's side and pointed to his hands. His knuckles were bruised and bloodied.

How had he hurt his hands? Had he been in a fight?

The girl was asking about his injury, showing interest. Classic pick-up. And she'd bought him a beer. Gracie admired her tactic. Not shy. Not fawning. Get the guy to talk about himself. See if he's interested.

For his part, Dusty looked like a deer in headlights. She watched with growing amusement as Agent Leif McAllister tried to find a graceful way out of the conversation. He hesitated over a few pleasantries, smiled, sweated, and then motioned toward Gracie and said, "I'd like you to meet my good friend Grace."

The brunette with a killer tan—probably good Italian genes—looked over. Gracie waved with a sprig of mint squeezed tight between her fingers.

The woman didn't seem embarrassed or uncertain. She smiled. "Hi."

Gracie finished making the pina colada, put the slip on the waiting server's tray, and approached the girl.

"Hi," she said. "What can I get you to drink? On the house, because if you've had to deal with this guy, you deserve compensation."

Dusty put a hand to his chest. "Now, Grace, I'm a little hurt you wouldn't give me a higher recommendation."

Ah, stupid fair skin. She could feel herself turning lady-you-have-no-idea-how-good-he-is red. Followed by angry-emoji-face red.

The brunette's eyes bounced between her and Dusty. She shrugged. "I'll have a gin and tonic."

Wow. A straight shooter all the way down to her drink. Gracie made the drink and slid it over to her.

The straight-shooter took it, raised the glass in thank you, and clinked it with Dusty's bottle. Dusty nodded and then took a long sip. The woman turned and walked away.

Gracie watched her go. How cool would it be to never turn all shades of red in a somewhat awkward situation? The light played across Ms. Cool's shimmery silver cocktail dress as she skirted the dance floor.

Her drink hand came up, and there was a flash and boom that lifted her and drove her across the room.

Chapter 40

THE BLAST SENT PEOPLE AND DEBRIS FLYING ACROSS the dance floor.

Gracie thought she was fast, fast with quick reactions. She studied martial arts. She liked to run. But shock, it turned out, could keep her rooted in place. As the explosion—fire and noise and smoke—punched through the air, she froze.

And then she was on the floor, behind the bar, under Dusty's heavy, protective weight.

She struggled to get up, feeling ice cubes under her back and heat on her front. Dusty held her down. His voice was insistent. "Stay down."

There was another explosion, followed by another—the sounds muffled to her stinging ears. Shards of glass beat across them like hot spikes.

Looking up, Gracie saw a roadway of smoke driving across the ceiling and pushed her hands against Dusty's chest. "Fire."

He rolled off her, helped her to her feet.

Blood ran down his face and neck. His expression was calm, his eyes dead serious. He quickly ran hands up and down her body, stopping at places she'd been cut. "Are you okay?"

Surprised to see buds of blood pooling on her arm and rolling down, she nodded. Beyond the bar, panic, like the blast wave, sent people racing, stumbling over bodies, shoving toward the exit.

The front doors quickly became choked with the pressing mob. Smoke began to compress the air. Gracie's furious mind considered a thousand options in a thousandth of a second. Soon the sprinklers would go off, increasing panic. People would push to escape, trample.

The emergency system would already have called 911, but they wouldn't get here in time to stop the crush.

She needed to create another way out. The stained-glass windows. The ones that had symbolized Sheila's vision for this space.

She got on her tiptoes to better reach Dusty's ear. "We need to break the stained-glass windows, create other ways out."

He nodded and shouted, "I'll get the one in front."

The big one. The one that would be harder to reach with the mob surging to the front door. Before she could object, he vaulted over the bar, grabbed a barstool, and made his way through the layers of smoke toward the front of the club.

Climbing over the bar, she landed on the other side almost on top of a guy and a woman curled on the floor. A tug on the woman's slender forearm got her to look up, eyeglasses broken, nose cut. "You okay?"

The woman nodded, and Gracie pulled her to standing. Together they grabbed the man's arms and helped him up. He staggered against the bar and held on. Tipsy or concussed? Hard to tell.

Coughing, eyes burning, Gracie picked a barstool up by the legs and lifted it over her head. Though she nearly lost her footing with the debris on the floor, she made it to the window, hauled back, pushed out from her hip, and tossed it. The stool smashed the glass but stuck on the leaded frame. *Fudge*.

Hacking, she grabbed another barstool and with a burst of energy that started as much in her desperate heart as in her right leg, she let the power and the scream rise up and out and hurled the heavy chair.

With a crash, the barstool tore clean through, dragging the first stool with it. Gracie nearly sagged with relief.

Someone scrambled up to the windowsill and began kicking out the remaining glass. Soon he had it clear enough that other people started climbing out.

At the other stain glassed window, the guy she'd helped held a barstool over his head. He sent it crashing through. And then the woman with the broken glasses climbed onto the windowsill, kicked out glass. Soon both windows had people scrambling out of them.

The sprinklers went off.

Water soaked people in seconds, making things slippery. Gracie fought her way through the overturned tables to the people struggling to get at the front door. She turned people around, got them to go out the window.

Once enough people began to see a clear, easier way out, the tide turned toward the windows, easing pressure on those at the front door. *Good*.

Gracie was guiding more people out when she remembered her chefs, Jack and Jenna.

Her heart pounding a thousand hopeless fists against her chest, she jumped back over the bar, ran through the walkway, and jerked to a halt in the kitchen.

It wasn't on fire? Smoke drifted about, but nowhere near as bad as in the main club. And the sprinklers, which went off only in areas where the temperature reached a certain degree, weren't on. Something wasn't right.

Jack and Jenna weren't in sight. Easy to see why. They would've had no problem going out the back. And, considering the smoke out front, would've had little choice.

A moment of relief followed by a crash of dread. *Victor*. Earlier, she'd let him upstairs to look at security footage. She sprinted across the kitchen and through the swinging doors into the back hall.

The lighted pad by the upstairs security door blinked with an error code. The door was programmed to unlock during a fire when someone unchipped was upstairs, but that shouldn't produce an error code.

Removing her Beretta from the secret compartment in the green bench in the hall, she pulled the heavy door open, took note that it was indeed unlocked, and ran up the stairs.

She glided through the hallway, calling on the smooth and measured training, the deep and pointed focus that had been with her since childhood. All the security pads along the hall were blinking.

How had three layers of back-up failed? Not right. Awareness locked on every shadow, split-second analysis of potential danger while dismissing the throb of alarms against her ears.

In the first room, the operations center, she found Victor. Calm and emotionless as a robot, she moved over to him and checked his pulse. Alive. Someone had knocked him hard on the head. So said the lump on the back of his skull.

She breathed a sigh of relief. He'd be okay. Squeezing his hand, she continued out and down the rest of the hall. Checked the server room and her office. All empty.

Her mouth grew dry. One room left. Weapon drawn, she stalked into the small hall that led to her apartment.

Her heart charged like a warrior intent on battle. She spun through the doorway, scanned. The bookcase that hid the elevator was open.

She moved deeper inside, toward the kitchenette, alert, ready to check behind the breakfast bar. At the last second, someone jumped out low and tried to grab her by the waist.

Using an avoidance technique, she slid to the side. Without any body to grab, the man fell. When he tried to get up, she brought her gun down across his masked face. Her sprinkler-moistened grip slipped and the gun glanced off his temple. Not hard enough. His head only jerked.

He leaped toward her, grabbed her gun hand, twisted. With a cry, she lost her weapon. Using her free arm, she sent an elbow into his nose. Fast. Hard.

He dropped to his knees then charged, grabbing her waist and shoving her backward.

Grasping the sides of his face, Gracie jabbed her thumbs into his eye sockets as her soaked feet refused purchase. He smashed her into the breakfast bar. Her back seized with the sharp jolt of pain. Air left her in a rush.

Fighting for breath, she forced one thumb into his eye. He cried out, pushed her off, slapped his hand to his eye and bent over.

Regaining her balance, she grasped him by the neck, drove his head down and hammered her kneecap into his face again and again.

Slam. His head jerked. *Slam*. His nose cracked. Blood soaked his mask. *Slam*. He made a sad, futile grunt and went boneless. She let go. He dropped to the floor.

She staggered away, the pain in her back making her

feel queasy. A sound alerted her to someone behind. She shifted just in time to feel the solid and unexpected whack of metal against her neck, followed by the sharp sting of what felt like a million volts of electricity from a stun baton.

She dropped to the ground, convulsing. Her teeth slammed together. Her eyes rolled back and into darkness.

Chapter 41

After stopping to help another person from the floor, Dusty picked up a barstool and pushed his way through the throng. The press of people, the heat of dimming fire, the cries of panic, and the driving urge of survival instinct forced him to use his size and strength to make his way forward.

If he'd been twenty pounds lighter, he'd have gone down for sure. Shaking water from his face like a dog, he sucked in thick, black smoke, coughed and hacked up phlegm through an already-aching throat.

Someone grabbed his belt from behind. With a chair held over his head, all he could do was look down. A woman. Using him to help get through the crowd, the way someone might follow an ambulance to get through traffic. He kept moving.

By the time he made the front window, he had a mini conga line trailing. No time to waste, he pitched the stool as hard as he could through the large stained-glass window. It shattered. The noise was lost to the alarm, screams, and gush of water.

The people behind him broke for the opening he'd just made. A few take-chargers took the lead and began directing others out the window. The crush at the front instantly lessened as people turned for the new exit.

He saw the flashing lights as a fire truck pulled up out front. Firemen started to haul people through the broken window as others with axes began to free people trapped at the front door.

Hacking into the crook of his arm, he pushed through the crowd and headed back into the club. Thick globules of wet drywall dropped from the ceiling and onto couches, where they burst apart like piñatas, spilling fist-sized chunks.

The ceiling? He looked up. *Damn it*. One of the explosions had come from the decorations.

He stepped over debris and scanned the club. Where the hell was Gracie? There was no way she'd leave until everyone else was out. Not while her staff and people were in need. *Her staff*. *The kitchen*.

Wiping water from his eyes, he vaulted over the bar just as a splintering crash sent a fighter jet decoration slamming onto the spot where he'd just been.

He loped through the hall and into the kitchen.

Smoke drifted about like fog, but it was clearer back here, easier to breathe. Nothing like the nostril-burning quality out front. And no sprinklers. What was going on?

Wiping soot, snot, and water from his face, grateful the bouncer had allowed him the weapon, he bent down and removed his Remington .380 from his ankle holster.

His mind alert, his body coiled with tension, he made his way through the kitchen and to the back hall. No one around, but the security pad on the door leading upstairs was flashing.

He crossed the hall and heard more than saw the club's back door being thrown open and a couple of firemen burst inside.

Slipping away, he opened the security door and climbed the stairs on the balls of his feet. At the top, gun drawn, he crouched and scanned the hall. *Empty*.

Stalking forward, he checked the first room and found a body. Male. It took him a moment to place the guy. He knelt and checked the guy's pulse. Alive. He patted his cheek. "Victor?"

Victor's brown eyes opened then widened with recognition. "Rescuing me. Got a thing for Latinos?"

"I got a thing for redheads and one in particular. Seen her?"

Victor shook his head, groaned, closed his eyes. "Stop fucking with her."

Guy was out of it. "We'll talk later. I'm giving you a pass."

Victor's eyes shot open. He tried to sit up. "Did you give Tony a pass?"

What? A slight press on Victor's shoulder kept him down. "Stay down. You hit your head."

The swish and clink of metal announced the fireman a second before his booming voice. "Fire and rescue. What we got here?"

Dusty hid his weapon. "Looks like a concussion."

Victor cursed. The fireman muscled in and Dusty retreated as the guy bent to Victor. Dusty left and made his way down the hall.

Where was Gracie? Had she gone out? No way. She wouldn't have left Victor up here. What had Victor been doing up here?

He quickened his pace down the hall, searching rooms as he went. A room with computer servers. An office. White. Clean. Sparsely decorated. Gracie's office.

Every door had a dead security pad. Turning the corner at the end of the hall, he saw the final door. Again security pad flashing error.

High alert surging in his blood, he stalked forward, pulled the door open, and saw her struggling from a seated position to her knees. After taking a hot second to make sure no one was in the apartment, he rushed over to her. She'd gone from kneeling back to sitting. "Where are you hurt?"

Grabbing his arm, she squeezed. "Dusty. The escape route, behind bookcase. Quick. Close it."

He looked over and saw what she meant. The bookcase was open to reveal a secret compartment.

Not bothering to argue with her—didn't know her well, but knew her well enough—he went over to the compartment and shut it. An elevator. An escape route? Was that how those who'd attacked her had gotten in? And if so, how the hell did they know this was here?

He turned back to ask her when two firemen came into the apartment.

The lights from emergency service vehicles, police and fire and ambulances, strobed across the back of Club When? The madness from inside had switched to the outside.

Injured people sitting on the ground, being tended at ambulances, walking around aimlessly. Less injured people crying, hugging, talking at each other as much as to each other.

Some people just standing around in shock. And lookie-loos gathered at the edge of the parking lot, still in their pajamas, watching the whole thing with curiosity.

Dusty guided Gracie over a fire hose as they exited the back of the club, then tried to steer her toward an ambulance.

She shook him off. "I don't need help. I need *to* help."

There was that upbringing of hers again. "You're going to be looked at first."

She began to argue, walk away. Dusty caught her by the forearm and held her for a moment. "Watch."

Her head swiveled, noted the ambulance that drove past and came to a halt in the parking lot, squeezing in between the fire truck and another ambulance. Two techs climbed out, rushing to meet a man carrying an injured woman. She had a tourniquet on her bleeding leg.

Gracie made a sound of grief so heavy and unexpected, his stomach turned sour.

He looked closer at the woman, her dress and dark hair. *Shit*. The woman at the bar, the one who'd been flirting with him. The one Gracie had given a free drink to.

Half of her right leg was missing.

Gracie's face scrunched in anger, tears dropped from her eyes. "This is my fault."

His heart broke for her. He leaned down. "Steady. It's not your fault."

"I should've known something like this might happen," she rasped. "That's my job."

"Grace, violence happens. It's not always easy to predict when. Don't convict yourself."

She looked at him. Broken. Hurt. Tear-stained. "How can I fix this?"

Fuck.

He folded her into his arms, gathering her up, so damn grateful she was okay, so damn grateful she let him hold her, hoping his strength could muffle some of her pain. He kissed the top of her head, swallowed over the bricks of anger stacking like a barrier, the Great

Wall of China, in his throat. "We are going to find whoever is behind this. It's that person's fault."

And he was done chasing his fucking tail when he already knew exactly who it was he needed, wanted to protect.

Chapter 42

Early morning, hours after the fire, Dusty walked through the surgical-white hospital corridor. The smell of smoke seemed to have taken up permanent residence in his nostrils. Probably better than the smell of hospital antiseptic.

With an apology for almost crashing into them, he veered out of the way of a woman with an IV bag walking with a nurse's aide in a candy-striped uniform.

He'd been up all night; so had Gracie.

He'd never seen a more determined person in his life. After he'd insisted Gracie be checked out—took nearly every bit of charm and convincing he had, stubborn woman—she'd gone nonstop. Helped out with the ambulances, talked to injured, consoled those in shock, talked with a few angry fellows Dusty had wanted to take down, but she'd handled it with...well, grace. She'd been interviewed by police and fire, insisted on coming here, checked on her staff, Victor, any available injured.

He'd been by her side through all of it, but she'd left him to speak with the hospital administrator about taking care of the bills, so he was on his own. And since he'd wanted to talk to the guy privately, because he sure had acted funny when Dusty had visited with Gracie, he turned into Victor's hospital room.

Victor sat up in bed. His dark eyes were pinned to a

television tuned to the news, which currently showed clips from the club fire.

Dusty rapped on the doorjamb he'd already entered. Victor looked up, waved him inside. Dusty purposefully kept his eyes off the screen. "You'd think that'd be the last thing you'd want to see."

Victor squinted one eye. "I'm just trying to catch up on what happened. I was knocked out through most of it."

He'd been unconscious because Victor had fought back—not only did he have a concussion, but a broken clavicle, a couple of broken ribs, and one hell of a shiner.

There'd been two men, and they'd wanted into the computers that Victor had been working on. Apparently, he'd been looking through some old surveillance footage of the club's exterior.

"Is it helping any?"

"Mostly it's just speculation on the Parish family's bad luck. Bringing up the drone attack earlier this year. No one's asking the obvious questions yet. Easy to see an explosion without a raging fire isn't amateur hour."

"Yeah. That's why I'm here. Trying to find out who is after Gracie."

Victor picked the corded remote off the guardrail where it hung, cringed in pain, rested his head back, and flicked off the television. "What is that?"

Now that he'd bothered to give Dusty his full attention, he'd noticed the flowers.

Dusty shrugged. "Wasn't sure of the protocol."

"I would've preferred a naked picture of your girlfriend."

Huh. This guy wanted to wave a red flag in front of a bull. "You're a lot less friendly now than when I was in here with Gracie. Heck, less friendly than the guy I remember from Mexico. And you were in a lot more pain in Mexico."

"Pain is a chronic condition when you get involved with the Parish family. You might want to write that down, tattoo it on that generous bicep, and walk away now."

Dusty walked over to the windowsill, put the flowers into a vase with other flowers. A little crowded, but he hadn't thought ahead. Sunlight streamed through the metal blinds and across the burgundy vinyl lounge chair. He sat, put his elbows on his knees. "Why are you so pissed at me?"

Victor turned his head to look at him. His eyes held the glassy sheen of medication, which explained why he seemed a tad slow to answer. "You need to be honest with Gracie. She might seem tough, but she's—"

"Not anyone I want to mess with. I got her. And I even get why you'd think poorly of me, but she knows why I'm here. She knows everything I'm about."

Victor lifted his head from the pillow, then let it drift back. He closed his eyes. "She knows about Tony? About his death?"

"I've been totally honest with her. And I'm no longer working my job."

That opened Victor's eyes. "So why are you here?"

A nurse came into the room to take his vitals and ask him a bunch of head-injury questions. Victor flirted outrageously with her, and she tossed a maybe-smile in his direction before leaving.

When she closed the door, Dusty continued their conversation. "Someone is after Grace. She tells me you've been helping her out. I'd like in on it."

His hand shaking, Victor picked up a Styrofoam cup

of water, missed his mouth twice with the straw, then finally managed a sip. "You know the players?"

"Rush and his family, specifically Porter. John and El."

Victor put down his drink. His eyes seemed to clear. "Specifically Porter?"

So the guy was going to feel him out first. "Yeah. Mukta has been using Gracie's existence to bribe Rush for thirty years."

Victor pressed the button on his bed and sat up straighter. "So why not Rush Senior?"

"Well, he's been dealing with Mutka for decades. He's got no reason to balk now. More likely the son, the campaign manager who would've had to vet his own father, discovered what was going on and decided to put an end to it."

"Seems like you got it all worked out."

"Come on, Victor. Get over whatever bug flew into your sweet tea and remember this is about Grace."

Victor scratched at an itch in a somewhat obscene place. "John and El have a money market account. One of them took out fifty thou last week and put it into an offshore account. A similar transfer of money happened right before Gracie was shot at."

That was an odd coincidence. But Dusty didn't buy them as perps. Still, a niggling voice told him there was something there. "Anything else on them?"

"I spotted his wife, El, taking pictures of Gracie's club."

"The wife?"

"She has a history. Got into a fight with another girl over her ex-boyfriend a dozen years back. She might've used those photos to help someone plant explosives."

"Outside the club? Doubtful." But if she'd been

looking for an architectural detail—could she have spotted something that would lead her to the elevator?

Victor shifted, made a face.

Dusty stood, reached out a hand. "Thanks. I'll get out of here."

Victor ignored the hand. "Don't ask her to choose between you and her family. It's not right."

Dusty dropped his hand. "Get some rest."

Out in the hall, Dusty considered the brick of truth that Victor had just lobbed at his head. He was right. He couldn't ask Gracie to make a choice between him and her family. The choice was his. So could he stand by not just Gracie, not just her family, but her mother?

He honestly didn't know.

Chapter 43

As the summer storm neared, the sky became a field of gray-blue. The wind picked up and whipped the late-blooming white flowers from the olive-barked Amur maackia. They drifted across the road, like petals cast before a bride on her way down the aisle.

Gracie usually loved this time of year, the magical drive through the flower-strewn country road that led to campus. Today, those petals reminded her of ash.

And lost limbs.

Including Victor, eight people had been injured badly enough to require hospitalization, though none as seriously as that woman who'd lost her leg. The straight shooter. All the way down to her drink.

Gracie closed her eyes, kept them closed. Pain pressed against her chest like a boulder.

Dusty drove, steadfast and intent behind the wheel of her car. They'd been awake for days, not just hours. And in that time they'd shared a lifetime. A heat like nothing she'd felt in her life, a connection, and then a crash back to reality. The anger and sadness when he'd admitted the focus of his investigation was Momma had been crushing. And then the explosion. He'd thrown her to the ground, saving her from worse injury. He'd then risked himself for those in the club and had stuck beside her afterward.

And if she was honest with herself, as much as it

scared her, she was so glad to have him here, to have him by her side.

Gracie opened her eyes and shifted her head toward Dusty. He had healing cuts from shattering glass along his handsome face. He caught her looking, winked. "Looks worse than it is."

True. And the explosion, as bad as it was, could've been worse. She was fairly certain it had been set to distract from whatever those two people who'd broken in upstairs were looking for. What *had* they been looking for? Had they known about her servers?

Dusty stopped at the elaborate wrought iron gate of the Mantua Academy campus. A security guard came out, checked the trunk, took their weapons and Dusty's bat-belt, checked credentials, did a pass under the car, waved them through.

He looked over at her as he accelerated through the gate. "Hate to think what happens when someone who's not family shows up."

She smiled. "They don't mess around."

They paused at the first stop sign. She looked right toward the school, lined walkways, spires, and brick buildings framed by marble pillars. It hurt her heart to see it so empty. Since the drone bombing a few months back, students hadn't been allowed to return.

"Which way?"

Gracie tried to answer but found her tongue stuck to the roof of her mouth. She was doing it. She was bringing him to the house. Yes, he was no longer working on the case, but still…"Left here, right at the next stop sign, and then up the hill."

He followed her directions up the big hill with the

big house at the top. *Big*. It wasn't just a McMansion or even a regular old mansion. It was the size of a palace.

It had to be to hide the operations center for the League of Warrior Women deep below ground. Hidden not just by earth but by a system that sent a false signal to any thermal imaging. Stealth technology that was closely guarded by her wealthy family. Because the idea behind the League—to help women—was simple, but the means to help them often complex.

She saw Dusty take in the huge home as they crested the hill. He looked over at her. "Bigger in person."

He'd meant it as a joke, but a thread of alarm worked its way down her spine. Should she have brought him here? Her family was unlike any other in the world. This place. Her siblings. It could be overwhelming. John had hated coming here.

Dusty pulled around the fountain and parked in one of the empty spots opposite the large stone mansion.

Disconnecting her cell from the car charger, she got out. Dusty grabbed her suitcase from the back seat and followed her.

At the top of the stone steps, both massive front doors were thrown open. Between them stood Momma, with her sturdy body in a light blue business suit and matching niqab, and her arms spread wide in invitation. Gracie moved quickly up the steps.

Until that exact moment, she'd never known what it felt like to arrive here, like so many of her sisters had, broken and in need of respite.

For the first time, she understood exactly how this home, these grounds, would seem to those kids. A sanctuary, a place that called out, "Here. Put down your burden. You are safe. And welcome."

She walked into Momma's waiting arms, which came around her soft and secure. Momma smelled like Une Rose and home. She whispered, "It will be all right."

Gracie didn't realize she was crying until the second set of arms came around her. Leland. Then there were more arms. And she sobbed and lost herself in the feel of her large family.

She couldn't see them with her eyes shut tight and trying to stop the tears. But she felt the love and warmth.

And then reality broke in.

"Stop stepping on my toes." A scuffle. A shove. And some angry words in a foreign language. Chinese.

The group broke up, and everyone piled into the house. She sensed Dusty walk through the threshold behind her. Momma turned to Dusty. Her dark eyes, already so mysterious when framed in her niqab, narrowed. "Aren't you the young man who is investigating me?"

Sugar. She knew?

Chapter 44

Dusty had to admit it was a mite awkward, standing in the most lavish entranceway he'd ever seen, a multi-million-dollar mansion, while a family of rescued kids hovered on the stairs. And the woman he'd been intent on taking down for the last few years stood there, smooth as the silk covering her face, accusing him, pretty accurately, of spying on her.

Gracie's head spun between him and her momma. His hand grew sweaty against the handle of Gracie's suitcase. "I'm not investigating anyone right now."

"What's that mean?" one of the older family members said from the steps. He looked up at her, and she looked back, brazen as all hell. The woman in her twenties had a blue stripe in her shiny black hair and a tattoo along her neck that he couldn't make out.

He heard Gracie whisper, "Troublemakers."

Momma turned to the woman who'd spoken. "That is a good question, but not yours to ask." She shooed everyone up the stairs. "Please find something else to occupy your afternoon."

Once they all took off, Leland said, "I'm not sure I like him being here at all. There's a lot we need to discuss."

Dude's voice was as rough as his attitude. Though he knew the guy from photos, they hadn't even been properly introduced. Dusty squared his shoulders; being big had its advantages, like letting this guy know he wasn't going anywhere. Not without a fight.

Mukta and Leland exchanged a long, wordless glance. Then Leland nodded and stepped back. What was that? Mind readers?

Gracie's momma turned her gaze back to Dusty. "You both look exhausted. Why don't you help Gracie to her room? I assume you'll be staying together. We can talk when you've had a chance to rest."

Mukta took Leland's arm. They turned and proceeded down the long hallway.

Gracie watched them go with her lips pressed tight. She turned to Dusty. "I wonder how much they know or suspect."

He wondered too. "Why don't we follow their suggestion and get some sleep before we go kicking at a hornet's nest?"

Despite wearing all her worries and her lack of sleep on her beautiful face, she gave him a small smile. "Good point."

Together, they turned and headed up the elaborate three-story staircase, wrought iron railing decorated in gold leaf.

Somewhere above, hidden by the sweeping turns of the stairway, kids chattered. Their differently accented voices echoed. Probably weren't many places in the world where this was possible. A regular Tower of Babel. But they seemed to make it work.

At the second landing, the floor branched off in a couple of directions. They turned right and then down the first hall on the left. "This," she said, "is known as Spice Girls Corridor. It's where Dada, Justice, Bridget, Tony, and I grew up."

"Spice Girls? Bet Tony loved that."

"He hated it. But we'd already had the name by the time he arrived. Momma had planned for our unit to have five. No one could've figured the last one would be a boy."

Planned? This was a bit of Parish culture he'd never heard before. "She plans the group size before adopting the kids."

"Yep. Momma is big into details. Of course, sometimes it doesn't work out. One unit, known as the Troublemakers Guild—the dark-haired girl with the blue streak is of that unit—was supposed to have five. But those three are enough to handle on their own."

"Units are divided by age, not when you're adopted, right?" Something crossed her face, but he couldn't decide what it meant. Anger? "Does it bother you that I know that?"

At her door—marked with her name in painted scrolling calligraphy on a beautiful hand-carved white-and-pink plaque—she stopped, shook her head. "No. Actually, makes it easier. And yeah, it goes by birth year. I was the first in my unit."

Her voice sounded smaller, as if she had reached into the past to retrieve it. "I can remember each of my siblings being added. Tony was twelve. The last one. The day he came marching down this hall with a new backpack, we were all waiting outside our suites. He looked so angry. I was so excited, so happy. I told Justice, 'We're complete now.'"

Dusty's breath came faster than it should. His head hurt the way it always did when he thought of Tony. *Leave it be, man. Leave it be.*

They walked into her room. Not a room. More, as

she'd said, a suite. There was a sitting area, a wall of windows, and a round table with a colorful mandala painted on top. The suite had been freshly made up, but still had the feel of a teen. Posters, teenage memorabilia, and photos.

There were a series of inset bookcases filled with books and model planes and a couple of Muay Thai trophies.

Gracie walked over to the table. "Knights of the Round Table," she said, picking up a red-framed photo of her unit from the center.

A tear fell from her eye. She put the photo down. He could feel her starting to close down, growing quiet. She turned and, without a word, went down a hallway leading off from the large sitting area. He followed past a huge closet and small bathroom. She stripped off her clothes, socks, bra, and tossed them willy-nilly onto the floor. She was losing it.

He placed her suitcase in the closet and picked up her clothes as he trailed behind her.

By the time he got into the bedroom, she was curled up on her side in her undies, on top of the blankets.

The bed was an exact match of the one he'd seen in her apartment. A huge bed with a wood canopy. Made him a little claustrophobic. But for her…

He took off his own clothes and put them, along with hers, on a chaise by the floor-to-ceiling windows. Beyond the windows was a park of a backyard with shrubs crafted to look like animals, walkways lined with flowers, and multiple seating areas.

He tugged the blankets out from under her, climbed into bed, gathered her to himself, and kissed the tears from her cheeks.

Chapter 45

Twenty hours after they'd arrived, Dusty awoke. For a moment, the panic of his dream changed into the panic of not knowing where he was. And then as he realized where he was, who was curled up in his arms, relief swept over him.

Just a dream. He'd dreamed Gracie was trapped in a burning building. He'd broken down door after door only to find himself faced with another door. Unable to reach her, he'd rammed his fists against the walls, trying to beat them down.

It had felt so real. Now with her warm and tucked up against him, he breathed deeply and said a prayer of gratitude to his Lord. And he made a decision. He'd do whatever he could to keep Gracie safe. Even if that meant allying with her vigilante family and the head of that family, Mukta Parish.

He kissed her lightly on her cheek. Warm. Then on the side of her lips. Heat. This woman had no idea what she did to him. She did enough that he was going to meet with her mother, ask her straight out about the digital recordings of Sheila. He needed the truth before he brought it up to Gracie.

He rolled out of the bed with care. Tired as she was, Grace didn't stir. He grabbed his jeans, T-shirt, and boots, took a pit stop in the bathroom, got cleaned up—bathroom was as well stocked as a posh hotel—and dressed. On his way, he grabbed an apple from a giant breakfast spread on the round table. He chewed as he went to find Mukta.

Though he'd never been here before, Dusty knew nearly every inch—well, every inch aboveground of the Mantua Home. The bureau had done a great job of taking photos and videos when they'd been here a couple of months ago.

The interior of the home was what his mother would've called a hodgepodge. Some folks called it eclectic. Mukta had done her best to incorporate a little from each culture in the decor. There was an almost comic mix of artwork in the wide hallway, with large floor lamps, ornate furnishings, tapestries, and thick hall furniture.

What he hadn't known from those photos and reports was what he now found most interesting. The smell of the place, clean and floral. The way all these cultures and personalities meshed. How did Mukta get them to feel such loyalty and kinship? The way they'd hugged Gracie. Still made his throat go tight.

He jogged lightly down the front interior stairs as the sound of kids playing drifted up from the indoor gym. Though Gracie's room had seemed a quiet oasis, the main part of the house was filled with laughter, teasing, and games.

Couldn't get over the fact that they had a gym off their elaborate front corridor. Four open doors, molded with dark wood, showed two teams playing a game of dodgeball.

The one male Parish, Gracie's younger brother—Romeo—played the role of referee. He had on an eye patch and was doing a fair Steve the Pirate from the movie *Dodgeball*, saying things like "Bollocks," and "Gar, this sucks."

Funny kid. He passed the gym and continued along the corridor with its hand-crafted red velvet gold-filigree designs.

The kind of money here…was insane. He drew up short as a little girl came running down the hall.

He called to her, "Where can I find Momma?"

She ran past, shouted, "In the library."

Russian accent?

Farther down the hall, marble pillars marked the grand entrance to the even grander library, with two-tiered walkways and books from floor to ceiling.

The library was downright charming. Colorful, with statues of fairies and imaginative ornamental globes. Two large chandeliers of winged pixies with tiny colored mirrors reflecting light—like twinkling stardust.

There were several seating areas and tables for private or group study. Mukta sat at a long table with a bank of Mac computers. She rose and came around the table. She wore a pastel pink business suit and matching niqab. She shook his hand. "Welcome. Welcome."

She had a good voice. Sort of whiskey and syrup. Sweet and strong. "Thank you. And thanks for your hospitality."

Her dark eyes never wavered from his. A direct woman. "It was the least I could do to repay you for being there for Gracie. Come sit." She sat and patted the seat beside hers.

Okay. He sat. The chair was a little small for him. Awkward. Seemed to be a family trait—keeping a man off-balance.

Her folded hands rested comfortably on the desk. It

was the most skin she showed. Those age-lined hands. "So you work for the FBI, are investigating me, and are sleeping with my daughter."

A lot awkward. "That your idea of an ice-breaker?"

She laughed; the brush of air fluttered her veil. "Being direct saves time. Time is precious and who I share it with greedily guarded, as that person takes from my family. Something I despise."

Well, that cleared it up. "You're worried about Grace."

The edges of her eyes creased. "Yes." She slowed as if counting her breaths, this pause in time, and found it worth her while. "Grace."

The heat rising in his body kicked him in the face. Calling her Grace and not Gracie had been stupid. Might as well have told the woman that, for him, it was more than sex.

He rested his hands on his knees. "My uncle always said there's no greater waste of time than an inauthentic man. The kind of guy that'll piss on a toilet seat 'fore lifting it up. So let me just state, flat out, I'm not here for you. I'm here to protect Grace, and if that means protecting you, so be it."

He let that marinate and soak into the exact meaning it needed, what he was offering, before he put out his demand. "I've been told you have a tape of Sheila Hall making accusations against Senator Rush. I need to authenticate it."

Mukta shifted in her chair. This obviously hadn't been the way she'd expected this to go. She composed herself quickly. "Why?"

"Because there are altered digital versions of that tape. Ones that suggest you have been blackmailing multiple officials with the same ruse. I need the original tape to prove the other versions are fake."

She leaned forward. "We obviously have a lot to discuss, but I have to ask. Did you tell Gracie about what her father did?"

His body washed with warmth. Woman hadn't even asked about the charges. She wanted to know about her daughter. "No. Wasn't sure she knew. Wasn't sure about the tape. Wanted to talk to you first."

She leaned back, as if satisfied. "We can discuss what kind of access I can allow you after I speak to Gracie, but if you don't mind, before we continue I'd really like to ask you another question."

"Okay. Shoot." Probably not the best colloquialism to use with a vigilante. *Suspected* vigilante. *Wink, wink.*

"What sparked your investigation into my family?"

Whoa. Lady knew how to strike at the heart of a matter. "I think that's Grace's story to tell."

Her eyes widened. "So she sent the email."

Fuck. How the hell…? Gracie wasn't going to like that he'd accidentally ratted her out to her momma.

Chapter 46

Gracie felt Dusty kiss her and get out of bed. She wanted him to stay so much it hurt. She could feel it in the center of her chest.

That scared her. What would happen between them now that he was here?

She waited for him to visit the bathroom and make his way out. After the click of the suite door, she threw off the blankets and picked up her clothes from the chaise.

Aw, he'd folded them.

Ignoring the bathroom to her left, she turned right into the closet. Had Dusty noticed that the bathroom he'd used only had a tiny shower? He must've. Man was big.

She flicked on the recessed lighting. The wide, shelf- and drawer-lined space lit up and was reflected in the wall of mirrors at the end. Pulling open the laundry chute, she dropped her clothes in, then pushed the glass wall open, revealing a secret room, and walked into the large, bright bathroom.

Covered in multihued stone, the bathroom had a spacious vanity, sauna, computerized multifunction toilet and bidet, and a set of long steps that led up to a six-person Jacuzzi. The bath overlooked the family grounds.

She went to the panel by the doorway, pressed the temperature and settings for her bath. She was sorely tempted to press *start* but set it to start in 120 minutes.

She dressed in black yoga pants and matching tank from her well-stocked closet. Out in the anteroom, she ate from the generous breakfast spread, poured some coffee. Pulling her laptop and cell from her bag, she set to work at the round table.

An hour later, she shut her laptop and wiped the tears from her eyes. That had been a rough series of phone calls. She'd contacted the hospital, checked on the injured, and made sure she was covering all of their hospital bills; she'd checked in with her employees as well.

She'd also called the police, the fire marshal, and her insurance company. Repairs might not be that awful, and could begin immediately. The investigators had expeditated the collection of evidence. Thanks, she was certain, to Momma's influence. Not that that had stopped her family. She wondered what they'd discovered while she'd been sleeping.

Time to find out. She headed downstairs. It hit her as she descended the staircase what she missed most about this place and why she enjoyed the nightlife of her club so much. The noise.

In total, fifteen of her siblings lived here. The house was filled with love, laughter, and arguments. Usually the arguments were between girls. After all, Momma had adopted only two males. And one of them was gone.

Oh, Tone. Miss you.

But when he'd been here, Tony rarely argued with anyone. So it was weird to hear a guy arguing with someone.

Gracie spotted him in the center of the gym. Romeo was openly arguing with Cee.

Gracie strolled toward the high-pitched conversation.

Romeo's voice strayed higher. "I think this has gone too far."

"What's gone too far?" Gracie said.

Romeo's head shot up. Cee spun around, a hand-in-the-cookie-jar look on her face.

Seriously, that's spy-craft 101: watch your back.

Romeo stepped forward to stand beside Cee. They wore the gym uniform—black workout pants, black tees, and bare feet. They couldn't have looked more like a team if they'd each had a lacrosse stick in their hands.

Even though she also wore black—force of habit—she definitely felt like the outsider.

"What's going on?"

"Nothing."

Both at once. It must be something. Could it be the case that Cee had talked about? "Come on, guys. I'm not the enemy here."

They stared at her, with thin bodies and thinly veiled guilt. She didn't like it. The two of them were up to something. And where was Jules, Romeo's twin and the third in their trio?

Okay. Fine. She could push them, but that wasn't going to get them to open up to her. "Let's go." She beckoned with her fingers to Romeo.

Romeo cast a glance around the gym as if for understanding. "What? You mean training?"

"Tony and I were the most advanced Muay Thai instructors. And Tony, our dear brother, is gone. So maybe I can catch you all up."

To her utter shock, Romeo burst into tears. *Crud on a cracker*. Shouldn't have mentioned Tony. He and Romeo had been close. Not only had Tony mentored him, but when Romeo had first come here, he'd been Tony's shadow. Tony had taken it as a compliment and had seen the need in the kid, a space he'd tried to fill.

Fudge. He was really crying. He needed a hug. She sucked at hugs. Putting her arms out, she walked forward like a short, red-headed Frankenstein's monster. Why couldn't Shelley have named the monster?

She heard Cee snort something that sounded like "Tin Man."

She wrapped her arms around the tall boy. Someone with a good sound effects machine should definitely start making rusty-hinge noises. He bent over, putting a weight on her that she hadn't expected. He was tall, like Tyler. She wrapped her arms tighter around him. "I'm sorry. I miss him too."

The kid sobbed harder. She felt her own throat grow tight. What had they done by telling these kids Tony was gone, but never having a funeral? When all of this was cleared up, she was going to insist Momma have a memorial service. They obviously hadn't processed their grief. And she included herself in that.

He pulled away, wiped at his eyes. "It means more because you suck so bad at it."

Gracie burst into laughter that met her own tears. That was a Tony quote. He'd said it as encouragement, as if the thing they were worst at, just because they tried, was worth so much more.

She'd been wrong not to come here, wrong to try and distance herself from them to win John's approval. She wiped her eyes. "I love you guys."

Their turn to look shocked. Cee looked down at the floor. "I'm sorry about your club, Gracie. I really am."

Aw. That was sweet. Romeo clapped a hand to his eyes, obviously embarrassed. “Me too. I mean, I’m sorry too.”

These kids. She wanted to get to know them well enough that they’d trust her with their secrets. Like Romeo had trusted Tony. “I appreciate that. And it sucks, but you know what, it got me here. And I’m glad I’m here.”

Cee perked up, smiled in a way that seemed triumphant. She rushed over and gave Gracie a quick, awkward hug. Gracie hugged her back. Two hugs in one day. She might get good at this.

Cee pulled away. “Definitely better the second time.”

Gracie had to laugh. “Okay. Let’s get to work. It’s not Muay Thai, but I’ll show you a move Tony taught me years ago. It’s saved my life twice.”

Chapter 47

ENTERING GRACIE'S SUITE, DUSTY SAW THAT SHE'D been up and busy. Her laptop, cell, and a stack of papers were on the round table.

He called out to her, but she didn't answer. He went to the bedroom area and couldn't find her. She must be somewhere in this huge home. Great. He'd have to send out a search party.

He turned to go back out and then heard it. Water running?

He followed the sound through the hoity-toity closet to the back wall of mirrors. Yep. Water. Another bath? He knocked on the glass.

"Dusty, if that's you, come in. Anyone else, go away."

Made a man feel special. He pushed, and the glass glided open. And who should he find sitting up to her perfect pink nipples in jetted bubbles but one Ms. Gracie Parish. "God, you're beautiful."

"Take off your clothes and get in. This is going to make your day."

He was pretty damn certain of that fact.

Dusty set the land-speed record for undressing, then climbed the stairs and dropped into the water. Thing was almost a pool. The heat loosened his muscles.

He drifted across the water to where Gracie sat. She had her head against the cushions and her eyes closed. He settled on the seat next to her, kissed her on the cheek, licked water off her neck, collarbone, sucked the lobe of her ear and then, "How was your morning? You okay?"

Her eyes still closed, her hand went between his legs and began to stroke. He sucked in a breath. Obviously didn't want to talk right now. He'd already been hard, but the hand job increased the pressure and pleasure. "Nice way to change the subject."

She laughed, opened her eyes. "How long do you think I can hold my breath?"

Before he could answer, her head dipped under the water. Her lovely ass floated up as her mouth slid around his cock. Holy hell. He grunted at the feel of her tongue working hot water against his hard-on. That felt incredible.

Her ass, damn near irresistible, bobbed in the water in front of him. Make that irresistible. He gave it a gentle spank. And beneath the water, Gracie went wild, dipping and sucking, and quickening that talented tongue.

Fuck. He fought to keep from coming, fisted his hands. She came up for air. Just in time.

The moment Gracie surfaced, out of breath, with her bottom still tingling, Dusty was on her. One of his hands squeezed her cheek, his mouth devoured her neck. He whispered, "That ass. None finer. None. All I could do to keep from reddening it properly."

She inhaled sharply at the thought, pressed her core against his hardness. "Yes to that."

He groaned, switched from devouring her neck to devouring her mouth. He kissed her like they had been apart a thousand years. And she was kissing him back with the same hot intensity, loving the feel of his strong, sure lips and tongue against hers, the needy way his hands ran along her body.

Her own impatient hands traveled over the heavy muscles of his arms, thick deltoids, biceps, traps, as she straddled him, and with barely a moment to reconsider, grabbed his length and slid down onto him. Her breath whooshed out in one startled rush.

"Careful there, Grace," he whispered into her mouth. She was tired of careful.

Grabbing his shoulders for support, she began to lift and lower along his hard length. As she rose up her butt broke the surface of the water, and he gave her a solid, stinging slap. The sound echoed in the room and sent heat along her skin. She moaned in approval. "Oh. That feels good."

"Goin' to make me come," he protested. But each time her butt rose above the surface of the water he delivered another. The rise and fall of her hips increased in speed, and she watched his handsome face fight for control as her breasts bounced in front of him. "Grace. Please."

The pressure built and built. She moaned against his forehead, into his ear, against his cheek, into his hair. And he held back his release, held back while her voice rose into sharp, desperate cries. Her body tensed, tightened, coiled, and exploded in a rush.

She came with a cry, muted by his shoulder as she bit down, but she still heard his quiet proclamation, "Watching you come…breathtaking."

Her head slumped forward onto his shoulder, her body paralyzed for a moment by how incredibly good that had felt.

He kissed her cheek, rubbed her backside. "You okay, darlin'?"

"Mmm," she managed, and he lifted her up, turned her, so she could kneel on the seat, facing the window. She braced her arms on the cushion. Head resting on her forearms, she looked at him, positioned to enter her.

Not a hint of playfulness, he told her, rough and sure, "That apple on your tattoo, I'd bite it a thousand times without a moment of regret. You're worth damnation."Her heart filled with warmth.

Brushing away wet strands of hair, he bent over her, kissed the back of her neck, moved a strong hand around her hip, down her stomach, down. His confident fingers teased her clit, dipped inside her softness. She instantly arched back, pumped her hips. Felt so good.

And because he was Dusty, and probably could talk a stone to dust, he told her about how hard he was, how deep he was going to enter her, how fast, until she gyrated her hips in rhythm with his hand and begged, "Yes. Please. Do that."

He chuckled. "Happy to oblige."

Removing skilled fingers, he grasped her waist, pushed deep inside. Her body responded instantly. Heat burst along her core. Tingles danced inside. Her need became urgent. She pushed back to meet every forceful stroke.

The slap, slap of their bodies, the splash of water, the whir of the jetted bubbles couldn't compete with her cries of pleasure.

She called out to him as the fever built inside and broke across her in tremors that wracked her with mindless rapture. Panting, she tried to catch her breath.

He bent forward, snaked a hand under her stomach, lifted her hips and thrust hungrily. She could feel every inch of him, sense his skin start to tighten, feel the electric explosion that rocked his body through the heat that spread through her core.

He came with a fierce growl, a sound so animalistic she was sure he'd gone back in time, all the way back to his caveman roots.

He pumped into her for long, greedy moments. And then his hips slowed. He dropped back, settled on the seat, brought her, quaking and as malleable as putty, onto his lap.

He snuggled into her neck. She moved to give him access. She was pretty sure that saying "in like a lion and out like a lamb" referred to Dusty. He sure did like to cuddle after.

He kissed her forehead. "Grace," he breathed hard. "Didn't just make my day. Made my life."

Hers too. She kissed his swollen lips. "Where did you go earlier?"

"Uh..." He stopped kissing. His eyes opened wide. He cleared his throat. "'Bout that..."

Dusty at a loss for words? This wasn't going to be good.

Chapter 48

Leland and Momma's dual office was on the ground floor of the Mantua Home. Their styles were so different, the room practically had a line drawn down the middle of it: Momma's whimsical, bold color palette and Leland's no-nonsense cowhide and earth tones.

Gracie and Dusty sat side-by-side on midnight-purple chairs, watching a screen that had lowered from a compartment in the ceiling. Momma and Leland sat across from them on a recently acquired designer showpiece. A multicolored couch that looked like a quilt, like it had been sewn together from dozens of bright fabrics. Kind of like their family.

Projected onto the screen was Gracie's mother, Sheila. This wasn't the woman Gracie remembered. The woman who'd been sick.

When this had been recorded, her mother had had a thin, girlish body and a guileless look. Thus far, the interview had concentrated on why she'd come to the United States, how she'd gotten involved in politics, and how she'd met the would-be senator.

But then an off-camera female interviewer asked her to describe the night of the "incident."

The story came out haltingly. How candidate Rush took opportunities to speak with Sheila, make her laugh, and how he'd offered her a ride home one night. He'd insisted on walking her up to her apartment and once there had asked for a drink of water. Inside, Sheila had toasted water-filled glasses with him to a bright future.

She described seeing the candidate to the door, beginning to say goodbye, feeling fuzzy. She'd mumbled, tried to grab the door handle for stability, and the world had gone dark.

Though her heart ached on hearing these details, the logical part of Gracie could see how this tape could've been altered to have the questioner ask different things, making it look like her mother was speaking about a different man. The questions were very leading. The interviewer doing her best to make it easy on her mother.

Thirty years ago, it might've been difficult to alter the tape, but nowadays, video was easily manipulated. The interviewer asked questions like a talk show host, leading the narrative, filling in blanks.

But Gracie could see the honesty of it. There wasn't a question in her mind what her father, Senator Rush, had done.

On screen the corners of Sheila's eyes tensed as she paused her story, obviously trying to keep control of her emotions. She fiddled with her necklace, whisking the cross back and forth along the chain. Her eyes filled with tears.

"Are you okay?" the questioner asked. Sheila's hand stopped and her cheeks grew pink. She nodded, swallowed, then shook her head.

The interviewer changed her line of questioning. "Are you okay to go on?"

Sheila's caramel-brown eyes lifted. She drew up her shoulders. So young. She nodded.

"Can you tell me what happened to you next?"

She dropped the cross as if it burned, balled her hands into fists on her lap as the tears slipped from her eyes.

Gracie could feel Momma and Leland across from her, ready to pounce forward and rescue her from this truth. Dusty put his hand on her knee, squeezed. It steadied her.

Sheila remembered nothing else of the night. She'd woken up the next morning on the couch. Alone. Her body hurt.

Not just her "front part," she said, wiping the tears, "but the back too."

Gracie tensed. The interviewer very gently asked, "Were you a virgin?"

Sheila lowered her head, nodded again, and broke into sobs. The tape winked to black. When it started again, Sheila had a tissue balled up in her right hand.

"I didn't go to the police. It'd be him against me. I didn't even have citizenship. I wouldn't matter."

"You matter," Dusty told the girl on the screen.

Gracie's heart opened even more to him. She did matter. All of the women and girls who were discounted and not believed, who were taught playing a role or playing by the rules would keep them safe. And then had those rules, that very role—the one that didn't let them question a senator or act rudely toward him—be the thing that doomed them. She mattered.

Gracie stopped the playback. The rest Momma had explained to her. Her mother had made friends with one of the Parish girls, a sister Gracie saw more on TV than in real life. She was an international reporter. Back then, she'd just been starting out and had been reporting on the campaign.

Sheila had confided in her. Maybe hoping this reporter would believe her. She had. But she hadn't taken it to the police. She'd taken it and news of the pregnancy to Momma.

And Momma had done what Momma did. She'd sought justice. Gracie didn't even hold that blackmail against her.

She delighted in it.

She hoped Rush had squirmed all these years, fearful. She hoped that he'd doubted his safety, doubted his choices, regretted his decisions. She hoped he'd spent years looking over his shoulder, checking the locks on his home, years terrified of what might happen.

Just as her mother had done.

Momma turned from the screen and focused on Gracie. Her dark eyes were wary. Maybe sad. "Do you have any questions, daughter?"

She had a thousand questions. About why she'd never been told. About who else in the family knew. About all the different ways Rush had been blackmailed. About...a thousand useless things. Because right now the important question was...

"How do we take Rush down? Not just stop him or whoever is after me, but stop that creep from becoming president."

She saw Leland smile a that's-my-girl smile. Darn tootin'. Questions could come later. When she could go back to fixing her club, making it up to the injured, perfecting her creeper detection software, expanding the underground railroad, protecting any women who might think, like her mother had thought, they didn't matter.

Then she would ask her questions. And make it up to Momma for sending that email.

Momma looked to Dusty. "And what of you? Are you interested in joining us?"

Her heart in her throat, Gracie swiveled in her seat to look at Dusty. She flinched at the uncertainty on his face. She tried not to feel the sharp ache in her chest. After all, he'd come to take down their vigilante organization, not to join it.

Leland made a disparaging sound. "We can't trust him."

Dusty met Leland's straight stare with one of his own then squared his broad shoulders. Gracie wondered if Dusty knew just how intimidating that looked.

"I appreciate your concern, Leland, I do," Dusty said, crossing his arms and making himself look even bigger. "But if I wasn't already all-in, I wouldn't be here, revealing company secrets, breaking the law. I'm hesitating because I'm not sure you will let me do my job."

"Your job as an agent investigating my family?" Leland said in a tone that had as much bite as growl.

Dusty's legs were flung out in front of him and crossed at his ankles. Casual. Except for his crossed arms and the storm in his eyes. "That's the issue, ain't it?" He was laying the Southern on thick. "I'm gonna need in on everything you got information-wise on Rush. On the blackmail. Anything that will help me identify the real threat and work with you to figure out how to end it. Something tells me y'all aren't prepared to give me what I need."

Gracie fisted her hands, dug her nails into her palms. Dusty had basically asked for proof of the family's vigilante activities and the blackmail. He'd asked them to trust him, take him not just into this house, but into the inner circle. The exact thing he'd explained to her that he'd wanted when he'd first contacted Tony.

Leland nodded as if this confirmed his suspicions. "We have a whole organization here. Trained people who've been on hiatus and are itching for work. We don't need you."

Gracie took a deep breath. Let it out. "You're wrong."

Momma and Leland gave her their attention. She held her head high and took the leap of faith. "We need him. He has valuable information, and more than that, I trust him."

A brick of silence crashed into the room. It thudded down, kicked up dust, and sent Momma's and Leland's eyes rapidly blinking.

She chanced a peek at Dusty. He smiled at her, smiled like a kid on Christmas morning. His heart, as the saying goes, in his eyes.

"See there," Dusty said. "Always knew you had good instincts." He addressed Leland and Momma. "And I think a good family. So if you can't offer me the same trust, maybe you can trust the facts. Facts are, I got no reason to go against you right now. I'm off the case. Punched out my boss. Sleeping with the enemy."

He winked at Gracie. She shook her head, bit back her smile.

Leland and Momma exchanged another long look. And though it was subtle, Gracie saw a signal pass between them, a tip of Leland's chin, an acceptance.

Momma clasped her hands together. All business. Except for the jingle of the bracelets on her arm. "What do we know so far?"

For the next forty minutes the group exchanged information. The flow of ideas and facts set the energy in the room buzzing. It reminded Gracie why she needed a team. Why no one person could do this on their own. And she was genuinely grateful to them, her team. For seeing the things she couldn't, for using their talents and skills to aid her.

Though, of course, that didn't mean they'd always say things she wanted to hear.

"Although I dearly respect Victor," Momma said, after Gracie told her that he'd been helping her on the case, "how focused could his investigation be when still recovering from severe injuries and simultaneously picking up the slack for his partner—now overseas with Justice."

The implication was obvious. *He isn't Superman. We need to reevaluate his research on the Rush family.*

Leland, as was so often the case, picked up the ball Momma had started rolling and ran with it. "Tell me what you've learned about Rush's family. All of them, including the wife."

Another long discussion of the facts, in which Dusty added that the odd coincidences around John and El couldn't be discounted, but his money was on Porter.

Momma nodded. "Porter is a good place to focus our attention." She fiddled with the series of gold bangles on her wrist. "But not just him."

She looked at Leland. "I don't know, but the attempts on Gracie's life, they feel…personal."

Leland cocked his head to the side. They stared at each other and simultaneously said, "The sister."

"Layla?" Gracie said, the shock in her voice obvious. That was not where she'd thought this was headed.

Dusty whistled like he'd had an epiphany. "She has multiple degrees in computer engineering, including as an artificial intelligence programmer," he said. "Would've been able to mess with the security at the club, allowing those guys who broke in access through the tunnel."

True. But how would she have known about the tunnel?

"She could have altered the video," Momma added. "Maybe her brother gave her the copied video, the one we sent to Andrew years ago. Maybe they are working together."

Layla? Could it be? Could she want her father to be president that badly? Or was this something else, anger over being ousted from her role as the one and only Rush girl?

"She's rich, too," Gracie said. "And Victor says she has millions of Twitter followers."

"No one easier to manipulate than someone with a bit of hero worship," Dusty said.

As soon as the idea was out there, they began to build on it, on how Porter and Layla had conspired. The ease with which they tossed out different hypotheses drove home the fact that the group had grown comfortable with each other in the last hour, if not certain of each other.

In the end, Gracie's head was swimming. "So we have some theories here, but not anything concrete. If Layla did set fire to the club in order to get information, she made a big mistake. The servers dump anything incriminating automatically when 911 is called. But I'll take a closer look at Layla. And if it's her, I'll find her weakness, a point of attack."

If Layla thought she could out-hack her, she was dead wrong. Emphasis on dead.

Leland, who'd taken out his iPad and was typing madly on it, said, "Evidence that she doctored those videos would come in handy."

So would a confession. Sheesh. "Is it possible for me to use the computers down in internal security?"

Leland eyed Dusty, shook his head. "No. Much too risky right now. Not only because of the FBI investigation, but we have reason to believe the NSA is directing satellites toward the house. We can do nothing that will send a signal from that area."

That made it harder. "Fine. I'll head back to the club tonight—"

"Tonight?" Momma said. "But what of dinner?"

"Tomorrow then. The upstairs wasn't damaged and my computers will more than do the job."

"And since they're eager for the work, I'll assign someone from internal to do a thorough investigation of the other Rush children just so we are certain."

"I'm going to take a closer look at John and El," Dusty said. "Something is definitely not right there. Too many coincidences."

And like that, the group had their marching orders. Find proof of who was after them and stop them. Hard.

And now that she was focused on it, and not on keeping secrets from Dusty and Momma, now that she had a team, she knew everything would fall quickly into place. As long as whoever was after her, betting money still on Layla and Porter, didn't have anything else up their sleeves.

Chapter 49

WEARING A BORROWED SUIT FROM WHAT LELAND called "stock," Dusty took in the immense dining room. It was dominated by a giant table long enough to bowl on. Above, gnarled wood beams crossed the fifty-foot high vaulted ceilings, graced with a shiny row of assorted chandeliers.

The table was set with blue crystal goblets, gleaming blue plates, and vases of blue roses running down the center.

Swanky didn't cover it. The same little girl he'd seen earlier ran past him and into the dining room, shouting, "Gracie's here!"

His heart echoed her shout as he spun to greet her.

Good Lord, that wasn't fair.

Blood exploded through his body like a hot, painful grenade.

Grace. Had dressed up.

She wore an off-the shoulder sapphire dress that swathed around her hips like a second skin. Her hair was down, kissing those bare shoulders. The swing of her stride, in heels that showed off every sleek muscle, set his heart racing and dried his tongue.

She came to a stop before him. Her eyes traveled down his body. "You look handsome all dressed up."

This was the point where he knew language should come out of his mouth, something spectacular that let her know exactly how positively gorgeous she looked—and how he'd worship every inch of her later tonight. And every single night thereafter.

All he could manage was a restraining hand to his chest, because she'd shot him dead center.

Her face warmed with heat. "You like?"

He liked. If only he knew sign language, he'd tell her just how much he *liked*.

Aw, hell. He put his hands on her waist and pulled her so close the heat of contact drew a hiss from his mouth. And then he kissed her, a slow torture that spoke every phrase he really wished he could say.

He drew back, and she, as if she'd heard every word, whispered to him, "I hope that's a promise."

He found his voice. "It's the start of a promise." A bit rough, but he'd found it. "You get the rest later. So eat up now. You'll need nourishment."

She blushed a heart-revving red, and they turned to find seats at the table—the giant dining table where every eye was now turned on them.

Including her mother's and Leland's.

Aw, damn, he'd forgotten where he was.

Completely unfair.

After giving him the sibling tour, Gracie led him to the head of the table where they sat near Leland and Mukta. Much to his surprise, Leland and Mukta spent dinner acting like regular parents. Talking with kids. Telling others to take a seat. Keeping people in line. Helping Bella, the little Russian kid, cut her steak.

Bella had made a good choice with the steak. His

was damn good. The whole night, so far, had been damn good.

And although Dusty had been around two other Parish kids, being with a whole bunch of them was a totally different experience. The thing he noticed most, besides the sense of unity and inside jokes, was the swearing.

Though Momma had reprimanded a few people close to the head of the table for swearing at dinner, in general it was allowed. He supposed raising kids from shit situations all over the world, getting them to heal, feel trust, was probably higher on the agenda than etiquette. Not to mention raising proper ladies was probably at odds with raising vigilantes. So he had to know.

Swallowing a sip of water—seemed a sin to wash down even the memory of that steak—he leaned over and whispered to Gracie, "Seems like your whole family cusses." He nodded toward Bella. "Pretty sure I heard that five-year-old swear in Russian. So what gives, why don't you ever cuss?"

She scooped up a forkful of potatoes. "Growing up, I was a multilingual curser." She lowered her voice. "Except for the b-word, of course."

Did she mean bitch? Wasn't that *the* girl word? They all used it. "Help me understand that 'of course.'"

She swallowed the potatoes. "That word…it's like, I guess, a trigger. A lot of my sisters came from situations where that word labeled them. It described their femaleness as lesser. A wrongness. It's taboo. Hurtful."

He looked around the room at the kids eating and laughing. Decided right there and then he'd never use that word again. "So you used to cuss, but not that word."

"Yep. Until I had a baby. John hated my cursing. He

wouldn't let a *damn* pass without comment. And really, he was right. I mean, who curses around a baby, even if it is in another language?"

Practically every adult he'd ever met. "So I get why you stopped, but you still don't swear."

She looked down at her nearly finished plate. "Yeah. Well, it's my way of still being a mom. And my penance for letting Tyler go."

She meant her way of never forgiving herself. Damn. Hurt his heart. "Remember that story I told you about me getting sick and my uncle coming into my dad's ministry to get me out?"

She put down her fork. "Yeah."

"My mom called him. She called him to come get me and take me out, even though she knew if she'd tried to go with me, my dad never would've let me go."

Her eyes widened.

"Yep. She gave me up, so my life would be better. That's what you did for Ty. Given the choice, you sacrificed yourself to keep someone you love safe."

A tear slid down her face. She let it sit there, exposed and raw. He brushed it away for her. "I know you wish you could take back that time you weren't there," he said. "But you have to realize you did what you did out of love."

More tears. This time, she wiped them aside. Then tipped up her head and kissed him on the lips.

Dusty jolted. Not just from the kiss. At the pinch. He adjusted himself and looked down at Bella. The corners of her dark eyes squinted in anger. "Don't make Gracie cry."

Gracie laughed.

Aw, hell. These kids. Tugged at a man's heart. "Yes, ma'am. Sorry 'bout that."

Chapter 50

After dinner, Gracie was ready to skip dessert and head to bed. She was nervous about tomorrow, about leaving the safety of campus and going back to her club. But then the dessert trays were brought out and she caught Dusty's gaze, and knew she'd be staying for dessert.

He leaned over to her. "I grew up with an aunt who could make a mean pecan pie, but this is Cake Boss–type material."

She kissed him on his cheek. "For such a strong-looking guy, sometimes you're just a big kid."

He grinned at her. "Who doesn't like cake?"

The servers carried the artful cakes around the table as her siblings oohed and aahed.

After everyone had a chance to appreciate the cakes, they were taken to a serving station. One of the servers, a big guy with an easy grin and a Pacific Islander tan, took out a gleaming silver knife, and with a flourish that sent the kids clapping, began to cut pieces.

Gracie decided on the Mantua Home's world-famous cheesecake and Dusty had red velvet because he'd never had it before. Once he'd made this announcement to the table, the kids around him watched intently as he took his first bite.

It was kind of adorable. Gracie watched too. Dusty, the adorable show off, exaggerated with a raise of his eyebrows, then he closed his eyes and declared it, "Good enough to make the angels sing."

With the addition of sugar, the conversation at the table reached earsplitting levels, a near deafening sound broken when Momma stood and clapped her hands twice. The room echoed her claps. Then silence. She nodded in approval. "It's time for us to share a story."

Gracie startled. They were doing that tonight? She grabbed Dusty's arm. "Let's go to bed."

"You sure?" he said, sounding as if he wanted to stay.

Momma passed behind them on the way into the other room. She put her hand on Dusty's shoulder. "I'd like you to hear this. It's my story. The way this all"—she waved around—"came to be."

Fudge. Gracie looked down as she heard Dusty tell Momma he was "Looking forward to it."

Gracie wasn't sure...scratch that, she *was* sure. She didn't want Dusty to hear this, but she had no idea how to stop it without causing a huge scene.

The girls left their dessert plates and headed over to the room with the large hearth visible through an arched doorway.

Her heart hammering, Gracie escorted him into the paneled room. They watched as the girls took seats around the brick hearth, plopped down on blue-and-gold pillows, and formed a circle. Unlike at the table where everyone sat with others their age—their units—the girls mixed it up. Older girls called the younger ones to sit beside them.

Dusty grabbed two cushions and they settled on the floor.

He put one arm behind her, leaned on it, so that her entire side warmed with his large, comforting presence. "So this is a big deal?"

"Yeah." She put a hand on his arm. She at least owed him a warning. "It's another way we stay close. Each person here has a story that tells us about them, where they came from. Even me. Our stories are told in second person, read by a professional. The idea is that you feel the others' stories, and that we join and know one another that way. Tonight, it's my mother's. It's kind of brutal."

"And the kids are okay hearing it?"

She looked around at her siblings. "They've lived it, Dusty. And just so you know, we don't ever let strangers hear these stories."

"Never?"

She nodded, gestured at the room. "Not even the staff is allowed."

"So this is—"

A recording whispered out at them from audio speakers. Everyone went silent as a soft female voice spoke.

You walk into the Red Cross tent with feet chalked white from the dust and dirt of the road.

Your head pulses with a thousand painful fires. Rejection. Regret. Injustice. Thirst.

Sliding onto the hot stool by the entrance, you wait to be noticed. It doesn't take long. A woman gasps, grabbing at the loose-sleeved olive shirt of another woman. "Karen," she says, forcing her to turn around.

Their colored eyes, specks of blue and green and yellow, float over you. Like flower petals adrift in a bowl of water. You can't help but be drawn to them as they bloom with pity.

The second woman, Karen, comes to you without hesitation. She scoops you from the chair, murmuring words you cannot understand. And yet they comfort your ragged thoughts, tucking in grief with their plush softness as she places you upon a plain, narrow bed.

Her words seem kind, soothing. But under that softness rests a pallet of ripe anger, a frustration born of centuries. You recognize the sound. It has been with you since that far-off day, before your very first moments of true pain. That day, your mother whispered to you, "They will cut you here," and placed her warm hand between your legs, "because we must pay the price of desire. No charm comes without a chain."

"Who did this to your face?" Karen asks, speaking English now. Her oddly accented words sound clipped and tight.

You say, "A man."

As the story continued, recounting Momma's pain, humiliation, and being rejected by her family, Gracie watched every emotion that crossed Dusty's face. She saw the sympathy, the disbelief, and anger. And then she saw him change, grow tense and uncomfortable.

The story finished up with Momma being adopted by the women in that tent—a lesbian couple, one of which happened to be the daughter of the wealthy Coleman Bell Parish.

It stopped there, with the happy ending.

Dusty's face looked anything but happy. She had watched his darkening facial expressions like they were the most important thing she'd ever see. Maybe because it felt that way. She'd paid such close attention that when he stood from their cushions on the floor and said, "I'm gonna get going," she knew.

He didn't understand. He was going to leave, like John, and never come back.

With her heart aching, she got up from the floor too. Around them, her sisters cried and spoke and shared their own stories in the quiet aftermath. A wave of love for them enveloped her.

Did he see? Did he see how the story helped them share their own pain, how they felt less ashamed? Did he see how children from all over the world suddenly came together as one loving unit, a family? Momma's story had become their story. Just as each of their stories became the family's story.

His eyes were shocked and bothered. No, he didn't see. Looking around, he'd taken in what she'd seen but reached a completely different conclusion.

She hardened her heart and her voice. "Can I walk you to your car?"

His eyes settled on her, on her tell-a-tale face. He opened his mouth, closed it, swallowed whatever he'd been about to say. "Sure."

After saying good night to Momma and Leland, Dusty took her by the arm, and they walked in silence through the hallways until they came to the front doors.

Dusty turned to her. "Grace, I don't actually have my car."

She knew that. "You said good night to Momma, told her you weren't staying. I'm sure she directed someone to bring a limo around for you."

He looked toward the front doors. "Kind of her."

"That's Momma."

He shifted. "Grace—"

"Don't," she said. "I can see it in your face. You don't approve. Trust me, I've been here."

That got a reaction. His eyes widened, he leaned closer. "No. You haven't. That's not this. Not me."

"Yet you're leaving. I saw your reaction during the reading. I saw it."

"What you saw is complicated. Not so much disapproval as—" he ran a hand through his hair. "It got me. I'll admit that. Reminded me of my childhood, of the way my dad would manipulate people."

"This isn't like that. You've met my sisters, seen the tape of my mother. Why is it so wrong for us to talk about what we've been through, to share with other people? Why are you so bothered by our truth?"

"Fuck, no." He shook his head. His honey eyes were angry, intense. "It's not about that, about you. It's about me. The fucked-up way I was raised. You get that? I just need time to process. Can you give me that?"

Of course. But she was still worried. Her family had revealed a lot to him. She wanted him to understand and accept them. She placed a hand on his arm. "I know the storytelling feels manipulative, but it's not. We can't understand each other's story, each other's pain, unless it feels like we are experiencing it for ourselves."

He let out a long breath. "Give me the night, okay? I'll see you at your club tomorrow. I'd like to take a look around."

She understood what he was asking, but it still hurt. It still felt like rejection. "Sure."

He bent and kissed her on the lips. "Night, darlin'. I'll see you tomorrow."

She watched him leave. Tomorrow? She didn't believe that. Not for one minute.

Chapter 51

INSIDE THE LAVISH SITTING AREA OF HIS SPACIOUS InterContinental Hotel suite, Porter Rush ended his phone call and placed his cell on the stack of files in front of him. His palms were sweating. He shouldn't be doing this. It wasn't him. He didn't do intrigue. He didn't manipulate government agencies, make them his lap dog. And he sure as hell didn't lie to his father, play him, in order to make him look innocent to the FBI.

His father came out of his room cleaned up, dressed for the dinner, and looking at the index cards his speech was written on. The man had to get more comfortable with a teleprompter. "Porter, who are the main donors at our dinner tonight?"

This was it. He stood up. "Dad, remember when I told you about that investigation into Mukta Parish?"

His father's eyebrows drew together. "I thought you were going to make that go away."

Porter's stomach turned. This "going away" was not an option. The only option was to play the hand dealt. "Why would you want this to go away, Dad?" It was a lifeline. "You're a victim fighting back. For years men have been wrongly accused, blackmailed and made to dance because a woman decided to lie. Enough."

His father's face changed from calm to fury. The difference between day and night. "Don't try to spin my own life to me, Porter. I know what happened. And you seem to think this is going to be easy. It's not. You have to weigh the cost here. One cabinet position versus being dragged through the mud."

"Dad, the FBI investigation into Mukta Parish all but guaranteed we were going to be dragged through the mud. You saw what the file said. Your voting record. The funding… But these tapes change all of that."

The tapes would shield his father from the worst of it and send the ire toward Mukta Parish. Ire she rightly deserved after years of torturing his father, holding this over his head.

"Awfully convenient," his father said. "These tapes."

Not one muscle on Porter's face moved. "What is it you say when we're given donations from questionable sources, Dad? Don't look a gift horse in the mouth?"

His father pocketed his index cards, went into the kitchenette, opened the fridge, and took out a Perrier. He opened it with a snap. "Porter you're putting unnecessary energy into this strategy." He took a sip from the bottle. A bottle big enough for four. "It's almost an obsession with you. Once elected, I'll be nearly untouchable. Let's focus on getting there. Not on this sideshow."

The man had no idea. He was that clueless. That self-confidence was great, most of the time, but right now it rankled. His dad honestly thought this would just go away. Porter knew better. Knew enough that he was risking everything on what would happen in this room in the next few moments.

There was a knock on the door. Porter let out a breath. "It'll be okay, Dad. Just answer the agent's questions honestly."

His father looked toward the door and back to Porter's guilty face. Slamming his bottle onto the counter, he stormed across the room and grabbed Porter by the lapels of his suit jacket. "What have you done?"

The knock came again. "Let go, Dad. I need to answer it."

His father let go, but Porter saw that his hands shook. Taking a steadying breath, Porter crossed the room and opened the door. The FBI agent stepped inside and Porter introduced him to his father.

He approached Porter's father without hesitation. "Your son said it would be okay, Senator, if I took a small moment of your time."

His father cast Porter a wounded look. "Of course. Let's sit."

Porter couldn't sit. He paced, watched as the two men took seats on the suite's stylish couches.

The agent wasted no time. "Senator Rush, it's recently come to my attention that you may have been a victim of a scam that Mukta Parish has been running on influential men."

His father visibly relaxed. "It's been many years. I'm not interested in pressing charges."

The agent's eyebrows rose to his hairline. "With all due respect, sir, whether or not you want to press charges isn't why I'm here. I'm here to ask you if you know of any reason someone might want to murder your illegitimate daughter, Gracie Parish."

His father shot to his feet. "What? She's dead?" His gaze swung from the agent to Porter, his eyes filled with genuine regret. "I didn't..." He stepped toward Porter. "You have to believe..."

Porter's relief was so intense his legs almost gave out from under him. His father had done good. Better than he could have expected. He went to his father, grabbed and hugged him. "Dad. You weren't listening. He didn't ask if *you'd* killed her."

He stepped back from his father. They exchanged glances. "And no, she's not dead."

His father visibly composed himself, as much as he could, and plopped back down in an unsteady lump.

The agent leaned forward. "Sorry that I had to test you like that, sir. I had to make sure. And now that I know, I want you to know I'm on your side here. It's going to be okay."

His father, ruffled feathers soothed, said, "I'm sorry, Special Agent… What was your name again?"

The trim man with the plain face smiled. "It's Dillon Mackenzie. Mack for short."

Chapter 52

WEARING A CHARCOAL-GRAY PANTSUIT BUTTONED UP OVER A white cami, with her hair pulled back into a tight bun, Gracie speed-walked through the hospital corridor. Her heart kept time with her sharp-heeled footfalls. The click and pound echoed across her jangled nerves.

One more room to visit.

Noting the numbers on the doors, she counted them down like a doomsday clock. When she arrived at the correct room, the door was closed. She took a deep, fortifying breath. Using a single knuckle, she rapped politely.

The door was opened by an older man. Thick black hair, still black eyes, the memory of smiles lined a face darkened by the heritage of desert sun.

His questioning gaze ran over her, over her suit, then settled on the vase of flowers. His heavy eyebrows bunched together. "Can I help you?"

He had a mild Middle Eastern accent. Gracie let out a breath. "I'm Gracie Parish." She swallowed. "Owner of Club When? I'm here to see Delilah. Is she available?"

Using his body and the half-opened door to block her view, he turned and looked back into the room.

Someone inside spoke. "Let her in, Poppa."

He gave way with a pointed look that said he'd throw her out at a moment's notice. And the vase suddenly felt heavy and slippery in her sweaty hands. She walked inside. The private room was packed with flowers. They lined the windowsill above the radiator, stood on extra wheeled trays, and were even on the floor beside the many chairs in the room, chairs filled with people.

Gracie had never seen so many people squeezed into one room, and considering her family, that was saying something. She almost made a joke about it being a fire hazard, but she tamped down that horrifying thought fast and hard.

Reclining in the bed was the woman from the bar. The one Gracie now knew was named Delilah. Half her leg was missing. She had bandages across her face. Her eyes were sunken and bruised.

The people in the room were silent, watching Gracie. "I wanted to come and say how sorry I am," she said. "And to see if there is anything I could do to make things easier for you."

One of the men in the room spoke to one of the women in Arabic. She didn't understand the words, but it felt like a condemnation.

Delilah flashed her dark eyes at them. A warning? Agreement?

Gracie swallowed. She stepped forward with the flowers, never feeling more inadequate in her life. It reminded her of a poem she'd once heard about bringing a cup of water to the ocean. Flowers. What a meaningless gesture.

Her eyes strayed to the blanket, to the missing part of Delilah's leg. Her heart fell to her stomach, making it pitch like an unsteady boat.

Delilah shifted forward in the bed. "Could you leave us?"

Gracie startled, her face growing hot. She stepped back. And then the other people in the room began to rise. Oh. She'd meant her family should leave.

The people began to rise, move from their positions

holding up the walls, and shuffled out. As they did, one of the women said something cross to Gracie in Arabic.

From the bed, Delilah answered in the same language. She seemed to reprimand her. The woman left with the others.

"Excuse her," Delilah said. "She moved from Iraq to get away from things like this."

The sharp sting of guilt pierced her chest. "I'm so sorry."

Delilah shook her head. "It's not your fault."

It was.

Delilah held out her hands for the flowers. "They're beautiful," she said. "And my favorite."

Gracie's too. She handed her the vase of lilies.

Delilah sniffed them. Sliding over the hospital phone and a Styrofoam cup of water, she placed them on her nightstand. Delilah's eyes creased with concern. "Don't look so… You didn't do this."

That wasn't true. She had known that someone was trying to kill her. She should've shut down the club. She should've gone home, hidden behind the gates, told Momma the truth sooner, and organized sooner.

"I'm responsible. I've come here to tell you that. I'm taking care of all of your hospital bills, and I'm working with your attorneys to get you the money you need to"—she bit back the word she'd almost used; recover wasn't an option—"rehabilitate."

Delilah closed her eyes. "I know."

It wasn't enough. Not nearly enough. "Is there anything else I can do for you?"

"You can tell me about him."

"About who?"

"Your man. At the bar. He's so hot."

Dusty? She wanted to hear about Dusty?

She opened her eyes and read Gracie's hesitation correctly. "I'm sorry, that must seem weird."

Gracie shrugged. "Kind of."

Delilah flopped exasperated hands down by her sides. "I'm just so tired of conversations about pain and fear. About lawyers. About interviews for television news and calls for justice. My leg hurts. My back hurts. And I'm bored and anxious. My family barely leaves my side. I had to have the nurse throw them out yesterday. They mean well, but they're making it worse."

She wiped a tear from her eye. Oh. Gracie got it. With one single act, Delilah had been blown out of normal life and into abnormal life. She wanted to feel normal again, to talk to someone about everyday things.

Sitting in the closest chair, the burgundy vinyl still hot from the last person, she put her purse on the seat next to her and began her story. "I met him in Mexico."

Delilah's gaze sharpened. "On vacation?"

Uhm. Well… "A wild trip, for sure."

She shared as much of the story as she could—the heat, her first glimpse of him, the banter, and him unexpectedly showing up at her club months later. She waxed on about his Southern charm and his way of making everything better. When she was finished, Delilah thanked her. Gracie squeezed her hand, took a business card and a pen from her purse, wrote down her personal number, and told her she could call any time. Day or night. Then she apologized again and left.

As she slipped out of Delilah's room, she felt worse than when she went in. Twenty-six. Delilah's entire life had been dramatically changed at twenty-six.

Should've closed the club.

In the hallway, she spotted the man she now realized was Delilah's father. He stood by the nurse's station.

She acknowledged him with a nod, and he approached her. She tensed, fisted her hands, waited for him to say the club should've been more secure, for him to ask how she could've let this happen, for him to ask—as so many in the media now did—if her family had enemies.

He stopped in front of her and said, "Stop blaming yourself."

A sob escaped her, and much to her shock and horror, tears flooded from her like water over an overwhelmed dam. He gathered her in a hug. He smelled like tobacco and spiced tea.

He let her cry. "It's okay," he soothed. "There are fields where we run and fields where we crawl. And Allah looks over them all with eyes tinged in joy."

Gracie pulled away, wiped her eyes. "I'm so very sorry about your daughter."

He shook his head. "You confuse empathy with guilt. You are not responsible. This is something I have learned. Others will use what you hold dear to commit crimes. They are not your crimes. They would make you feel responsible, like you caused their bad actions. Don't let them deceive you. Fight them in this. Fight them where they would lay roots."

He tapped his head. "Here."

And tapped his heart. "Here."

Fight them. He was right. Fight them she would.

As she left the hospital, Gracie found him exactly where

he said he'd be. Sleek, dark hair and roving, dark eyes, Victor sat on a bench outside the hospital doors, his right arm in a sling to help his clavicle heal. He wore black-and-white checkered slacks and a white shirt, unbuttoned enough to see his naturally tan skin.

She sat beside him on the white wooden bench, leaned over and kissed him on the cheek, avoiding his sling. "Got your text. Seems an odd place to meet though. I thought you'd been released."

"Came back for a checkup. Figured you might be around and was hoping to talk with you for a minute. I was so out of it the last time we spoke, I forgot to ask you about the Tony stuff."

"Tony stuff? What are you talking about?"

Victor's voice dropped low. "FBI didn't tell you?"

Blood rushed to Gracie's suddenly pounding head. "What is this about?"

"The security footage you gave me." He made a fist. "You know how I'd been looking through it for anyone suspicious?"

She nodded.

"Well, after I'd spotted El, I kept looking. That's when I spotted him. At first, I couldn't believe it, so I asked to see more footage. Hoped I'd see him again. Sure enough, I did. Got up close. Double- and triple-checked. It was him."

He'd spotted someone at her club? What did this have to do with Tony? Chills ran up and down her spine. "Tony's dead."

Victor shook his head. "Where's his body?"

She opened her mouth and shut it with a snap. "Dusty. Dusty…buried…"

More chills. As if she'd plunged into Lake Michigan in November. *Had* Dusty buried Tony? How would she know? She wouldn't. She hadn't examined Tony's body. Hadn't tried to stanch a wound. Why would she? He'd been poisoned. Or so they'd thought.

How hard would it have been for him to have taken a drug that night that mimicked death? Not hard. And it would've been easy to fool both her and Justice. Everything had been so chaotic. Emotional.

Her stomach soured. Tony was alive? Her heart leapt with joy. Tony had faked his death—with Dusty's help? Her heart thrashed with anger.

But she had no more tears left. Not for the relief she felt. Not for the grief. Not for the rage. Dusty. Her hands curled into fists.

"I'm sorry, Red. Fuck. I should've told you sooner."

"Don't do that, Victor. You won't put up with me blaming myself for the club, and I'm not putting up with you blaming yourself for not telling me sooner."

Her mind raced. Was Tony working with Dusty? Was he providing the FBI with information on Momma? Was the family in worse danger than she'd suspected? Had Dusty been collecting information on her family, on Momma, on her, last night?

Tony was alive. Anything seemed possible.

She'd been an idiot. Dusty had asked her, in bed no less, if he could meet Momma. And then what had she done? She'd brought him to the house. That had worked out great. He'd shown disgust when he'd listened to Momma's story.

Stupid, Gracie. So f'ing stupid! "Can you let me be the one who tells my family? It's my responsibility."

"Sure." He squeezed her knee. "And if you want, I'll kick FBI's ass for you."

Standing, she slung her purse over her shoulder and said, "I'll kick it myself. Thanks."

Chapter 53

WATCHING WHERE HE STEPPED, DUSTY PICKED HIS WAY through the burnt debris, staying out of the way of the remediation workers who—given the go-ahead by the authorities—were loudly breaking things apart and clearing Gracie's club.

Not much to salvage as far as the front part of the club went.

The furniture had been singed with fire and smoke and soaked with water and foam. The walls were covered in soot, the decorations destroyed.

He'd be interested to read the reports, to see what the authorities and what Leland and his crew had found in here. Clearly a professional job.

Three explosive devices had been planted around the club, near the dance floor, sitting areas, and bathrooms. They'd been designed to keep the action out here, so that whoever had tried to access the servers upstairs could do their job without interruption.

He gave the bar a thank-you pat as he moved past. It had served as a buffer for him and Gracie during the explosion. The same kind of buffer her family had provided when they'd rolled onto campus a few days ago. Damn.

He shouldn't have left her last night. That mistake had cost him a good night's sleep. He'd realized, sometime between midnight and four a.m., that Grace had been right. The kids needed to share their stories to connect. He'd seen that connection.

Truth was, his problem hadn't been with the sharing, but with how the story had made him *feel*. At first, he'd been moved by it, but then he got to analyzing, interpreting, remembering. Then it had felt like manipulation, reminded him of his father. It had felt like being herded.

He'd sworn to protect people from lunatics like his father.

But—and this was the thing that let him finally get some sleep—Mukta wasn't his father. He'd seen the care she'd taken with her children. And not one of Mutka's children was afraid of her. Respectful, yes, fearful, no.

That was the difference. His father wanted power over people, wanted and needed them to fear him, see him as a god, so he could take their money and live off them.

So as soon as Gracie walked in this morning, he intended to sit her down and apologize for leaving, explain why he'd walked out.

He headed toward the back of the club. He stopped at the burnt-out hallway, the area that had once had a door separating the club from the back of the club. This spot had taken the brunt of the explosion. It had been some kind of miracle that no one had been entering or exiting the bathrooms.

He squatted by the blackened closet across from the bathroom. The door had been torn clean off and the contents inside turned to ash. He reached into the back, to the ash-darkened wall, and wiped his fingers through the soot.

He rubbed his fingers together under his nose. A chemical smell. A controlled explosion. That would take some money.

Grace had security cameras back here. But he doubted

whoever it was had been sloppy enough to be caught on film. Still, Gracie had given the security footage to the inspectors and a copy to Leland. If there were any valuable clues there, they'd find them.

He stood up as the back door to the club opened with a creak of dry hinges. A blast of morning light and Gracie walked inside, pulling her hair from a tight bun and shaking out her head. Sun-blinded, she didn't seem to see him, but he saw her…unguarded and in terrible pain.

His fists clenched, his heart sank. He needed to go to her, try and make it okay. He stepped from the shadows.

The moment they made eye contact, her face reddened into a volcano of anger. Whoa. Time to make this right. "Grace. I'm sorry for leaving last night."

Wearing a gray suit that seemed to highlight the fact that she meant business, she stalked toward him. She wasn't messing around. She definitely would have her say, but he also sensed she was considering throwing a punch. He'd been in enough fights to recognize *that* intention.

"Sorry!?" She wiped a tear from her eye.

She was crying? His heart started to pound. His nerves jumped to careful attention. "Darlin', what's wrong? What happened?"

"You are a liar. You lied."

Her accusation slammed into him hard enough to wind him. Made him want to babble, explain away whatever had caused that anger, but he had no idea what she was talking about. So he stood there, mute for probably the first time in his life.

The back door to the club opened again. Dusty's eyes shifted from Grace to the door. *Oh. Shit.*

Chapter 54

In the back hall of her club, hands fisted at her sides, Gracie wanted to know what had caused Dusty's eyes to widen as if the devil and the grim reaper had walked in behind her.

She spun on her heels, ready to fight or flee. Entering her club was the last person on earth she'd expected to see.

John?

Power-walking through the corridor, the hard set of his jaw a clear rebuke, John avoided the construction equipment and tools. He wore a black suit, black as his mood. Must've come from work.

He stopped a few feet from her. "I need to talk to you." His eyes traveled to Dusty—whose *Lyle's BBQ* T-shirt was snug against his huge chest. All his American Ninja Warrior fierceness was on full display. John's eyes widened a little. "This is private."

Dusty crossed his arms, biceps bulging, and leaned against the wall. She could feel the weight of him, the weight of his protection. It was as if he was saying to her, with the absolute strength of his body, that he was the one she could trust.

Liar. Liar. Liar. Trust no one.

"What's this about?"

"Gracie Divine..." John cracked his neck, as if he had the weight of the world on his shoulders. "It's about Tyler."

Tyler? Where was privacy? Her ground-floor office was filled with construction equipment. But the upstairs was fairly safe. And thanks to the fire marshal's request to leave the security door open, accessible to him. Heck, to everyone.

"Let's go upstairs."

As they moved to go upstairs, Dusty followed. "Grace."

She turned to him. Anger surged through her chest. "No. This isn't about you."

He jerked, looked sincerely hurt. And confused. But he was an *f'ing* special agent of the F.B.-tootin'-I. She had no doubt he'd figure out why she was so pissed.

Pulling a Jolly Rancher from her pocket, she slipped it into her mouth and led John upstairs.

Chapter 55

Gracie stopped and turned to John. The hallway upstairs of Club When? was private enough. "What's going on?"

John glanced down the row of open doors. She gave him a get-on-with-it stare.

He did. "Where's Tyler?"

"Ty's missing?"

"Stop it, Gracie. I know you were supposed to meet him today." He looked down the hall again. "Is he down there? Is he in your apartment?"

Why would Ty be here? "I haven't been talking to Ty. I wouldn't go behind your back like that. Why are you asking me this?"

"Look, we both know that's not true. You lied to me for years."

So not the time to dig up those old wounds. "John, is Ty missing?"

"Yes."

For a moment, as his dark eyes drilled condemnation and anger into her, panic washed through Gracie's body, but that was quickly replaced with her training. A detached calm, cool and capable, focused her mind and sent her into action.

She led John into the computer room, kicked the chair out of her way—sending it spinning on its wheels. Dropping her purse onto the desk, she booted up the computer. If Ty had his cell she could track it from here.

The sound of fans and technology coming online filled the room. "How long has he been missing?"

"El went into Ty's room early this morning to ask him if he wanted to hang out at the station while she performed her radio show, but he wasn't there."

He'd been missing for hours, then. It was after noon. "Is that normal behavior? When was the last time you saw him? Have you called the police? Did he have his phone?"

"What's normal? He's a teen. El dropped our other son off at daycare and went to work, figuring Ty would show up eventually. She called him a few times but no answer. She came back around ten to check on him and found his cell in a drawer. That's when she really started to panic."

No phone. That made it difficult. "Have you called the police yet?"

"If you cooperate, I'm hoping it won't come to that," John said.

Again he focused his rage on her. The space between them suddenly felt too small. She took a step back.

He noticed, stepped forward. "I know what's going on, Gracie. After El found his phone, she called Ty's girlfriend. She said Ty has been communicating with your sister Cee. And that Cee had set up a meeting between you and Tyler for today."

"Cee? My Cee knows Ty?" No. That made zero sense. And… Tyler wanted to meet her? Her heart jumped. *Focus. Focus.* "If Cee is involved, I know nothing about it."

"If?" He looked mildly nauseous. "Don't you have some kind of tracking system for your people?"

He was right. "Yeah." She turned back to the computer and its still-dark screens. Was this due to the fire? Had something been damaged? Leland had said the security was working, but she hadn't asked to have the computers checked. *Crud*.

"As soon as the computer kicks on, I can access family GPS information from here. It should only take me a minute or two to figure out where they are. Until then, anything else you can tell me?"

Now John looked uncomfortable. "Years ago, Momma set up a money market in my name for Tyler. I don't really think about it except at tax time. Today, El searched Ty's room looking for clues as to where he went and found bank statements he'd been intercepting."

Ice rolled down Gracie's spine, straight over her feet, freezing her to the spot. Never once had she considered the idea that *Tyler* had been taking money out of that account. "So there was money missing from the account and you think Tyler took it and gave it to Cee?"

"It makes sense, doesn't it? Cee is…" He trailed off. But she understood what he hinted at. She was a Parish. A broken kid taken from the streets, who didn't play by the rules. She pushed aside her annoyance at that and concentrated on the facts.

Cee didn't need money. Unless… *"Please let me do the job. Please."* Had she wanted to fund her own shadow League? But where did Tyler fit into this mess? Had she contacted him for the money?

Crud. She went back to the computer, checked her connections. One of the screens blinked on. Finally. She began to type in her access codes to bring up the GPS locator.

Nothing she typed showed up on the screen.

She tried again and a video of her mother, Sheila, popped up. Dumbfounded, she listened as it played. Her mother was giving the exact same testimony she'd given about Andrew Lincoln Rush, except the voice asking the questions wasn't asking about Rush.

This was what Dusty had told her about—one of the other versions of her mother's recording. How the heck was it on her screen?

"Gracie Divine?" John stepped back from the monitors. She glanced over her shoulder and saw him looking like he was getting ready to run, straight to the police.

Tyler. She needed to focus. Find Tyler.

Gracie fished her cell from her purse to call Leland. Her cell rang in her hand. She looked at the screen. *Victor*. So not a priority right now. She sent him a "Can't talk right now" text.

She dialed Leland.

He picked up on the second ring. His voice was military gravel and too many roughly-barked commands. "Gracie, how'd it go today?"

How'd it go? Oh, the hospital. "Leland, I've got a situation. Can you ping Cee and tell me where she is?"

Leland must've heard the anxiety in her voice, because he didn't even question. "Hold on. Let me get to the right computer."

She bent and continued to try and get control of her computer system. After a moment, Leland said, "She's on campus. In her room."

Her room? Thank God. But then where was Tyler? "Are you sure? She couldn't have taken her chip out?"

"No. We've finally figured out a way to program the

chips to go off if removed, without making them vulnerable to hacking or easily destructible."

Gracie let out a breath. She mouthed to John, *"She's there."* And then to Leland said, "Can you get her? I need to talk with her."

"I'll have home security run her down. No problem."

"Thanks."

The video of her mother was now on every monitor. Playing over and over. Each one with a different time stamp and a different man being mentioned. She squeezed her cell between chin and shoulder and continued to type commands, but nothing was happening.

The click of a call coming through her cell buzzed in her ear. She ignored it, let it go to voice mail.

Someone had taken control of the system. Someone had blocked her.

How…?

The fire. They hadn't been searching for something. They'd been planting something. *Fudge*. This was bad. "Leland."

"Hold on." She heard Leland talking with someone, then come back on the line with a gruff "Security searched Cee's room. She wasn't there. They found a chip."

"You said it couldn't be removed."

"This one was clean. Not a speck of blood. She must've had a duplicate made."

"Wouldn't there then be two signals for her?"

"Not if she wore a device that blocked one of those signals. In that instance, the signal on the first chip might drop for a moment in the control center, but then we'd have pinged her and picked up on the second chip."

"What about her cell?"

"In her room."

She felt panic rising. Why would she do this? What game was Cee playing? Could she have anything to do with the attempt on her life, the club fire?

Tony was alive. Dusty was a huge liar. Anything seemed possible. Besides, Cee had gotten into the club when Gracie hadn't been there. She could've planted explosives. Could've used the money from Tyler to get them made. Could Cee's need for payback extend to her? Had she lured Tyler away to hurt Gracie? "Tyler is missing too. John is here. Says Ty and Cee have been in contact. Why would she do that?"

"I don't think we're going to get an answer on that unless it's directly from her. But I'm going to work on how."

"You think Rome…?"

"I'm going to go talk to him now."

"Thanks. I'm on my way over."

She hung up. Her cell rang again. She ignored it. Turning to John, she braced herself to tell him she had no idea where their son was, tell him that the family he had feared—had rightly feared—had taken Tyler.

Chapter 56

It wasn't so much a dirty main street as a poor main street. Boarded-up businesses, like missing teeth, were interspersed with open businesses—an old-fashioned pharmacy advertising the lowest price on cigarettes, a thrift store, and a corner market that smelled like pickle brine.

Having traveled by bus an hour from his home, Tyler stood in front of the store, eating the beef jerky he'd just purchased with cash. He lowered his baseball cap. This didn't seem the type of city to have high-tech cameras, but he'd been told to avoid cameras. He had on special sunglasses that blinded facial recognition software, but he could still be filmed, so his hat came down.

He put his hand in his jeans pocket, feeling the smooth steel of his folded pocket knife. A gun would've been better. But his family didn't have one. And he'd only ever practiced with one once. His friend's father had taken the two of them to a range. And though Tyler's father had told him to "Just observe," Jake's dad had let him fire a couple of rounds.

When his hand grew slick against the knife, he took it out. Felt like he'd been waiting for this moment forever. And here it was.

A shiny limo pulled up to the curb. A big guy with a nose that had been broken once or twice rolled down the window. They'd sent a limo? Tyler leaned on the open window. The man inside said, "Your mom sent me. Time to go."

He hesitated. Then remembered not getting into a strange car were instructions you gave little kids. They didn't apply to a six-foot covert vigilante.

Besides, it was a limo. Why would they advertise if they intended to hurt him? He opened the door and slid into the back seat, shut the door. The cold temperature in the car was a relief. It smelled good in here, a new-car smell. The partition between him and the driver slid down. "Help yourself to a drink," the man said.

There was a fridge. Awesome. He took out a grape soda from the small fridge. The inside was lit with a blue light. Neat. Flicking open the silver tab, he took a long sip. Tasted incredible. His parents never stocked soda or any sugary drinks.

There was food and candy in an inset cabinet, too. Shouldn't eat the candy. That was for kids. But since the driver had lowered the divider, he asked, "Do you know where we're headed?"

Duh. Of course he did. He was driving. *Nice, Tyler*. You'll make one observant spy.

"Yes, sir," the driver answered as if Tyler hadn't just said the stupidest thing in the world. "We'll be arriving at our destination in two hours."

Two hours? A phone rang out through the speakers. The driver must've accepted the call, because suddenly he heard Cee's soft Spanish accent. "You've made it. You are officially one of us."

A burst of joy raced through his chest, making him want to shout. He'd done it!

After all the jumping through hoops. He'd stolen

from his parents—well, technically, taken money from a trust that was his without them knowing. But he'd lied to his parents, visited the dark web, planned, plotted, snuck around, and now he was going to meet his...Gracie Parish. "That's great, but two hours is a long time. You told me not to bring a phone, so how can I let my parents know when I'll be back?"

His mom would freak when she found him missing. Luckily, it was summer, so she probably wouldn't discover him gone for a few hours.

"We'll text her for you. Even make it look like it came from your phone."

"You can do that?"

"Your mom can. Now settle back. You'll be there soon enough."

Ty relaxed in his seat. They'd taken care of everything. This was what it meant to be part of an elite covert group. So cool. He rested his head back. Took another sip of his drink. He suddenly felt so tired. His eyes drifted closed. And the world went black.

Tyler woke up in a bedroom that was and wasn't familiar. He struggled to place the light-blue walls, the Mario lamp on the nightstand and matching curtains, and then it came to him. He was in his bedroom at the family cabin—far from home. So thirsty. He licked his dry lips, tasted like chemicals. His head hurt. What had happened? What time was it?

He sat up in the bed and fought back the sick that rose into his throat. His stomach turned. He reached into his pocket for his knife. It wasn't there.

"You're okay."

He turned to the doorway, to the person there. Cee. Taller than he'd expected. But he'd only ever seen one photo of her, and it had been blurry. Her long, dark hair draped around a pale face. She wore dark sunglasses that were way too big for her face. "Cee. What's going on?"

She shook her head, began to cry, covered her mouth.

"What's wrong?"

He tried to get out of bed but found the weight of his head nearly tipped him over.

"I'm sorry," she said. "I thought… I didn't realize what she had planned. I'm so sorry."

What was she talking about? He wanted to ask, but his lips felt numb and his body so heavy. A flat-screen television was in his room—where had that come from?—and was playing a video. Fighting to keep his eyes open, he watched.

It took him a minute to understand the images, but when he did, he began to scream.

Chapter 57

STANDING IN THE DEBRIS-STREWN CORRIDOR OUTSIDE THE kitchen of Club When?, Dusty watched as Gracie and John headed up the stairs. What had just happened? Gracie had been so angry that she'd shut him down and had gone upstairs with John because he needed to talk "privately."

And he was sure John did have something to say, but he was also certain it wasn't going to make Gracie happy. Judging by the pain written all over her sweet face when she'd walked in, she'd already had a bad morning. Seeing her like that… Nearly killed him.

But then she'd caught sight of him, and her pain had changed into rage. Why was she so angry at him? It couldn't be about last night. Yes, she was upset, but when she'd texted him this morning she'd seemed distant, not angry. And he got the impression she was giving him her schedule, so they could meet up later. She'd told him she was going to the hospital to see some of the injured and meet with Victor before coming to the club.

Victor.

Could he have said something, made some comment against Dusty? He took out his cell, searched for and found Victor's number, then dialed. He put the phone to his ear.

A couple of the construction workers came in through

the back entranceway, carrying equipment. He nodded to them and stepped out of the way.

"Cops are here," one of the guys said as he went past.

Dusty turned to find Mack in the back doorway. Victor answered the phone with a "Yeah."

He had a half second to make the decision. He shielded his phone and whispered, "Call Gracie. Tell her to take the escape route. Now."

Wearing a black suit and sporting a bruised nose and dark circles under his eyes, Mack entered the back hall of Club When? like he owned the place. He had two police officers with him. Dusty flexed his slow-things-down muscles. He approached Mack as if a dear friend, held out his hand. "Mack."

Mack ignored it. "Dusty."

Dusty dropped his hand, shoved it into the pocket of his jeans. Casual-like. "What's going on?"

Mack held out a folded paper. "We have a warrant to search the upstairs and confiscate evidence."

Dusty's hackles rose, along with his temper. He set it to simmer. "What's that all about?"

"You wanted proof. I'm here for proof." He hitched a thumb toward the steel door that led upstairs. "Proof that Gracie and her family are involved in blackmail and extortion. I have reason to believe it's contained on a computer upstairs."

Gracie had told him whatever was left on the servers was harmless. "What specifically are we talking about?"

"I have the destination for a file that will show that Gracie Parish has taken part in a series of blackmail schemes against elected officials and business leaders."

Evidence? "Don't do this, Mack."

Mack shook his head. "We follow the facts where they lead, Dusty. You know that."

Sure. "DNA, evidence, facts—none of it will make a lick of difference if you've decided to toe Rush's line. And he doesn't need your help. Kind of control people like him have over information—whole media empires dedicated to his spin—isn't likely facts will ever play too large a role."

Mack smoothed the lapel of his suit jacket. "Not sure what you're talking about. You laid the road for this drive. Now, is Gracie Parish here? Because I also have a warrant for her arrest."

Dusty squared his shoulders. "On what grounds?"

Behind Mack the two officers tensed, exchanged a get-ready look. They didn't stand a fucking chance. But no reason to make them wary. He unhitched his shoulders, gave them both an all-good-here nod of his head.

Mack took it all in stride. Seemed to be enjoying himself. "The exact things your investigation uncovered: blackmail and human-trafficking. Add to that arson."

Bullshit. His stomach churned. Mack was determined to shield Rush, even if that meant fabricating evidence. "You have evidence of her involvement in *human-trafficking*? *Arson*?"

"The fire marshal has plenty of proof it was arson. Know how long it took someone to set these devices? Hours. Not something some guy can come in and do on his lunch hour. She lives and works here. You telling me she wouldn't have noticed the devices being set? Besides, I wouldn't be surprised if we found evidence of purchases to make those devices when we search."

"Why would she want to destroy her own club?"

"She obviously knew we were onto her and tried to burn her club down to destroy the evidence. A lot harder to get evidence off a burnt computer than a wiped computer. And you were there when she turned on her partners in Mexico."

Oh, sure, and the area upstairs where the evidence is just happened to be unharmed. He blinked at Mack for one dumbfounded moment. Gracie had been set up. "This is my case, Mack. I'm not going to let you railroad her."

"As we've already discussed"—Mack ran a finger over his still-swollen nose—"you are no longer on this case."

Bastard. Although Dusty knew the records showed why he'd started his investigation, he hadn't proven Gracie and her family had been in Mexico on a vigilante mission. Could what he had put in his reports be misconstrued to support Mack's theory?

Maybe. Especially if Mack had other information to guide the narrative. Time to stall. "I think Gracie's in the front of the club."

"Not here," said one of the construction guys, carrying a halogen work light and an extension cord through the hallway. "Maybe upstairs."

Dusty closed his eyes, counted to three, and tried another tactic. "Let me go up and get her. There's only one way down." He pointed at the door. "It'll be easier. Then you can go up and search for your evidence."

Mack shook his head. "You've gone too deep on this one, pal. Take a step back. It'll save what's left of your career."

Mack turned to go up the steps. Dusty stepped in front of him. "You've got her life in your hands, Mack. Rush will know exactly where she is and how to get at her."

A tinge of disappointment seemed to weigh down Mack's shoulders. "Give me some credit, Dusty. I checked it out. He wasn't even aware of the attempt on her life."

He wasn't? "Did you check Porter out too?"

Mack ignored him, walked past him and started up the stairs, cops in tow. Dusty followed them, tried again. "You bringing her to jail makes her a duck in a shooting gallery. How easy would it be for Porter to get her there?"

His loafers making gritty sweeping sounds as he ascended the steps, Mack shook his head. "Trust me. That won't happen."

"I'm going to fight you on this, Mack. You are going to look like a fool."

Mack stopped, turned. "Not if I get Mukta to confess."

Confess? "Why would she do that?"

"I'm pretty sure she'd do just about anything to get her daughter out of jail."

Mack continued up. Dusty stopped in his tracks. Of course, Mack was right. Mukta would confess to blackmail to get her daughter off of worse charges. And Mack was smart enough to let Mukta pick her poison. Confessing to the blackmail—a white collar crime—would get her a few months in a cushy club fed.

Mukta might do that, if it got Gracie out of the more serious charges, and if she had no other choice. But she did have a choice. So why not send a team of lawyers today and have Gracie out of jail in a heartbeat?

As he started back up the stairs, Dusty stewed on this, picked it apart like a dog picks meat from a bone, bit by bit. And as he broke from the relative darkness of the stairwell to the light of the upper floor, it hit him. Mack was going to take Gracie to a black site. Once there, there would be no way for Mukta to get Gracie out.

Mack could keep Gracie there, in that limbo between being arrested and being set free, for weeks. Gracie would be a prisoner, tortured—no matter what they called it, not letting someone sleep, sit down, piss, was fucking torture—until she confessed too.

The thing was, Gracie wouldn't confess. No matter what they did to her. He'd seen her stubborn and it ran straight down her spine and deep into the earth. She'd die first. Dusty's heart cracked open with the thought. Wouldn't be the first to die in that kind of place.

Mukta would confess, do anything to save Gracie from that. And so would he.

He was taking her out of here, hiding her until he found a way to clear her name, use Mukta's influence to clear her name, and put Mack in his fuckin' place.

Now to signal Grace, give her the heads up. They had one shot. Surprise. And overpowering Mack and two cops would be a lot easier with the two of them on the same page.

Chapter 58

IN HER COMPUTER ROOM, WITH JOHN MAKING FISTS AT HIS sides and her heart starting a *For Whom the Bell Tolls* gong in her chest, Gracie faced John. "There's a chance that Cee is with Tyler."

"A chance? What's going on, Gracie Divine? What did Leland say?"

"Cee isn't there. She's missing too. My brother—"

"Tony?"

For a flash her brain faltered as the competing thoughts "Tony's dead" and then "Tony's alive" rushed through her head. "No—"

Her cell rang again. *Victor. Why did he keep calling?*

"Different brother. He's at the house. He might know something about where Cee and Ty have gone. I'm headed over there. Do you want to come?"

"To the Mantua Home?" His face said he'd rather eat a bug dipped in dog poop. "Yeah. If we can take my car."

Her cell rang again. *Victor again?* She picked up.

"Red, escape route. Go now."

Gracie looked at the monitors still playing her mother's confession, confessions. She looked at John. "I have to go. I have…"

She headed out of the room and down the hall, cell held to her ear. John followed a step behind, asking, "What? Where? Is this about Ty?"

"Victor, what's this about?"

"No idea. Message is from Dusty."

She stopped dead. *Dusty?* What was he up to? John pulled up beside her. "What are we doing?"

We? Stay or go? Stay or go? Could she trust Dusty? "He didn't give you any hint what this is about?"

"No. Didn't say a word but what I just told you. And I know you have some serious issues with him, but if I have a vote, I say go."

"Thanks, Victor." She hung up.

The sound of a leather gun belt alerted her. She turned as a fed and two cops appeared at the other end of the hall. She took off at a run.

Voices commanding her to stop echoed down the hall. She picked up her pace. A weight slammed into her, drove her to the ground. They went down in a heap.

John's voice came tight in her ear. "Stop. It's the police."

No way. She couldn't help Tyler from a jail cell.

Not the first time she'd been pinned, Gracie's training took over. She elbowed John hard, rolled. A businessman whose main source of exercise was running, John was no match for her. She was up and freed in one and a half seconds.

Not fast enough. Another body slammed into her, drove her back. And another set of hands, grabbing at her. She dodged and swung, punched, kneed, and grappled.

The limited space in the hallway made it harder. She was surrounded quickly. She seized balls, sent Cop One to the floor, and threw a sharp elbow into Cop Two's neck. He went down gasping. Then she was face-to-face with the fed and his gun, which was trained on her.

"You are under arrest," the fed said. "We have a warrant to search the building and remove evidence, including your servers."

She stood, breathing heavily, hands up. Her servers? "Evidence of what?"

"Evidence that you and your mother have been bribing numerous elected officials and businessmen and using the money to fund child sexual exploitation."

She blinked at him. Someone had planted evidence, including those videos, on her computer servers. Her security had made hacking into her system without being detected impossible, so someone had decided to go old school, just come here and plant evidence in person. It was kind of crazy. And on any other day, she might've taken a chance, fought the good fight legally. But not this day. She needed to get out of here and find her son.

John had gotten up. He had a red just-getting-started bruise on his cheek. He looked around like his head was attached to a swivel. Back and forth. Back and forth. "I think she took my son. She lured him away, got him to give her money too."

What the hell? *A-hole*.

Her eyes came up and found Dusty's. Dusty was here, sneaking up behind the fed.

The moment froze in time. His gaze locked with hers. Her face grew so hot, so quickly her cheeks stung.

But his unflinching honey eyes tried to communicate with her, tried to send a message. If she'd had Momma and Leland's ESP-like bond, she would've said those deadly serious eyes said, "Trust me."

Toots. Not likely. She cursed the day she'd first seen those eyes, the pull they had on her. Those eyes lied. Just like the rest of him.

One of the officers, not the guy moaning on the floor with his hands covering his scrunched scrotum, took out cuffs and the fed intoned, "Grace Parish, you are hereby under arrest for bribery, extortion, human-trafficking, and arson."

Chapter 59

By the time Dusty arrived, Mack had a gun on Gracie. He moved quickly and quietly behind them, tried to get her attention. For a moment her eyes lifted to his. He sent her the signal, what he hoped she understood—that this wasn't happening. No way.

Her eyes were wide and her face red with anger when she looked away. Did she think he had something to do with this? *Fuck.*

Why was she so mad at him? The sound of handcuffs being taken out unlocked inaction. *No. Fucking. Way.*

He came up behind Mack, thrust his arms under Mack's upraised ones, got hold of his gun, twisted it up, and lifted. Mack shot into the ceiling. Dusty tossed him at the cop who'd taken out the cuffs.

They crashed into the wall and fell over each other, landing on the floor in a heap.

The final cop—Dusty liked to think of him as crushed balls—stayed down. That left John. And wouldn't you know, that fucker tried to grab Gracie. She chopped his outstretched arm down, spun away, and ran on. Atta girl. Dusty was a step behind her but took a moment to slam John into a wall and hiss "Fucking fuck" in his face.

A bit childish, sure, but it felt good, knowing the guy didn't like cursing.

Dusty rounded the corner. Mack shouted at them to

stop. *No can do*. Gracie raced through her apartment door and he followed.

The moment he sprinted through the door, she slammed it closed and ran quick fingers over the trackpad, securing it.

Steel pins slid into place a blink before Mack tried to turn the steel handle. He beat on the door. "There's no way out. Open up."

Pushing away from the door, Gracie turned to look at him. Her expression, one of distrust and confusion, hit him straight in the chest. It felt like someone had taken the business end of a pickax and slammed it into his breastbone. Hurt like a son of a bitch.

"You rescued me."

Not yet. But he intended to. "Does that elevator still work?"

She looked toward it. "Yeah. It does. But it's just for one person."

He nodded. Fine by him. "Go to your Momma's. Lawyer up. Call me when you're safe. I'll let you know what I know. Till then, I'll sit here and negotiate with Mack. Keep him busy."

She looked at the elevator again, then at him. "My son…someone, my sister Cee, has taken him."

Her sister? What the hell? Dusty pulled a hand across his face. "We'll find him, darlin'."

Her spine stiffened with the endearment. "You're a liar."

Mack began pounding on the door. "You're throwing away your life here, Dusty."

Dusty looked at her, waited for her to absorb this moment, what he'd done, what he would do, because it was the only testimony he could give since he had no idea why she was so pissed off. Her face folded into confusion. She took a step away from him, turned toward the elevator.

That pickaxe was drawing blood, but he turned toward the door. Why had she called him a liar? "Mack, we're going to want a couple of concessions before we open this door."

Behind him, he heard the elevator rise and open. He glanced over his shoulder. She'd climbed inside. She paused. "You know you can't open that apartment door without me, right?"

Nope. He didn't. He shrugged. Eventually they'd get someone here to open the door. Judging by the security system she had, it would take a couple of hours.

The elevator door started to close but she stopped it. "First half of the elevator code is on page seventeen in *Of Mice and Men*. First seven letters going down. The other half is on page three hundred of *Anna Karenina*. The last letter of the first six lines of dialogue." She let out a breath, a tear on her cheek. "I'll see you at Momma's."

She let the elevator door close. And Dusty had the most inappropriate sensation he'd ever had in his entire life—relief. Relief, despite being trapped inside her apartment with his SAC on the other side of a steel door, knowing he'd lost his job and was probably going to go to jail.

Though he could always plead crazy. Wouldn't be the first agent to blur the lines during an undercover operation. Yes, sir, he might just end up in a mental institution. And that shouldn't make his heart light and put this smile on his face, but there it was. Because Ms. Gracie Parish, despite whatever her head had told her, had just decided to follow her heart with him.

And he intended to see she never regretted that decision.

Chapter 60

SLAMMING HER HANDS ON THE ARMRESTS ON EITHER side of Romeo's chair, Gracie growled, "Stop ignoring my questions."

The mood inside Momma and Leland's sun-streaked office drummed with tension. Momma and Leland watched uneasily from their distinctive desks.

The only person who seemed immune to this palpable stress was Romeo himself. Cool as he was unmoved, handsome, and young. This close, she could smell his deodorant and see the acne on his chin. He shifted.

First sign that she was getting to him. Uncomfortable with someone invading his personal space? Good. She leaned in closer. "Look, Rome, I get it. Cee convinced you to help root out this group, this fraternity, acted like everything you did was related to that, but clearly something else is happening here."

Silence.

"Did you know she'd reached out to Ty for money?"

Silence.

"Do you know where she's taken Ty?"

Silence.

Come on, kid. "Why involve Tyler? Did she need his money? Or was it just some way for her to get back at me?"

Romeo's eyes snapped from staring at the wall to Gracie. "Why would she want to get back at you?"

Was that disgust in his voice? "Just because you said you didn't want her to become part of this family and live here?"

"So she's talked to you about that?"

Romeo's eyes narrowed. "Do you know what she's been through?"

She did. She'd interviewed the kid extensively. And Cee's story, each and every horrible, gut-churning detail, had come pouring out with an anger that had been chilling. Not sadness. Anger. That's why Gracie hadn't wanted her to come here. Cee was the kind of angry person the power of the League could warp.

Pushing off the chair, Gracie leaned back against Leland's desk. "I know."

"Then you know that she's not soft. The fact that you didn't like her or didn't want her here didn't matter to her."

It obviously mattered enough that she mentioned it to Romeo. "So why reach out to Ty? Why lure my son to…wherever? Why have him deposit money into an account? Did she use that money to set the fire? Did she hire a hit man to kill me? What is she doing with Ty?"

"She didn't do any of that." Romeo slammed his hands against his thighs, lurched forward. "That wasn't her. They were supposed to meet, but not what you're saying."

Oh. Man. This was just sad. "I know it's hard when people lie and abuse your trust, but I'm telling you she did."

He dropped back against the seat, cast his eyes down with a sigh that said it was all futile. He started to pick at the seam on the side of his jeans, making a flicking noise that rode down her spine like a nail. "She wouldn't do that. She loves us."

Kneeling at the side of his chair, she softened her

voice. "Look, my son is in danger. The feds are after me. They have a warrant for my arrest, charges include sex-trafficking and blowing up my own club. Somebody set me up, and I'm running out of time. I need to know everything you can tell me about what Cee was working on."

He flinched. "I'm sorry about all that. But why aren't you worried about Cee? She's out there. She rates as much as your son. Doesn't she?"

What? Gracie's stomach turned. Good thing she hadn't eaten anything today. "Are you saying Cee went to meet Ty, but somehow she's in danger too?"

"Yes." He straightened up. "That's what I've been saying. She went to meet Ty, that part's true. But she was supposed to pick up a burner phone and contact me. She never called, never got in touch with me. She wouldn't disappear like that. She wouldn't do that. Not to me. Not to Jules. Not to the rest of our unit. And not to you. She wants you to like her."

She blinked at that. It took her a moment to recapture thought. "You think Cee wants me to like her?"

Anger dive-bombed his face like a kamikaze. "What, just because you're afraid to trust and love someone you think Cee doesn't want to be loved?"

Jolted by his anger, Gracie stood up. "No. I—"

"You're never going to convince me of that. Never. There's something else going on here. You're not listening."

That hit her like an open hand. Warmth spread from her cheeks and down to her chest, a steadfast certainty. He was right. There was something else going on here. And her fear, the one that told her it was logical not to trust—not Cee, not Dusty—was preventing her from seeing that truth. Relaxing shoulders that had risen to her ears, she said, "Okay. I'm listening now. So tell me."

Romeo pressed hands to his lap and wiped his palms across his jeans. "Cee wasn't the one to reach out to Ty. Ty reached out to us about the fraternity."

Her brain stuttered for a moment; a thousand questions pushed forward then landed on, "Cee told me it was a student at the Mantua Academy who told you about this fraternity. That's not true?"

"*Plus minusve*."

Latin for more or less. "Explain that."

"Jules got an email right after the drone attack from a school email address, from a student who goes to the Mantua Academy. She told her about a girl who'd been victimized and that no one was helping her. We began to do research on the dark web on the girl and on the group."

Leland stood too, came around his desk and stopped beside Gracie. "You went undercover on the dark web?"

Romeo, looking a little less cocky, nodded. "Yeah. We managed to get into the group, and then get into their online…uh"—his eyes lowered—"red room."

Leland slammed his hand on his desk, causing the cell Cee had left behind to jump. "You bypassed school security to visit the dark web. Then used school computers to go to a site that live-streamed coeds being drugged, tortured, and raped?"

Romeo held up his hands, shifted back in his seat. Gracie didn't blame him. She rarely saw Leland so pissed. His voice had dropped to an ominous rumble, like an earthquake. She was pretty sure the ground shifted under Romeo's feet. Even though she knew

Leland would never *ever* touch a hair on their heads, Leland angry was scary.

Romeo shook his head emphatically. "No. No. The security here is too complex. We went to Starbucks, used their Wi-Fi, an anonymizer, and a laptop I purchased and stored off campus."

These kids. Gracie rubbed her face. "Anonymous isn't the same thing as secure. A laptop could serve as some damning evidence. They don't differentiate between accessing those sites to help people vs. going to those sites to hurt people."

Momma, who'd been unusually quiet, took that moment to say, "Which is why we don't allow teenagers to conduct unsupervised operations."

Romeo didn't glance at Momma, but you'd have to be a robot not to hear the disapproval in her voice. He shifted. "We were smart about it."

Gracie waved that off. They obviously hadn't been smart *enough* about it, but she had bigger fish to fry. Like finding out where Ty fit in with all of this. "So you used the laptop, infiltrated the group, and Cee went after them in North Philly?"

"North Philly?" Leland echoed.

Whoops. She hadn't told them about that little incident. Honestly, she'd wanted Cee to like her too, to trust her. She gave him and Momma a quick rundown, then asked Romeo, "What happened after that?"

"A few days after Philly, someone reached out to us," he said. "Asked if we were the vigilantes who took down the North Philly house."

What? No. With this information Momma stood and moved to stand with her and Leland before Romeo's seat. Her hands were on her hips, a sure sign of agitation.

Gracie couldn't blame her. This was unbelievable. As in, something here was not right. Romeo's shoulders tensed under the tri-person scrutiny.

"The dark web is anonymous," Gracie said, talking quietly and gently. "What we do at the League is secret. Didn't you wonder how some random person online figured out what and who you were?"

"Of course. We asked."

"And?" Leland said.

Romeo fidgeted, looking only at Gracie. "He said he was your son. And that his father had told him about us. He said he'd taken over a school email address but was actually the one who'd given us the lead on the group. And that he had others."

That made absolutely no sense. Although Romeo would have had no way to know. She knew that John would never, ever have told him about her lifestyle. El, maybe. Ty, never.

Gracie put her hand against a stomach doing fix-this-now flips. Someone had set Cee, Ty, and her up in a very smart, very detailed way. "It wasn't Ty sending those emails. You were catfished."

Romeo shook his head, turned a healthy shade of shame. He started to stammer, protest, then accepting the information, began to talk: "Cee wouldn't tell me where she was supposed to meet Ty—said it was better if I didn't know—but I got the impression it was in the Poconos."

She swung her head between Momma and Leland, both of them staring past her at each other. It wasn't Ty. It wasn't Cee. It was someone drawing them together while pretending to be both of them. Someone with computer experience, enough to set all of this up. Someone with motivation.

Momma and Leland had been right. This time it was Gracie who named her first. "It's Layla."

Gracie's cell beeped. Her heart picked up its pace; she looked at the text. It was from Cee. Coordinates. And the words, He's here. Come alone. Or Cee, who's not here, will die.

She handed Leland the phone and he shared the image with Momma. Layla had them both, apparently at separate locations. Her eyes traveled across Leland's desk. And she'd used Cee's phone number—despite the fact that she was currently staring at Cee's cell sitting quietly on Leland's desk—to text Gracie.

She was good. She'd hacked Cee's phone—which had layers of security. There was no doubt she'd used that phone to spy, to listen in on conversations, to gain information, to manipulate. That's how she'd known about the elevator. She'd been listening in on their conversation, because unlike the Mantua Home, Gracie's apartment didn't have a countersurveillance system.

Come alone.

Fudge.

The desk phone rang. Leland reached across his desk and picked it up. He frowned. "Wave them inside."

He hung up. "Dusty and Victor are here."

Dusty *and* Victor?

Chapter 61

Dusty was done arguing with Victor, who'd been outside the club when Dusty had escaped through Gracie's elevator and tunnel. The man had a look of pure rage on his face. Though that could be from the pain of driving an Expedition with his arm in a sling.

"I could've driven your SUV, you one-armed bastard," Dusty said.

"I'm not trusting you with my ride. I saw him—Tony."

Not again. "I don't give a fuck what you saw, the man is dead."

Dusty rubbed at his aching eyes. The setting sun right in his face didn't help. His head throbbed. His stomach turned. *Leave it be, man. Leave it be.*

He bent forward to get away from the sun and massaged the sides of his skull.

Victor looked at him. "You okay?"

"Can we just leave this be? Let's worry about saving Gracie's son."

"You don't look good."

Going quiet, Victor drove the car to a place Dusty had never imagined would have more of a pull for him than the job.

Victor stopped the car at the manned gates of the Mantua Home. A guard came out, and after a rather surprisingly quick check of the car, waved them through.

They drove through the gate and over a new speed

bump large enough to jar his teeth. Still recovering from his injuries, Victor cried out, "Mother. Fucker."

Looked like the Mantua Home had themselves a new scanner. *Swanky*. "Pretty sure that motherfucker speedbump had a scanner in it that just weighed our balls."

Victor's eyebrows rose. "Could've bought me dinner first."

After passing through campus and up the hill, Dusty directed Victor where to park. He pulled into a spot and turned off his car.

Dusty climbed out of the SUV, his stomach in knots. He had no idea how this was going to go. For all he knew, Gracie would kick him right out.

He took the front steps two at a time. The door opened, and he walked into the Parish home and found himself greeted by...Gracie.

His heart gave a whoop of joy and a rallying cry of *Steady, man*.

"Feel for you," Victor said as he sidestepped past him, then nodded at Gracie. "Where's Momma?"

She pointed down the hall. He began to walk in that direction and threw back, "Go get 'em, Red."

Really? Dusty braced himself. He'd rather she hit him than look at him with eyes that screamed her pain.

Gracie stopped within feet, looked him right in the eyes. "What happened with Tony after we left?"

He startled. "What? Tony?" He tried to think, tried to remember what had happened at the end. His head ached like someone tried to split it open with an ax. He cringed, put his palms over his eyes. *Leave it be, man. Leave it be*.

He had no choice. He relaxed, let it go, lowered his hands, and blinked at her. "I have no idea."

Her eyes looked strained, hurt. Wait. Hurt not *by* him but *for* him? She moved forward and put her arms around him. Why couldn't he remember?

A thread of sharp alarm winged up his spine. He wrapped his arms around her soft warmth. "Grace, I can't explain why, but I don't remember what happened at the end with your brother."

She shushed him. "I know. I know."

Again that sharp slice of alarm. Something was fucked there. He felt what must be her tears soak into his shirt. "You do?"

She stepped back, wiped her eyes. "We have a dire situation here. I need your help. And I don't have time to explain M-erasure to you, the levels of mind wiping, or what a complete and total Moby Dick my brother Tony has been to you. So can you trust me on this?"

He found his throat swelled with emotion. She was asking him to trust her? "Hell yeah."

He bent to kiss her. And when she lifted her lips up to his, he claimed them, tasted and rejoiced in them, in her. She moaned. His heart filled his chest. So sweet. She put a hand on his face and pulled back. She ran a thumb across his chin. "I love you."

He sucked in a breath. Damn, he was going to cry. He swallowed. "Love you more."

Chapter 62

LAYLA'S COMPUTERS WERE SET UP ON THE DINING TABLE IN the great room of the True family vacation home. The shades were drawn, the room was dim. Just like Layla liked it.

Though, as far as cottages went, this one was ridiculous, with Victorian couches and lamps and an old-grandma smell and feel.

She preferred modern furniture. Sort of like the upstairs office in Gracie's club. Another thing they had in common. Like computers and technology.

Despite its crowded and kitschy décor, this cottage was perfect for her needs. Far into the woods, secluded in the Poconos, and it abutted a whole lot of nothing. She typed another instruction into her computer, checking the images of the surrounding property on the multiple computer screens.

She directed a drone into place on the perimeter of the home. The tiny drone, an invention she'd named Huntsman, flew up, skirted branches, and when it reached the coordinates attached its talons to a tree branch.

The device weighed less than five ounces. Like the others, it was programmed to recognize and track human movement. And the best part? They weren't that expensive. So losing them in the fire wouldn't be a big deal.

One of the mercenaries on loan from her father's biggest overseas supporters—a rich billionaire with more sand than soul—walked in from rigging the underground propane tank to the detonator.

Privately she called these borrowed soldiers Thing One and Thing Two. It still shocked her that the Dubai businessman hadn't even asked what she needed them for, just handed her a couple of humans. Damn, that felt great. Perks of every step her father took closer to the presidency, living on this planet with no rules. Being rich was one thing. But living with no rules was what all humans really wanted. Just ask Mukta.

She turned to Thing Two. His pacing was making her nervous. "Can you check on the boy? Make sure he isn't up yet?"

So far her borrowed humans had been super helpful. Thing One, scratched cornea and all, was outside readying the tripwires. He said he could do it in his sleep, but she still trusted robots more.

"No problem," Thing Two said, swinging his stun baton around in a way Layla wasn't sure was smart. Thing Two was always trying to impress her. Kind of stupid when she was already fucking him. He took his Hulk-body up the stairs.

"Do you know the 'Little Red Cap' story?" Layla asked the girl, Cee, who was tied to a white wicker chair.

Despite the bruise on the side of her mouthy face, which had taught her just how far Layla would let an insult go, Cee leveled a fierce reddish-brown glare at her.

"Guess not. It's the Grimm version of 'Little Red Riding Hood.' A story that even at the tender age of two I hated. Because if you're so stupid you can't tell the difference between a wolf and your grandma, you fucking deserve to be eaten."

Cee's jaw tightened. She glared. Smart enough to get the insult anyway. Not her fault she was cyber-stupid. The wolves these days were in your own home.

Layla continued to type, occasionally checking the remote feeds on the screens, flashing night vision images of the cabin's perimeter and surrounding woods. It was all set.

Her hands were sweating. There was one element here that could screw this up. She trusted her technology. She trusted her remote operators, two tech geeks that had been following her since she'd gotten her first college degree in computer science at fourteen. But the human element… "What do you think, Cee? Will Grace come alone?"

Cee scoffed. "No. She will bring an army. And more guns than just those two men."

Probably not an army. Her surveillance of the woman said she was pretty much a loner and seemed to keep even the attempt on her life to herself. Porter. What an idiot. "Nah. I don't think so. This is another thing we have in common. I could've gone to my brother Porter, gotten help with this, but I didn't."

Given an opening, Cee wasn't going down quietly. "Momma will come with her. And Leland. And—"

Layla laughed out loud. Momma. That old bitch. Not likely. "At this very moment, the FBI is at the Mantua Home searching for your sister. No. If they were to send anyone, it would have to be someone *not* at the house. And your team is scattered. So that's not likely. Sure, there's a chance Grace will bring backup, but I think I've got it covered."

She could handle as much as three extra bodies. More

than that, it would get iffy. "Thanks, Cee. Sometimes you just need to talk these things out."

Layla toggled from drone image to drone image, checking the grounds. She'd have to pick up the long-range sensors and other valuable equipment, but there would be very little evidence left here. "Stop squirming, Cee. You can't untie yourself with me in the room. This isn't the movies."

The girl stopped shifting on the chair.

With the last of her drones in place, Layla turned to Cee. She looked terrified.

Maybe not so stupid. "How would you like your explosive vest, Cee, with a little bit of fringe or unadorned?"

Chapter 63

GRACIE LOOKED OUT HER WINDOW AT THE CRUMBLING edge of earth that separated the car from a long drop. Yikes. This was as rural as Pennsylvania got. The SUV had passed a defunct town a few miles back, but they hadn't seen anything resembling life or the remains of once-life since.

The higher they drove into this remote part of the Pocono Mountains, the rougher the thread of road became—and the thinner. Though moonlight brightened the night sky, the dense trees crowding the dirt road blocked much of it.

As he drove, Victor's headlights sliced a resolute triangle up the winding road. He cursed as the SUV rocked over the pothole-strewn road. Couldn't be easy with his injuries.

"Are you sure about your information on Layla, Victor?"

"I told you, Red," he said. "This chick keeps to herself. Is a control freak. She wants Cee here. Makes the most sense to get you all together, clean up the mess in one swoop."

Letting out a breath long and low enough to empty her lungs, Gracie tried to calm her nerves. What if Cee wasn't here? What if…

The big warrior next to her scooted across the back seat, put his strong, protecting arm across her shoulders. "Focus on the plan. On what you can do."

She leaned her head against his shoulder, getting a face

full of scratchy Velcro from his bullet-proof vest and a side full of weapons. Dressed all in black, including his hat and long sleeves, Dusty had a small armory on his person.

He was right. Concentrating on action would keep her sane. She'd checked her phone, which Layla had insisted, via text, that Gracie "had to bring."

No more messages from Layla. In fact, her phone read, "No service."

Dusty and Victor had no cells on them. They'd communicate via two-way.

Focus on the plan. "I approach from the front," Gracie said. "Distract Layla."

Dusty squeezed her close. "I swing around the back. We have the layout of the house. A good sense of the land." He meant they'd managed to get details on the house and property from online photos. It was forty acres square in the middle of wild brush-filled forest. The perfect family getaway for an angry psychopath to take her victims. "Not that I'd brag, darlin', but the woods and I are fine friends."

She smiled, though he couldn't see it. What with her face smooshed up against him. "Not that you'd brag."

"Never. But if I were to brag, I'd say you'd picked the right man for this job. You keep that psycho busy. When I get close enough, I'll switch on my jammer. It's got a good range, but a shit battery. Not to mention waiting until I'm close will give her system less chance to evolve past the intrusion. Once I flick the switch it'll slow down the signals to her security and her communications. Enough that I can ghost into the house. Get Ty. Get Cee. And—"

"Get out," Gracie interrupted. "I can handle Layla."

"You won't be alone," Victor said. "Whatever she

has planned, and I have no doubt she's got a couple of live bodies, the major thrust of Layla's execution will be electronic. That's her comfort zone. So when Dusty signals me via two-way that he's close, I'll break from my hidey-hole and head straight down the driveway. And *my* jammer," he patted the huge black box plugged into his outlet and to an external battery on the floor of the front seat, "has lots of juice. Thanks to your momma's technology we'll roll over whatever Layla has up her sleeve."

"Easy peasy," Gracie whispered, though her throat was tight with a ball of doubt and fear. What if Cee wasn't here? What if Ty… Damn Layla.

She was terrifying. Brilliant, with access to powerful technology and the darkest places on the web, through which she could reach the darkest of human minds.

They rounded another corner and started up the steepest incline yet. Trees crowded the thread of road like a threat. This was the final road, the one that led to the driveway and the cabin. She didn't want them to get too close. "Victor, stop and hide under the cold pack in the back, so she won't be able to read your heat signature." Assuming she was that prepared. And Gracie was assuming it. "I'll drive us to the spot she indicated and park there."

He pulled over, turned off the lights. "You sure we shouldn't try to get closer?"

"No. I'm nervous enough about bringing you guys." Momma and Leland had tried repeatedly to get her to let them organize a team. That would've been a disaster. The time it would've taken, for one. The risk for the family—this was getting beyond complicated with the FBI. And the personality dynamic. She had enough dealing with Layla. She couldn't add siblings hopped up on revenge to the mix. "We need surprise. So we'll do our best to make it look like we're following her instructions. She wants me to park my car two miles from the cabin, under a tree with a glow-in-the-dark *X* spray-painted on it, and run up to the house."

"Sounds like I'm going to be all kinds of comfortable," Victor said. He held up his two-way. "Until Dusty buzzes me that I'm needed."

"I'll try to make it fast," Dusty said. "It's a few miles through these woods on foot."

Her stomach twisted with fear. Was this a mistake? Should she have come alone? What if something happened to them? To Dusty?

Reading her mood, probably from the tension in her body, Dusty bent closer. "We're going to be just fine. You concentrate on your part."

She angled her head to meet his lowering mouth. She kissed him, open-mouthed and long and hot. The ache that shot through her body was as much emotional as it was physical. "Just be careful."

"Yes, ma'am."

From the front, Victor cleared his throat. "Do I get one of those? Either one of you can answer."

Dusty smirked and gave her a you-take-this wave as he climbed out of the car.

"You're staying in the car two miles from the cabin. Only coming at the last minute to a jam party. What could possibly happen to you?"

As she opened the door to climb in the front, Victor gingerly climbed between the seats, careful of his sling, on his way to the cold pack in the back. "Knowing my luck with your family, a bear attack."

The dirt road was an uneven, ankle-turning mess. Not easy to sprint on in thick boots in the dark. And though Gracie used her night vision goggles, they didn't help with the altitude. That's it. She was never taking such a long break from the gym again.

She came to the swing gate that marked John's property and slowed to a stop, sweating and panting.

Layla must be enjoying this. Gracie hadn't seen any cameras, but a little way back instructions had started appearing on her phone that let her know she was being monitored.

Normally, she wouldn't get service up here, but her phone had been taken over, admitted into some kind of Wi-Fi network. Layla had obviously done that. As Gracie caught her breath, her text alert beeped. She read it. Leave the goggles on the road.

She took a long look down the driveway, scanned as far as she could in the woods, before reaching up and pulling off her night vision. Her eyes blinked and adjusted as she bent and placed her googles on the ground before starting down the driveway—which was, thank God, downhill. She reduced her speed down the half-mile, mostly because she couldn't see very well.

When she saw the cabin lights, she slowed to a walk and did some recon. One person on the distant porch. Layla. She spotted no one else, but she couldn't see very far into the woods without her NVG. Surely Layla had at least one person covering her. Probably more.

She might not be in the best shape of her life, but Gracie still had above-average conditioning and her breathing quickly evened out. Too bad she couldn't control her sweating as easily. Her clothes, black cargo pants and shirt, clung to her sweat-soaked body. She wiped her face with her hand and swung at the swarm of gnats circling her head like a rain cloud.

"Stop right there."

Gracie startled and stopped. The disembodied voice had come from a small device attached to a tree.

"Strip."

"Is that necessary? You must have sensors."

"Strip."

Crazy person. Gracie pulled off her boots, struggled out of her sweat-drenched pants, lifted off her shirt, and stood there in her bra and panties. She twirled to show she had no weapons and wasn't wired.

"You have a tattoo?"

"Can I put my clothes back on?"

"What does it mean?"

The calmness of Layla's voice turned Gracie's blood to ice. This was a game to her. "Why do you care?"

"If you tell me, I'll tell you where Cee is."

Gracie's heart started to pound. Cee. Was she close? The yellow lights of the cabin fell across Layla, but she wasn't close enough to read the expression hidden by the woman's baseball cap. "I got the tattoo when I was fifteen. My sister Justice"—the one who shared no blood with her but was her sister—"and I snuck out."

"You ran away?"

"Yeah. For two weeks. And in that time, we got into a lot of trouble. I met a tattoo artist. She started the tattoo. It was supposed to symbolize my take on the world, grab the sin, the apple, the bad decision, and don't let go."

"Bold. You said *started it.*"

She didn't want to answer this lunatic's questions, but as long as she was calm and paying attention to Gracie, she wasn't paying attention to Dusty coming in the back way. "Yeah. We were caught, had an incident with a stolen vehicle. Anyway, I had it finished later."

There was a moment of silence. "Cee is in the woods. Does that make you feel better?"

It should. It didn't. "Is she alive? Injured?"

"Actually, she's been doing a good job of following instructions. And judging by where your friend Dusty is, he should come across her soon. She's wearing an explosive vest. It's a booby trap. I wish you'd come alone. That's going to be hell for me to clean up. Don't worry, though, I have a plan."

Gracie had to swallow over the boulder of anger that had avalanched into her throat. Cee was rigged with explosives? Dusty would have his hands full trying to disarm that device. And she wouldn't let herself think of any other outcome, but that meant he was out of the plan. Ty was at the house, and she had no idea if someone was guarding him. She also had to assume Dusty hadn't yet sent Victor the signal.

So she had no weapon. No idea of how many people were working with Layla—though she'd wager a guess the two big guys that had been at her club would probably be here—and she still needed to deal with the psycho on the porch.

Crud. She needed a new plan. Fast.

"Can I get dressed?"

"Yes. Please do. I'm starting to feel self-conscious. You can come the rest of the way to the house. I'm on the porch. I just want to talk."

Funny. Hysterically funny. "Good. That's what I want too."

And to kick your crazy ass.

Chapter 64

WALKING THROUGH THE WOODS ANY TIME OF THE DAY, BUT especially on an overcast night, was a skill. Dusty knew well the minuscule adjustments and awareness a person needed to avoid tripping or getting caught up in brush. He'd learned this from his Uncle Harvey, who'd had a negligent parenting style and a big woodsy property filled with old junk.

Once you've tripped over a car bumper in the dark, you learn to look after yourself in those woods. After his overbearing father, it had been a blessing to be alone. Uncle Harvey had understood that. Still, he'd gotten lost many times. Never once scared him, though.

But he was scared now. Adjusting his night vision goggles, he glanced at the small device in the tree. Some kind of drone. It had definitely spotted him. Too bad he needed the battery on his jammer for when he got closer to the house.

Despite himself, he was impressed with Layla. And incredibly freaked out. This was a different kind of war. One built not on knowledge of guns and warfare, but on technology and ones and zeros.

He'd do his best with the skills he had and hope he got close enough to use them to stop that lunatic. Wouldn't be easy without the benefit of surprise. Stalking forward with a quiet that said he expected her to send the cavalry or at least a big dog or two, he pulled up short when he saw the girl. A girl wearing a helmet. He knew her. Had met her at the house, at dinner. Cee.

He moved forward with cautious strides, scanning the area as he went. No one in the woods. Just the kid. The kid's helmet had a camera attached to it, and he'd guess some sensors.

As he neared, he noticed something odd about the way she carried herself. "You okay?"

She took a step back. Her lips tightened into a line of determination. "I'm"—she looked down at herself—"strapped with something."

Good Lord. Kid was rigged with explosives.

Dusty took a deep, steadying breath. He didn't know a lot about explosives, but a quick look told him that the wires and explosives were hidden inside the vest. Not easy to get at without setting it off.

No wonder Cee shook like a leaf despite the fact that it was as hot as hell. A hell Layla was doomed to spend eternity in.

Through his NVG, Dusty tried to get a better read on the wires and camera attached to her head. Not a timer. Not a wire trigger. Nope. A cell phone on the front said it was set to be remotely detonated.

Cee jolted, and he heard a sound from the helmet. Not Layla's voice. A man's voice. Couldn't make out what he'd said. "We have to leave the woods. Or else. If we get far enough, the device can't be set off. We don't have much time."

So some guy somewhere with an itchy trigger finger was in charge of this mess. Looked like his jammer was going to be needed a bit earlier than he'd intended. First things first. Figure out what kind of a visual this guy had on him. "Okay. You good to run?"

"We can't run. We have to walk. Or it'll be set off right away. And you have to walk in front of me. Keep your hands up."

Okay. He had no choice but to leave these woods, walking. That meant even if he could get far enough away to save Cee, he wouldn't make it back in time to help Gracie.

He followed her directions, scanning the dark for more of those drone cameras. "No problem. So do you know who's talking to you?"

"I—I'm not allowed to answer that."

That cleared up nothing. Fine. If there was one thing he was good at, it was a distracting conversation. "Ain't it just a nice night for a walk in the woods?"

He heard Cee make a small, pained sound. "I don't want to die. But if you can save yourself..."

She trailed off. Dusty's heart filled with an unexpected and heavy weight. This was one brave kid. He shook his head. "That's a nice offer and all but wouldn't really be much of a life knowing I abandoned such a fine young person as yourself."

She sniffed an obviously runny nose. "I should've known better. I don't deserve..."

Aw, damn. "Sometimes you can't outsmart Loki."

"Loki?"

"Trickster god. And he's got all sorts of minions. So sometimes you get tricked. Live and learn, my uncle Harvey always said. And then he'd tell me, 'People always emphasize the *learn* part of that, son. But it's really the live part that's most important.'

"I tend to agree. Live. Don't really matter if you learn shit. As long as you can greet God at the end of your short life and tell him you lived without fear."

"I think I want to do both. Live and learn."

"Fine by me. Uncle Harvey died from too much chewing tobacco, so you might have a good point there."

She didn't laugh, as he'd hoped. Instead, she said, with that soft Spanish accent, "I'm sorry for your loss."

This kid. He didn't know her whole story, but he knew she'd been trafficked. Mukta had rescued her. *Fuck.*

He'd been fooling himself. There was no blurry line of morality. This was right. Rescuing this kid. "No worries. Harvey lived a big life. But here's the thing—I'm pretty fast. Long legs and all. So you tell me if you have trouble keeping up."

He hoped she got what he was telling her. They might not be able to run, but they shouldn't be moseying either.

"Okay."

He picked up his pace. She didn't say anything. He turned and saw her keeping up.

Smart and brave. And now that he took a look at her eyes, alight through his NVG, he saw something else too. Yeah, she'd live and learn.

And use her knowledge to change the world.

Assuming whoever manned the controls on that thing wasn't herding them far enough away from the cabin to blow them up.

Chapter 65

THE DRIVEWAY FLATTENED OUT AS GRACIE NEARED the house. An old cabin with a stained rocker on the porch and the carcass of a bear would've been more appropriate for this scene.

But Gracie stood before a faded Victorian cottage, almost gingerbread in its cuteness, wide wraparound porch, wicker rocking chairs, and though it was too dark to see now, the online photos had shown a cheery lavender-and-royal-purple color scheme.

Large moths fluttered around the lights by the front door and tried to get inside through the screen door. Layla sat on a wooden footstool on the porch, a rifle with a scope pointed at Gracie. She looked very comfortable with the weapon.

Great. Apparently, her sister was a computer genius and had experience with weapons.

Up until that moment, Gracie hadn't been sure she could kill this woman, her blood, if it came to it. She realized now she probably wouldn't have a choice. She knew the look of a person way off the deep end, someone who thinks they are still totally in control.

Layla wore camouflage from head to toe. Her eyes were wide, almost horror-movie wide, as if someone else had control of her body and she fought them internally. Her smile was coy. Her posture eager.

All of this told Gracie a lot. This meant something to

her. It wasn't just about getting Gracie out of the way so that Layla's father could be president. No. She wanted this. She was enjoying this.

Layla's blond ponytail bounced behind her camo baseball hat as she tracked Gracie. "That's close enough. It took you a while to figure things out, huh? Even with Porter sending a hitman after you. Even though he'd made that mistake and put you on alert. Unbelievable how much I was able to mess with you. It kind of got boring."

Layla wanted to play games, brag about her genius. Of course. Gracie knew enough about the psychology of psychopaths—socially cunning, glib, high self-esteem—to know that this moment, this very second, Layla was thoroughly enjoying herself. "Where's Ty?"

"You're not much of a sharer, are you?"

"On the contrary, I'm glad to sit down with you and have a long talk, as long as you give a little to get. How is Ty?"

Her hands slick with sweat, Gracie could practically feel the heat from the red dot of a laser pointed at her head. Layla squinted through her sight at her. "Did you know you're who I should have been? You're her."

She'd been right. Helping her father and his career was secondary to the slight to Layla's ego. "Where's Ty?"

"Inside." She smiled, a wide, elegant grin, the kind of smile a politician would covet. "He's a good kid. Too bad you don't really know him. He says it doesn't matter to him. He says he's happy. That should mean something."

Layla was trying to manipulate her. Gracie knew she mattered to Tyler. She knew because that's how Layla had been able to abuse and manipulate his trust. "You're really enjoying this."

"Of course. This is why I did it. This moment right here. I could've just tried to kill you like my stupid brother. But this moment, this electric, delicious moment where you are helpless and I'm one step away from ending this nightmare has been worth all of my trouble."

Apparently Layla had seen the movie, the ending where the villain reveals the master plan, and decided that that was it, that was her big life goal. This too was the typical grandiose mindset of a psychopath. "I have to admit, I'm impressed. Brava. But if you don't mind, *sestra*, I want to see Tyler."

"Don't fucking call me that! You will do what I want. When I want it. You need to hear me."

The change in Layla's demeanor was instant and intense. A light switch being thrown in the dark. No longer casual and calm, but angry and determined and bent on revenge. Maybe Gracie could use this. Her plan, the one she'd just devised, required she get an invite into the house. She needed to get close enough to Layla to disarm her. "Look, I'm your prisoner. I will do whatever you want. Hands up. Lips shut tight. As long as you let me see—"

"I used analytics to track your son through the internet, to watch where he went, to gauge who he was. I tailored content to him, lured him into asking the question: 'Can I find my mom?' I even wrote articles about how to track down a birth parent. And he paid me for the privilege. Of course, he thought he was paying a private detective ten thousand dollars to find his mother."

Layla laughed. It was a light and tinkling sound, and it chilled Gracie's blood. It was a laugh coated in the delusions of a brilliant but unhinged mind.

"Once he knew who you were, I hired someone to follow him. To mimic you, what you were doing when you'd set out and stalk him in Manayunk, but to be a little more obvious. You're very good at not being spotted. I'm better. At everything."

Oh, God. No wonder Ty had waved. He'd paid for information, had tried to find out about her, been looking for her. The volcano of Gracie's skin stayed cold and under control, but inside, she was panicking. This nutter was devious. She'd gone out of her way to manipulate Ty. "Why would you do that? Why involve him in this?"

"Really? Didn't think I'd have to explain something that obvious. You've been stalking him. You contacted him. Got him to give you $60,000 to help fund your vigilantes. You set him up on an expensive laptop in order to get him to help you—the location of which will be anonymously sent to the FBI—you lured him out here, and then when he realized what a nut you were, he tried to defend himself. And shot you dead."

Cold swept down Gracie's body, freezing her to the spot. "You're going to kill me and make it look like my son did it?"

Layla tsked. "Simple minds conceive simple plans. He *is* going to kill you."

"Ty would never do that."

"Of course he would. You killed his parents. His mom. His dad. His little brother. Pretty awful of you."

She'd seen John a few hours ago. "They aren't dead."

"No. But I made it look like they were. Showed him a video and everything. He was very upset. I slipped him a little sedative to calm him down. And to confuse him."

Gracie's stomach rolled. *Oh, Ty.* "Seems to be a

family trait. Drugging people. I get why your father did it. I don't understand why you did this, risked this. You already set me up with the FBI to clear your father's name. If you'd done nothing else, I would've gone down for a crime I didn't commit. Or at least been charged with it and been embroiled in years of legal difficulties. Your father would probably be president before it was all said and done."

"Simplifying again. That was to take down your mother." Layla emphasized the word "mother" so strongly that saliva shot from her mouth. "But you? You don't get to fucking live. My dad has one daughter. One."

Rage glistened in her too-wide eyes. She looked like she wanted to shoot Gracie. She looked like murder.

"It's fine, Layla. It's all good. You *are* his one daughter. I honestly don't care. I have a family."

"Fuck you," Layla said. She raised her gun and shot.

Gracie dove to the side, a moment too late. She felt the sting of a dart pierce her leg as she hit the ground. A dart?

She reached to pull it out. Her hand felt like it belonged to the world's least coordinated person as she tried to yank it from her thigh. Missing the blurry end twice, she struggled against her drooping body, but found her vision beginning to dim as she looked up at the night sky.

Layla came into her view, bent over her. "Yeah. You see, that's the problem. I'm not his daughter. You are."

Chapter 66

THE SOUND OF LAPPING WATER GREETED GRACIE'S ears as she began to wake up. A toilet? She opened her eyes. Everything was blurry. She blinked. It didn't help.

Neither did trying to lift her head. So heavy. That sounded the alarm that sent adrenaline racing into her body, the shot of which sparked her blood and woke her up.

Where was she? The cabin. The woods. Layla. She needed to do something.

Her body delivered a staggered situational report. Dry throat. Pounding headache. Aching arms. Probably because her hands were tied behind her back to her legs. Trussed up.

She rocked, brought up her head. Her vision did a vertigo flip. Then settled. Her eyes watered. She blinked away tears and the room washed into focus. She was on the floor, half her body on an Oriental rug, upper half pressed against the scarred wooden floor of the cabin.

Layla must've dragged her inside. The water sound was a fountain on the floor. A meditating Buddha with water flowing from the center of a lotus flower nestled in his lap. *Disturbing*.

The room was old-lady-having-an-English-tea-party style, with Victorian seating and lamps and enough dust to make her nose wrinkle. It was dimly lit by one fringed lamp on an end table near the couch.

She turned her head to take in more of the room and saw him. Tyler. He paced the floor to her left, talking to himself.

"Tyler?" Her voice sounded as grim as she felt.

He pivoted in her direction. Gun in hand. Tears lined his face. "Why? Why did you do it?"

"Ty—"

"Why!" He pointed the gun at her.

Gracie's mind came online with a jolt. "What you saw was fake. Your family is okay. Listen to me."

He wiped tears from his eyes with the back of his hand, the very hand holding the gun. "Done listening to you."

Gracie's heart trampled through her throat like a bull through anyone careless enough to get in its way during the run of Pamplona. "Be careful with that gun. You're going to hurt yourself."

He snorted a desperate sounding, agonized laugh. "You want me alive, but you don't get it. I'm not alive anymore. You took them. You took me. You—"

His voice broke. He began to sob. The weapon went down, pointed toward his own feet.

"Tyler. No. Listen—"

"Shut up!" He pointed the gun at her again.

Realizing as the cold calculation of her training washed the panic from her body that she wasn't going to convince him of the truth, Gracie came up with a new plan. Ty was in no place to believe her. He wasn't able to distance himself from the beliefs that had been so carefully installed in his head. She had to try something else. "I'm sorry. I'm so sorry. Please. You're not a killer. You don't want to hurt me."

He laughed. The gun shook in his hand. He nodded. "You're right." He pointed the gun at his head.

"No!" A spasm ran through Gracie's body.

Tears streamed down his face now. "This is what you wanted. Me. You killed them for me. Now you get nothing. Spend your whole life in jail. Empty."

No, no, no. She had to stop him. She had to do something. Fuck! She rocked on the floor, tried to get closer to him. She couldn't even fucking move.

Something. Something. Make him angry. Make him point that weapon anywhere but at himself. Point it at her. "They deserved it. Those fucking idiots. Especially that little one. Stupid fuck. Kept asking for you. I enjoyed killing him."

Fury took over the pain in Tyler's eyes. He jerked the weapon away from his head, aimed at her, and shot and shot and shot.

Chapter 67

THE WOODS HAD A LOT OF UNSETTLING NOISES AT NIGHT, places a foot could be put wrong, but nothing made Dusty as afraid as this walking, getting farther and farther away from the woman he loved.

He needed to get that vest off Cee and head back to Gracie. He'd been able to take several glances at the device. It was held on by Velcro. Knowing he'd need to get it off quickly, no telling how well his jammer would work and what kind of intrusion work-around Layla might've setup, he'd already tried to get information from Cee about the device.

How much it weighed. If she could see a clock or certain wires. No surprise that she'd only been able to answer with "I'm not allowed to answer that."

Didn't matter. The questioning itself had given information—how closely they were being monitored. Verbally? Like a hawk. Visually? Not so much.

Because while he'd asked his questions, he'd altered his direction. He shifted course to the left and then to the right, subtly, not overtly. Whoever was monitoring didn't flag it or tell Cee to "Stay this course. Do this."

In addition, the guy had never asked him to remove his night vision goggles. Which probably meant he couldn't see him that well. And if he wasn't mistaken, there was a lag that had gotten a bit longer the deeper they went into the woods. Sometimes when Dusty asked his questions, Cee was able to get a whole word out before she'd then say, "I'm not allowed to answer that." So whoever was operating this rig wasn't close by. Good to know.

Dusty kept walking, talking up a storm, because he'd also noticed whoever monitored them seemed to get distracted by Dusty's talking. Always knew what his uncle had called Dusty's "chipmunk chatter" would come in handy one day. Voice had been a lot higher in those days.

He readied himself to put his plan into action, scanned up ahead, picked the perfect spot. Made sure there were no more mini-drones. There weren't. Layla only had those suckers closer to the house. Slowing his pace, he waited for Cee to catch up.

He glanced back, got a visual, made sure she was in grabbing distance before he put a foot wrong and tripped over a root.

She gasped, bent over his prostrate body. The moment she bent, he reached up and flicked up her camera, so it showed trees and darkness.

Her eyes went wide and terrified. He put a finger to his lips and worked the straps that held the device. Pulled the Velcro off as he spoke, talked loudly over the noise. In a sense, using his own voice to jam the signal. "Fucking root. Did you hear that snap? I think that was my ankle."

"Oh, it's twisted," she answered. "It looks bad."

Quick kid.

"Yeah. Can you help me up?"

"I need to step back. I'm being told..."

Too late. Dusty flicked on his jammer, got her out of the vest, tossed it and the helmet into the woods. He rolled and bounced up from the ground, picked her up, and ran like the devil himself was after him.

Boom! The blast sent him sprawling. As he fell, he shifted to the side to avoid crushing the kid.

They lay in the dirt. Gasping. Sore. She was up a

half second before him, looking around the woods as if expecting an enemy. "You did it."

He stood on slightly wobbly legs. She hugged him. He hugged her back, then held her away from him so he could make sure she wasn't injured. "You okay?"

She nodded, though he could see she was bleeding. Looked minor. "Okay, Cee. Gotta work fast here." He took off his bullet-proof vest, put it on her. "And take this two-way and these night vision goggles."

She tightened the vest. "But how will you see?"

"Take them and walk north. The two-way is set to the right channel, but don't use it unless you really need to. Whoever strapped that bomb to you might think you're dead, but not if they pick up your signal. You'll find a car there. An Expedition. The guy inside, the guy on the other end of this two-way, is named Victor."

She shook her head. "No. I'll go, but you take the goggles. There's tripwire set up near the house. I don't know where."

"How many guards?"

"Two. And one of them is huge." She pulled back a little. "Even bigger than you."

Bigger than him? Wasn't sure she could see so well in the dark, but he'd take her word on it. "Okay. I'll take the glasses. You take the two-way, call Victor."

Distant gunshots ended their conversation. "Go!" Cee shouted.

And he ran. His arms pumped. His body fought for speed. Every obstacle came into focus. He jumped branches, roots. His heart pounded. And he prayed. *Grace. Please Lord, give me Grace. Don't let me be too late. Please.*

Chapter 68

GRACIE'S BODY CONVULSED AT THE *THUCK*, *THUCK*, *THUCK* impact of each of the bullets being fired into the floor around her. They stopped. The echoes faded. And the smell of gunpowder filled the room. Gracie worked to unclench her locked jaw. Then she opened her eyes.

Tyler had lowered the gun. He stared at her. His face a mask of fear, confusion, and hope. He sucked in snot. "You said they were alive."

His voice sounded so young, so hurt. Gracie felt her own throat grow tight with tears. "Yeah. I promise. They're alive."

A brutal curse, a sobbed "Fuck. That bitch. She lied. She really lied?"

He began to tremble. The adrenaline backlash. She needed to get him moving and out of here before it got worse. "All lies. She pretended to be my sister Cee. Pretended to contact you on my behalf. I wouldn't have gone behind your dad's back, hurt you that way, inserted myself in your life that way."

Ty wiped snot from his face, blinked. "They're for sure alive?"

Oh. Kid. Goosebumps raced down her body. They needed to get out of here. Where was Layla? Was she close by? She had to be. She had to be watching what was happening. Was anyone else around?

"Yes. I promise. I promise you, Tyler. The scene was faked. You know how they fake stuff like—"

"Aliens or ghosts caught on video?"

"Yes. Like that. We have to get out of here." *Now*. "Okay? Can you untie me?"

The skin on his cheeks heated. He nodded and rushed over, dropped to his knees, put the gun on the floor. As he untied her, his fingers shook, so did his voice. "I saw what you were doing. When I put the gun to my head. I saw it. You'd let me shoot you. You'd let me do that if it meant that I got to live."

Grace couldn't stop the small, pained sound that escaped her throat. Or the tears. He saw. He saw her. "Yeah. I would've."

He loosened the knot and the slack was instant, releasing her arms. She rolled. Swinging her arms under her legs so they were in front of her, she began to untie the rope from her feet.

Ty watched her. "Do you think she's around here somewhere?"

"Yes. Layla, that's the woman you met, not my sister Cee, is around. And probably not alone. Did you see anyone else in the house?"

"A limo driver brought me here. Drugged me. After that I just saw…uh, Layla."

Discarding the rope, Gracie put a hand on Ty's shoulder and he helped her to stand. She wobbled. Ty put an arm around her. Shaking out her drugged legs, she said, "I'm okay. Can I have the gun, Ty?"

He retrieved it and handed it to her.

"Let's go." One hand on Ty's arm, making sure he moved so that he was always protected by her, Gracie used every bit of caution her slowly awakening body required, scanning the house for any sign of danger.

Adrenaline quickly heightened her senses, and she became sharply conscious of every pop and creak of the floorboards, the slide of Ty's black-and-white canvas sneakers, the way her boy held and released terrified breaths, the whooshing sound of water. *Water?*

Her eyes searched. Remembered. The fountain. The water inside was shiny, slick with rainbows playing inside it. And the smell. Why hadn't she noticed? Not water.

Pulling Tyler's arm, she yanked him forward, and shoved him in front of her. "Go!"

He stumbled against the front door, slamming it open, as he tripped onto the porch. A step behind, Gracie scanned the trees.

And then she saw her, no more than a shadow, a dark figure moved through the woods, raised her gun, intent on making sure Tyler and Gracie would be dead in a moment, their bodies burnt in the explosion.

Layla.

Everything unfolded in one horrible instant. A moment of brutality that seared itself into Gracie's horrified, witnessing mind.

As calm as a woman who has never lost a thing in her life, Layla stepped from the woods, weapon raised. No darts this time. An AK semiautomatic rifle.

Launching forward, Gracie shoved Tyler, propelling him into the air. She followed, her body covering his as they flew forward. Her one hand pushing him down, the other bringing up her gun, a panicked voice screaming in her head—*not fast enough, not fast enough*.

A *rat-a-tat* of gunfire erupted a split second before Gracie's finger depressed the trigger of her weapon. That moment played out in blinding clarity. The feel of Tyler's warm back against her palm, the smell of the summer woods, the startled silence of time standing still as the electric prayer fired through her brain as quick as the shot, quicker: *Please, God, keep Ty safe, let the bullets only strike me*. And then Layla's skull exploded, her body seized by the spray of bullets, as muscle, tissue, and brains were shredded on impact.

Ty and Gracie slammed to the ground with a thud and a whoosh as air was knocked from Tyler's lungs. She landed partially on top of him, spun off, scrambled to her feet, gun raised and ready. But Layla stayed down.

Made sense. She no longer had a brain. Movement. On the driveway. Gracie pivoted and brought her gun up as her pulse pounded in her throat, ears muffled and ringing from her not-fast-enough shot.

"Hold your fire, Red. It's me," Victor said as he limped forward, face pinched with pain, semiautomatic sticking out from his sling. "You okay?"

"Layla!" The cry tore from the woods, like the large figure. Rage and disbelief contorting his face as he charged forward, leveled his gun at Gracie. She screamed, swung her weapon around. Victor turned at the same time, and…

Another figure moved through the woods. Bigger than the first. He hit the charging man, slammed into his side like a fullback, knocked him to the ground.

Dusty held the man's gun arm down, while bringing his own gun down on the man's skull again and again. There was a *crack*, *crack*. A splatter of wet darkness shot up into the space between the man and Dusty. And then stillness. Dusty got off the man, lurched up. Scanned the darkness. "Cee said there were two of them."

A beat of definitive silence, as if for an entire heartbeat, or the skipping of one, the world went quiet. And then Gracie yelled, "Forget him. Explosives! Run."

Bringing his two-way to his mouth, Victor turned and ran. Tyler was on his feet running. A split-second later, Gracie was by his side. And Dusty too. Car lights appeared down the drive. Cee was driving?

Gracie made a looping gesture with her hands. Cee swung the vehicle around with a skid of wheels. Gracie jumped into the back seat and ended up between Ty and Dusty. Victor climbed in the front, his door still open as Cee tore down the drive. It slammed shut, caught him on his good arm.

He cursed.

The house exploded. The SUV lurched forward, like a giant hand had come up behind it and given it one firm shove. The people inside flew forward and then hit the back of their seats with the momentum.

And then a series of concussive blasts began to explode down the driveway, catching the trees on fire, and sending pockets of fiery debris raining down around them. Cee swung the car left and right like she'd been doing this for a living. Mad skills. Great teamwork.

Her body rocking back and forth between Tyler and Dusty, Gracie looped an arm through each of their arms. Unable to articulate a single word of the relief and horror crowding her throat.

The glow from the fire lit the night sky as the car pulled out of the driveway onto the road. Cee stopped the car so Dusty could drive. As he moved to get out of the seat, Dusty leaned over, kissed Gracie gently on the head.

And beside her, Tyler reached over, grasped her hand, and squeezed. "Thanks for rescuing me… Mom."

Chapter 69

STANDING GUARD AGAINST A HORDE OF TRESPASSERS AS THE summer sun scorched the ground, Dusty was beginning to think once again he had John McClane's *Die Hard*-brand of luck.

He wiped sweat from his face. They were outnumbered. The field, some called it a quad, was awash in red. The enemy hid everywhere. Behind the huge boulders that lined the field. Stationed atop the guard tower—a raised deck with telescopes the school used for stargazing. And crouched behind trees and bushes.

His crew now consisted of him, Gracie, and Ty. They were hunkered down behind a Dumpster hidden by a fancy wooden fence at the field's edge. Their team mates needed to be freed. But that meant getting across this field, across a field guarded at every conceivable ambush point. He'd seen episodes of *Game of Thrones* that were less messy.

"I've been in tighter places," Grace told him. He raised an eyebrow then grinned, because so had he, but that had been a lot more fun.

Maybe reading his mind, she elbowed him. "Here's the plan."

She outlined a pretty decent game plan, using some stones and Popsicle sticks to mark it out. It could get at least one of them through alive. Only needed one to free the other players.

Tyler watched them from the edge of the Dumpster.

Gracie beamed at him. "Got it, Ty?"

"Yep. Got it." He raised his paintball gun, turned, and ran out onto the field, screaming "Leroy Jenkins!"

Dusty shook his head. "Your son."

Gracie grinned. "Gotta love him."

She ran after him, firing randomly.

Dusty had a good mind to let them go it alone. *Naw*. What fun was that? He ran out balls to the wind, or what he liked to think of as Butch-Cassidy-and-the-Sundance-Kid style, a.k.a Leroy Jenkins.

The paintballs pelted the ground and their jumpsuits in no time. Tyler and Gracie were tripped up and went sprawling onto the grass together. He came up and fell on them, covering their bodies with his own. Paintballs slammed into him. *Hurt. No fucking kidding. That hurt.*

Grace pushed against him. "The paintballs are less dangerous than being smothered by you."

"Stop shooting," Justice called from her spot on the guard tower. "It's a fucking massacre."

He rolled off them, stood up, and helped Gracie and Tyler to their feet. The two of them burst into laughter. They high-fived each other. Made his heart do something funny, a bit of gymnastics in his chest.

He reached out and drew them both in for a bear hug, lifted them up. They complained mightily, but what was a man to do? They'd just survived a massacre together. Yes, sir, he was that damn lucky.

Chapter 70

THE MANTUA HOME CAMPUS LOOKED IDYLLIC IN AUTUMN. Trees filled with green, yellow, red, and orange leaves lined the campus lawns, streets, cozied up to brick buildings and park benches. The wind smelled of earth and a summer well spent.

Gracie's heart was light as she left the quad with Tyler by her side. The teams had broken up after the war games, and groups of people walked here and there. Dusty, Justice, and Sandesh strolled together, discussing the "fucking massacre."

It was still weird having the school so empty this late into September, but it sure made it easy to get around. They walked into the main road leading onto campus and toward the front gate. The sun was starting to set, spotlighting the tops of the trees with an orange glow.

Cee, Romeo, and Jules jogged past heading toward the house. One of Leland's rules for training. She remembered it well from childhood. *Don't walk, run*. Romeo bumped Tyler's shoulder as he jogged by. "Ask again."

Gracie yelled after him, "Don't encourage him. Remember who you're training with tomorrow morning."

Romeo turned around and spread his arms wide. "Dusty said he'd train with me."

She turned to look at Dusty, who gave her a sassy Southern grin, or at least that's how she took it, when he winked at her.

She didn't try to hide her smile. "You're lucky you're so cute."

"So, can I?" Tyler asked.

Letting out a breath, she grabbed his hand, held it as they walked. Yes. He was too old to hold his mother's hand, but strangely he never objected. "We've been through this, Ty."

"But Rome goes here. Why can't I?"

Oh boy. This was the third time he'd asked. And it made her beyond happy that he wanted to make a home here—even if it was just during the school year. She could see him all the time. Get to spend time with him, take him for ice cream, teach him about computers.

"School won't start until the end of October this year. There's a short holiday break. A shorter summer break. It wouldn't be easy. And I don't think your parents—"

Ty brushed slightly sweaty bangs from his green eyes. "No. Dad knows. I talked to him."

John knows? Surprising. Well, John and El had become a lot kinder to her since she'd saved Tyler's life. And all that other stuff with the authorities. John felt guilty after accusing her of kidnapping Ty. She shuddered. Tried not to think about it.

Truth was, she would love for Tyler to go to school here, but was that fair to the girls here? Ugh. What was she doing? She was making excuses. Sexist excuses. The kind that made Tony run away, fake his own death. Well, that and the fact that he knew if he'd stayed he'd have been M-erased. Man could run, but he couldn't hide. "I'll talk to Momma."

Tyler perked up, swung their clasped hands back and forth. "She'll let me in. Momma loves me."

Gracie's throat grew tight. "Yeah. She does."

As they neared the main gate, she could see John and El sitting in their car.

"Are you sure you talked to your parents about it, Ty? They won't even come onto the grounds."

He cringed. "Yeah. I talked to Dad. Mom, uhm, I mean—"

"She's your mom, Ty."

His face reddened. "Yeah, Mom's against it. She thinks it's too expensive."

It *was* expensive. El could've just been saying that, but Gracie was going to take her at her word. She was done feeling guilty or wrong about being present in her son's life.

Gracie grinned at her son. "Did you know that family goes here for free?"

Chapter 71

STANDING BEHIND GRACIE OUTSIDE THE NEW AND improved "Staff only" doors leading from the back of Club When?, Dusty tied the blindfold—a long strip of black silk—over her eyes.

Pretty as a picture in spiked red heels and a short red dress that laced up the back, she didn't object. The curve of her fine ass reminded him of an apple. Ripe. Juicy. Begging to be bitten.

One thing at a time. He bent forward, put his lips by her ear. "You ready?"

She tilted her head back. "I've been ready for weeks."

He had too. But the thing needed to be perfect. Taking a small nibble of her earlobe, the silk from the blindfold pressed against his cheek, he whispered, "Is that excitement or wariness in your voice?"

She laughed. "Excitement. If I hadn't promised, I so would've peeked in there to see what you've been up to."

"Have to say, I was impressed with your self-control." Especially since they were both living at Club When? now. It had taken all his powers of persuasion, after the club had been repaired to her specifications, to get her to allow him to take over designing the theme for the grand reopening.

He hoped she liked it. Hoped what waited beyond was their future.

"Good thing you hadn't peeked," he said, giving her

a light pat on the round swell of her ass. "You would've been in big trouble."

Grabbing her by the hips, fingers itching to pull that bow, he steered her through the doors, using his foot to kick one open. Lord, he was starting to sweat.

Inside, the ceiling of the club was draped in black fabric. Projected on that silk was an endless night sky, brilliant stars, the Milky Way's glimmering sweep of silver dust, and the ethereal pinks and golds of distant galaxies.

Sculpted white trees draped in lights perched along the perimeter of the dance floor. And on each of the white-linen-draped tables twinkled smaller handcrafted versions of the trees.

A light show of white shimmered slowly over the floors and walls. All along the bar were a series of glowing tall and short silver candles.

Mouth dry, heart pounding, Dusty fished out the remote and hit the button that started the music pouring out of the speakers. The sounds of the piano played quietly, and then Garth Brooks began singing what Dusty now thought of as their song: "Make You Feel My Love."

"Dusty?"

"One sec."

He tried to still his pounding heart, took the ring from his pocket. Dropping to one knee in front of her, he held up the gem that reflected the purity of his intentions and his undying love.

"You can take off the blindfold, Grace."

She reached up and pulled it down. Her hands flew to her mouth. Her eyes bounced around the room, glittering with the reflection of all those lights. By the time they settled back on him, tears streaked her cheeks.

He found his own eyes growing wet. *Aw, hell*. He adored her. "Grace Divine Parish, will you do me the honor of marrying me, making me the luckiest man in all of the universe?" She dropped to her knees, took the ring. "Yes. A thousand times. In a thousand ways. Yes."

Felt good to be back behind the bar of Club When? Especially when he was putting together his favorite, or at least his most cherished, drink. Dusty took in the growing crowd beyond. Still early, but looked like another banner night. He just hoped it went smoothly.

First week back, and Club When? was experiencing a bit of a hiccup. There wasn't a night this week that the bar hadn't had at least one fight.

Starting to feel more like a club bouncer than a bartender, he couldn't help but wonder if it had anything to do with the "costume change" as Grace called it. She'd loved the wedding theme—so said her enthusiastic yes—but later pointed out that they'd have to tie the theme to a specific date in history.

He'd considered it and decided a royal wedding was an historical event. What wasn't to like about Kate and William's wedding? Pomp. Ceremony. Crazy hats. Maybe it was the hats.

He passed the drink to the customer, telling her, "It's called Blood and Guts, because you need some to drink it."

She smiled, clinked her blue swirly drink with her boyfriend's beer. Squaring his shoulders, Dusty moved to the other end of the bar. He'd seen the guy come in earlier. Apparently the man didn't understand the "get lost" signal Dusty had been sending him. Couldn't really help the curl of his lip as he reached the end of the bar. Guy deserved a sneer. "What do you want, Mack?"

Mack nodded. He looked a little older. Nose a little less straight. His face a little rounder, like he'd put on a few.

"Guess you're wondering why..." Mack trailed off.

He wasn't wondering. Dusty knew exactly why he was here. Turned out the FBI didn't take kindly to agents using manufactured evidence against innocent people. Mack's case and career had fallen apart. But not before he'd taken the low road.

"Naw, I think I get it. You need a job."

Mack's eyebrows jumped, and he laughed. Just a little. He waved around the club. "Pretty romantic."

Yes, it was. Every time he walked in here, Dusty was struck by the overwhelming truth that he'd been given a gift. *Her*. He hadn't been sure she'd say yes. And he'd had nerves the night he'd asked her to marry him like he hadn't had in...well, ever.

The word *yes* had never sounded as sweet in the history of mankind. Made even sweeter by the sharp yeses he'd coaxed out of her fifteen minutes later upstairs in that big bed of hers.

"I came to apologize to Gracie Parish. It got messy there."

Messy? Fucker had arrested Gracie after they'd come back from dealing with Layla and her crazy vendetta. Dusty had gone insane trying to find Gracie. Fucking Mack. He'd had her transferred to a black site. Tried to get her to confess, hoping to salvage his career—and Rush's

Honestly, he'd never been more grateful for the Parish family pull than when they'd joined with him to help locate Gracie, and Dusty, Justice, and Sandesh had gone in there and busted her out.

Still made his blood boil. So, no, he wasn't going to be nice to Mack. It was all he could do to stop himself from punching the guy before forcibly hauling his sorry ass out of the club. He caught the eyes of the woman whose presence was currently stopping Dusty from following that exact course of action. Beautiful. "If you want to apologize to her, turn around. She's standing behind you."

Mack blanched and spun around. Gracie stood there, wearing her Club When? finest and looking hotter than any woman had a right to.

"Apology accepted," Gracie said. "Now if you don't mind, Dusty and I were just going to rewatch the shockumentary on disgraced Senator Andrew Lincoln Rush. Did you hear when the authorities finally came to believe my version of events and searched Layla's home, they found she had numerous videos showing the disgraced senator had drugged and raped girls? Including several recordings of him, drunk and slurring, admitting his despicable behavior?"

Mack nodded. "I did. Yes. I guess you just can never tell what people are like behind closed doors. Sometimes, people confuse you."

"Yeah," Dusty said, scratching at the beard he'd been growing, "it's so difficult to figure out that someone drugs and rapes people when you've seen the video of one of his rape victims telling you that she'd been drugged and raped."

Dusty eyed his old friend meaningfully. Mack had the good sense to stay quiet.

He began to walk away, turned his head back toward Dusty. "Your dad died. Did you know?"

He did. And he knew his congregation had tried to stay together, but in the end couldn't. He hoped they all ended up better for it.

Seeing Dusty wasn't going to answer, Mack took a deep breath and walked away. Dusty watched him go. *Good riddance*.

Gracie climbed up onto a stool, leaned across the bar, ran her thumb along the shadow of stubble on his chin. "You're still mad at him, huh?"

She looked worried. Like he'd hold that grudge forever. And he might. But how to explain to her? Those panicked, brutal moments of not being able to find her, then finding her and realizing she was locked up, taken somewhere where people could and did hurt her. Of the anger, and the lengths he'd gone to to rescue her. He couldn't. He wouldn't.

She had her own stuff to deal with regarding that mess. But she was here now. Safe. And—as much as she'd object, tell him the word meant ownership, though that's not how he felt—she was his.

Maybe seeing the thoughts playing across his face, Gracie swung over the bar, dropped down next to him, wrapped her arms around his waist. Aw, hell. This woman. He bent to her, kissed her for all he was worth, kissed her like a man who had almost lost the best thing that had ever happened to him.

And she kissed him back. Just as sweet and hot as every minute he spent with her. When they pulled apart from their kiss, it was to the approach of three twenty-somethings, who sat down and began singing with the music pouring through the club's speakers—"Going to the Chapel"—out of tune and without the correct words.

Gracie grabbed him by the belt hooks and moved her sweet ass to that god-awful song. Actually, now that he thought about it, he kind of liked that song. Might just be the company. Or the friction.

"Love you, Grace."

The singing trio whistled and hooted as Dusty bent and kissed his bride-to-be. *His*.

Chapter 72

Making their way through the corridor of the Parish Palace, as Dusty had taken to calling the Mantua Home, Gracie tried not to let her tell-a-tale face let Dusty know just how freaked out she was about what was going to happen. It was unprecedented, unusual, and scary.

Now that the lower levels of the League were back in operation, Momma was going to reverse the M-erasure that Tony had performed on Dusty. Unfortunately, it was much easier to hide a memory, as Tony had done, than to retrieve it, so they weren't sure it would work. But Momma was going to try and make him whole, give him back his memory.

They walked in silence, their footfalls resounding off the corridor walls as a soccer game echoed from the gym. She directed him left, toward the elevators. Though she pressed the up button, they weren't going up.

The doors to the elevator slid open. They walked inside. The doors slid shut. That was probably the longest she'd ever *not* heard him talking.

Dusty reached for the B—basement floor—but didn't press it. "Not really four floors, right?" he finally said.

"Not really." Gracie put her wrist up to the control panel. The elevator beeped. Gracie swallowed and said, "Subfloor 4B."

Another beep. The new system had added security that she thought was a bit too much. A small door on the panel slid open. She bent, let it scan her eyes. The elevator repeated the floor she'd identified and then said, "Grace Divine Parish. Welcome. Rider two, identify yourself."

Dusty turned his wrist over, eyeballed the elevator like it was a demon. "So I just..."

She grabbed his chipped wrist and held it up to the sensor. The elevator beeped. He bent toward the scanner. It read his eyes and said, "Leif Eric McAllister. Also known as Dusty. Also known as American Ninja Warrior. Also known as Southern Accent. Welcome."

He laughed in a way that was both amused and disturbed. He looked at her, honey eyes alight. "Rome?"

She nodded. He shook his head. "Kid's gonna pay for that."

Dusty reached for the indented handrails on the sides of the elevator. She intercepted his hand, pushed his arm away. "Nope. Justice would never let you live it down."

He smirked at that.

The elevator intoned, "Proceeding to Subfloor 4B."

"Well, I'm all about impressing your..."

The elevator dropped.

Fast.

Dusty jerked sideways, hit the wall, grabbed the handrail. "Shit."

Feet braced wide, Gracie stood her ground and grinned at him as he used the handrail to regain his feet.

"Got a lower center of gravity," Dusty muttered.

And that only made her smile widen.

The elevator slammed to a stop. Dusty released the white-knuckled grip he had on the handrail, walked away from the sides. Looping her arm around his, she didn't bother to hide her smile. "What do you think of Elevator-X?"

His easygoing grin gracing his too handsome face, he declared, "That's just not natural. That's what that is. Un…natural."

He bent and kissed her. His tongue moved into her mouth. The stubble on his chin scratched pleasantly against her. Heat rolled through her body and she grabbed his shirt, pressed herself closer.

As the doors opened, the elevator announced, "Subfloor 4B. Welcome, you are being monitored. Entering unauthorized areas will result in immediate expulsion."

He pulled back from the kiss, rubbed his thumb across her lips. "Sweet as you are hot."

Heart hammering with lust and a sudden fear, she really fucking loved this guy. She grabbed his hand, squeezed. "It's going to be okay."

"Hadn't been nervous at all until you said that."

Taking a right off the elevator, away from the misted glass doors of Internal Security—no way was she going in there—she led him to a door that meshed with the walls so seamlessly you had to know it was there. She held her wrist up to the hidden sensor in the wall. There was a beep. Dusty leaned over her and did the same. Another beep and, "You are cleared for access to Neuro Room 3D."

"Sounds like we're going to a holodeck."

She snorted. "You have geek in you?"

His eyebrows furrowed. "Gotta ask? Used to work for the FBI, remember?"

There was a rush of air as the door slid open. They were the last ones to enter the clinical-looking room.

Everyone else stood around looking anxious. Or that might just be her suddenly jumping nerves. Yes, the procedure was much safer than in the past, but… She let her thoughts trail off. Dusty had made the choice. He said he wanted his memories. Every one.

Dusty skirted the chair in the middle of the room, kissed Momma on her silk-lined cheek. She told him, "It will be quick and painless. I promise."

That did a lot to calm Gracie's nerves. She said hi to everyone—Justice, Sandesh, and Victor. Momma had said she needed as many of the people who'd been there that day as possible.

Leland was here for support, though he'd been instructed to stay silent during the procedure.

Momma pointed to the chair. "Would you mind sitting down?"

Dusty eyed the chair in the middle of the room with obvious unease. She couldn't blame him. It was a cross between a mad scientist's and a dentist's chair. A large arm connected to a helmet with wires and submerged sensors projected from the top of the seat. It was those sensors, that direct brain interface, that would, hopefully, awaken the hidden physiological data, helping restore Dusty's memory of what had happened with Tony.

Dusty nodded but didn't say a word. Not a good sign.

"It's going to be fine," she said as he reluctantly took his seat. She had to fight herself not to stop the whole thing when Leland began to strap him into the seat. She had to remind herself that he needed to be drugged and hooked up to the specialized equipment for this to work.

Instead of concentrating on the leather straps being tightened, she readied herself to take part in the drama.

A replay of the last minutes in Mexico—with each of the people here playing a part, recalling what they could from that day. Momma even had sound effects set up. It was being run by one of Leland's staff in internal security, who'd also be recording this session.

She dreaded reliving that day. This, in conjunction with the sensitive neuronal interface technology, should help unlock his memories.

If it worked, Dusty would be able to remember what had happened with Tony. If it worked, he'd be whole. If it worked, they'd hopefully be able to use that information to find Tony. And bring him home.

Acknowledgments

Before I'd gone through the extensive and exhilarating work of readying my novel for publication, I was unaware of how many talented and dedicated people would add to the shape and texture of my novel. I am so very grateful to all of them.

As always, a huge thank-you goes to my agent, Michelle Grajkowski, for cheerleading my work and being there every step of the way on this wonderful journey. A huge thanks to Ann Leslie Tuttle for her invaluable help with her developmental read for *The Price of Grace*. And to my wonderful editor, Cat Clyne, who gave me the time and encouragement I needed to make this novel its very best—thank you. A sincere, heartfelt bow to my publisher and Sourcebooks founder, Dominique Raccah, for taking a chance on her own dream and thereby allowing me to live mine. And for all the wonderful people at Sourcebooks and on my publishing team—with a special shout-out to my wonderful cover designer, Dawn Adams, and my intrepid publicist, Stephany Daniel—thank you for all that you do and continue to do to make books that really do change lives! I count myself beyond lucky to have had the benefit of your hard work, creativity, and guidance.

A big, sloppy virtual kiss and hug to my senior production editor, Rachel Gilmer, for your priceless insight and endless patience. Thank you, Rachel! And thank you to Gail Foreman for being a second set of eyes and asking the questions I never would've asked myself.

I also want to express my gratitude to Patricia Gussin, who not only read my work but championed me and my novel!

A sincere thank-you to all of the librarians and bookstore owners, big and small, who have taken a chance on this series and stocked it on their real and virtual shelves. And finally, my undying gratitude to all the avid readers who have picked up the Band of Sisters series and who continue to enthusiastically support the adventures of the League of Warrior Women. I consider it a privilege to be able to make this connection with each and every one of you.

About the Author

Diana Muñoz Stewart is the award-winning romantic suspense author of the Band of Sisters series, which includes *I Am Justice* and *The Price of Grace* (Sourcebooks). She lives in eastern Pennsylvania in an often chaotic and always welcoming home that—depending on the day—can include a husband, kids, extended family, friends, and a canine or two.

When not writing, Diana can be found kayaking, doing sprints up her long driveway—harder than it sounds—practicing yoga on her deck, or hiking with the man who's had her heart since they were teens.

Learn more or connect with Diana at:

dianamunozstewart.com

facebook.com/DMSwrites

@dmunozstewart